Lock Down Publications and Ca$h
Presents

I0637474

REMEMBER
EVERYBODY AIN'T
LOYAL

Written By
KEESE

Lock Down Publications
P.O. Box 944
Stockbridge, GA 30281
www.lockdownpublications.com

Like our page on Facebook: Lock Down Publications
www.facebook.com/lockdownpublications.ldp

Stay Connected with Us!

Text **LOCKDOWN** to 22828 to stay up-to-date with new releases, sneak peaks, contests and more…

Like our page on Facebook:
Lock Down Publications

Join Lock Down Publications/The New Era Reading Group

Visit our website:
www.lockdownpublications.com

Follow us on Instagram:
Lock Down Publications

Email Us: We want to hear from you!

Prologue

Aug. 26th

"Imani, ease back a lil' bit. We don't wanna fuck up this lick," growled Diesel from the passenger seat of a black-on-black Dodge Challenge SRT Hellcat. With a roll of her eyes, Imani slowed just a little to allow the BMW 750iL they were following to open the distance another two car lengths.

As she adjusted her speed, the butterflies in her stomach kicked up another notch or two. Still, Diesel didn't seem to notice as he slapped the thirty-round, hollow-point-filled magazine into his fully automatic MP-5 submachine gun sitting in his lap.

Imani was accustomed to the adrenaline buildup when it came time to put in work, and being eight and a half months pregnant wasn't enough to affect her driving skills. The two were iconic street legends, known for pulling off nearly impossible armed robberies on anybody out there that was doing too much. They lived by a couple of simple rules.

Rule one: anybody could get it, no matter who they were down with. His second was never to rob anyone of an insignificant amount of money because anything worth living for was worth dying for, so getting rich was first and foremost. The ski mask was their way, even though he never wore one. It wasn't needed when you left no one alive to testify against you.

Two left turns later, the BMW pulled to a stop at a red light with only one car separating them from their next big come-up.

It was exactly what Diesel had been waiting for. He quickly leaned over and gave Imani a kiss while placing a hand on her bulging belly. "Mad love, lil' man. This is for you as much as it is for us."

With that being said, Diesel yanked back the bolt on the MP5, loading a round into the chamber before exiting the car. Diesel kept the small machine gun held low behind his thigh as he approached the luxury sedan from the rear passenger side while keeping his eyes on the driver.

Just as Diesel raised his weapon to fire, he made eye contact with the driver in the rearview mirror. The seconds of shocked hesitation were enough to cost the driver slash bagman his life, as he was a fraction slower to react than Diesel was to squeeze the trigger.

The MP5 spit fire and 9mm hollow-point death, punching rounds through the rear window and into the driver's body, causing the expensive sedan to roll slowly into the intersection.

Diesel moved to his right while releasing another long stream of bullets that stitched the entire passenger side of the once pristine vehicle. When there was no more movement in the Beemer, Diesel then turned his weapon on the white Honda CR-V that happened to be the unlucky car in the wrong place at the wrong time. A short burst sprayed the elderly white woman driving the small SUV.

Diesel then made his way back to the BMW and snatched open the passenger door of the car, which revealed a scene straight from a John Woo movie. The driver's bullet-riddled body lay slumped against the driver's side door, with bits of brain, hair, and skull on the steering wheel. Blood and gore covered the dashboard, but Diesel cared about none of it.

He only wanted the briefcase on the passenger seat. No sooner had he fallen into the car seat with his prize, Diesel was penned to it as Imani stomped the gas pedal to the floor. The supercharged 6.2-liter Hellcat became a savage beast released from its cage when Imani spun the wheel, making the powerful sports car fishtail around the ruined Honda CR-V.

Taking them east of Tryon Street, Diesel tossed the briefcase in the back seat, then removed the spent magazine from his weapon and replaced it with a full one, slapping it into the MP5.

He was forced to grab the oh-shit bar as Imani pulled off some *Fast and Furious: Tokyo Drift* type shit around the next corner, cutting off a city transit bus. The sleek car ate up the roadway.

There was a look of determination on Imani's face as she whipped in and out of traffic, but that look on her face was enough to keep him quiet while she did her thing behind the wheel. There was no one he trusted more in life or behind the wheel than his ride or die chick, his street queen, his wife.

Five blocks later, Imani pulled into a parking lot beside Walmart, where they had stashed their second, less obvious vehicle. CTS-V married power and class in a package, almost as strong as the Hellcat, but more importantly, looked nothing like the Dodge Challenger the police were sure to have a solid description of by now.

While Imani took the briefcase and MP5 to the Caddie, Diesel used a window cleaner bottle filled with a mixture of baby oil, WD-40, and motor oil to spray down any and every surface of the Challenger that could retain a fingerprint.

It was an old trick used by car thieves. The baby oil mixture wouldn't allow the police forensic technicians to pull a usable print. He then removed a bag with his cut clippings from several barber shops and salons around the city and shook out the contents of the bag all over the interior of the Challenger. As Diesel walked away from the Challenger, he wished he could walk away from that lifestyle as easily, but he knew he never would.

Six days had passed since the robbery, and Imani was more than ready to be gone, but she knew Diesel was right about laying low until word of mouth was a whole hell of a lot more dangerous than being caught by the police. The person they'd stolen from was truly a man to be feared, and not even the police could protect them if he found them, so there they sat in a shabby, run-down motel room on the west side.

Imani was almost at the breaking point with the smell of piss and stale cigarette smoke when Diesel finally said they could leave. Diesel took point on the way to the car, and all was quiet. Nothing seemed to be out of the ordinary, and that bothered him most. There wasn't a lot of movement at street level, but that was one of the reasons he'd picked this little out-of-the-way motel, yet he felt he was missing something, something important.

The old drunk stumbling down the street away from them didn't raise his suspicion, so what was it?

"What's wrong, babe?" asked Imani, rolling down the window and also breaking his concentration, but one more look around revealed no threats.

It wasn't until he began to get into the driver's seat that his brain finally registered what his gut had warned him of, but his eyes had overlooked it.

Wait. Where were the prostitutes and all the homeless souls who always seemed to show up as soon as anyone hit the block?

"Get down!" Diesel yelled as the first gunshots rang out, slamming heavy lead slugs into the car. Imani quickly ducked down across the front seat, using her arms to cover her head. Diesel drew a bead on the first person to emerge from the alley across the street.

Using the open door for cover, Diesel sprayed his oncoming attacker and began firing in all directions as more and more gunmen came from everywhere. Diesel had been through way too much gunplay in his life not to know he couldn't win this, but he had to give Imani and his unborn son a chance to survive, knowing he wouldn't.

"Imani, open the briefcase, and tuck the diamonds and flash drive into your bra. Keep your head down and get behind the wheel!" he shouted over the gunfire and bullets striking the car.

Imani opened the briefcase to do as Diesel said, but then a stray bullet hit the lid of the case, sending diamonds everywhere, mixing them with the broken glass, so she grabbed the flash drive and shoved it into her bra.

The engine growled to life. "Come on, babe! Let's go!"

"I can't come with y'all, but I'll cover for you 'til you and lil' man get clear!" Diesel replied.

"No! Get in the car! I'm not leaving you!" Imani screamed at him as tears streamed down her face just as two slugs found a new home in Diesel's flesh.

One last look passed between them said more than a thousand words ever could. Diesel pushed himself to his feet and stepped away from the car door, firing wildly to draw all the return fire upon himself while allowing Imani the chance to escape.

With her whole heart breaking, Imani snatched the Caddie in drive and stomped on the gas, leaving Diesel standing in the street, firing, as she made her getaway. Imani took a hard right at the end of the block and was clear of the trap.

The bloody smile on Diesel's face may have been mistaken for a grimace of pain as he was shot repeatedly, but truth be told, it was pure happiness he felt, knowing his wife and unborn child would live. Diesel was still on his feet when the MP5's chamber cycled on empty. It was only the adrenaline pulsing through his system that kept the pain at bay. It wasn't until a bullet shattered his left leg that he finally fell to his knees, bringing the gunfire to a halt.

Men stood in a loose circle around him, guns still smoking, just outside the growing pool of blood. The two men in front of him stepped aside to allow a tall man he'd never seen to enter his line of sight.

In this man, Diesel recognized the same killer instinct that dwelt within his own heart. Diesel's smile widened because he knew Imani had escaped this ruthless killer.

As if reading Diesel's mind, his killer spoke.

"I know why you smile. It's because you think that you have saved them, but please let me assure you that your wife and unborn child will soon follow you into the afterlife."

Diesel spat a mouthful of blood onto the man's chest, unable to reach his face while on his knees. As his killer raised the gun that would take his life, Diesel looked straight on into the barrel. It took a few seconds for his mind to process what he was hearing.

It wasn't the expected boom of a gunshot, but the deep roar of an engine at high speed and the impact of bodies coming into contact with metal. Imani knew she should have kept going like Diesel had told her to do, but she just couldn't live with the feeling she'd abandoned him.

Their wedding vows spoke of 'til death do they part, and Imani had meant that shit then, and still did, so she'd turned around, hoping against all hope that maybe Diesel had found some way to make it through yet again. But as she fled from them, all her hopes were dashed at the sight of Diesel on his knees, looking down the barrel of a gun.

Imani knew that she couldn't save him, but she would send as many of them to hell with him as she could. The Caddie's response was immediate as Imani mashed the gas, launching the car from zero to sixty in 4.6 seconds and plowing through the men before they could react.

The powerful car sent men flying through the air as Imani sped through their ranks. She was more than a little pissed as the man pointing his gun at Diesel jumped to safety. In passing, Imani locked eyes with Diesel as the car flew by, watching as the light began to fade from his eyes.

Even at that terrible moment of her life, she was glad he was able to see she'd not completely abandoned him. After jumping from the path of the speeding car, Cerrano drew a bead on the rear window and began firing shots, hoping to score a lucky headshot at the driver.

Cerrano thought he'd done just that as the speeding car suddenly swiped two parked cars on the right side of the street, but the driver regained control in time enough to swing around the next corner and out of sight. He didn't mind so much, because he loved the chase almost as much as the kill.

Four blocks south of the shootout, Imani struggled to concentrate as every beat of her heart sent a wave of pain throughout her body. As bad as the physical pain was, it couldn't hold a candle in comparison to the mental anguish and sorrow she felt at losing Diesel, the love of her life; it was tenfold, and thoughts of their unborn son weighed heavily on her heart and mind as she passed out behind the wheel of the speeding Cadillac.

"Paging Doctor Mirren. Paging Doctor Mirren to the E.R."

"Lisa, what've we got here?" asked Doctor Mirren as she rushed step for step beside the stretcher. "Black female, early twenties with late-term pregnancy, suffering from a single GSW, a collapsed right lung, broken left wrist, and multiple contusions. Her B/P is 120 over 60 and falling fast."

Doctor Mirren shone a small penlight into each eye of the unconscious woman. "She's showing signs of anaphylactic shock, and we're at risk of losing them both. This baby's under a lot of duress and has to come out!"

"Operation Bay Five is ready. Take her there and tell the nurses to prepare for an emergency C-section!" Doctor Mirren called over her shoulder while rushing into the scrub room. Hours later, Erica Bates stood at the glass window of the newborn nursery of the maternity ward, looking at the small newborn wrapped in a light-blue blanket.

She didn't even notice when the lady from childcare services and Doctor Mirren stepped up to the window beside her.

"Excuse me, Mrs. Bates. I'm Ronda Lazoe with the Department of Social Services, and this is Doctor Holly Mirren. We're sorry for your loss." Ronda finished softly. "I see that you've been given your daughter's personal effects and belongings, and I know this is a bit soon, but by being his only family, I'd like to have you sign some papers of guardianship and..."

"No." The single word caught the other two women off guard.

"I want nothing to do with him," Mrs. Bates said, wiping a tear from her cheek.

"Mrs. Bates, you can't mean that. You owe it to your daughter and grandson to be there. If there's a problem of money, I'm—"

"I said no!" Mrs. Bates cut in rudely over the other woman.

"I owe her, him, or them nothing," said Imani's mother. "My daughter made her own choices, and we weren't close. She chose to run the streets with that thug. Then she married him against my wishes. She allowed him to ruin her life, and I refuse to let this child, who looks so much like his father, ruin mine. Put him in the system for all I care!" She then turned and walked away, but stopped after a few steps, and turned back, giving the two shocked women hope that she'd changed her mind.

"Imani once told me if she had a son, she'd name him Epic. Epic Anders. That was her wish, and now, I owe her nothing." With that said, she turned, walked away, and never looked back.

Chapter 1

Twenty Years Later…

"You like that, baby?" Kendra asked as she ran her tongue down the length of Epic's hard penis.

"Damn, shorty. You know I do." A very happy Epic moaned. Kendra bobbed her head while pumping his dick at the same time. Epic grabbed the back of her head while pushing his hips off the bed to feed her more of his meat stick. She knew exactly what he wanted and took his entire throbbing rod into her mouth, allowing more than half of it to slide deep into her throat without choking while gently squeezing his balls.

Epic couldn't take much more of the way Kendra was devouring his pole. "I swear, Kendra, yo' head game is the best thang going. It's the fuck off the chain. If you keep puttin' it down like this, you gon' make a nigga wife yo' fine ass."

Kendra rolled her eyes, knowing a nigga would say whatever when he had his dick in someone's mouth. Still, she added more suction on the very sensitive head of his dick, readying herself to swallow all he had to give. Kendra didn't even mind that she wasn't Epic's main chick, but she was willing to play the game as long as he kept giving her that paper. Epic kept that paper, fly ass whips, and hot gear with expensive ice.

Kendra was more than wet and wanted to feel his thick dick deep inside her, but his damn phone started to play 'Dirty Money' by Rude Bwoy, which meant that was the end of this fuck session for her. She'd learned early in the game, when fucking with Epic, if his phone played two specific songs, no matter if he was balls deep in her, he'd stop to answer.

One ring tone was 'Dirty Money', the other was 'Love of My Life', and she hated the fuck out of both songs now.

Shit, she even knew who each ringtone was for. 'Dirty Money' was assigned to his best friend and right-hand man, Payne, while 'Love of My Life' was for his main bitch away at school. If she only knew how he got down behind her back, that bitch would change that ringtone to 'A Nigga Ain't Shit' by Keke Boyd.

The thought made her smile.

Epic answered his phone with his signature tag line.

"Yo, what it do, my nigga?"

Kendra rolled over to the other side of the bed, reaching for the blunt of OG Kush in the ashtray on the nightstand. The session might've been over with Epic, but just like she wasn't his main chick, he wasn't her main dick, and as soon as he left, she would be calling her main thing to finish what Epic had started.

Kendra fired up the blunt, filling her lungs with the high-powered weed as Epic finished his call with Payne. After a long sigh, Epic told her what she already knew.

"Aye, check it. I gotta dip out to take care of some biz with Payne. I'll hit you up later if I can find the time, right?" he asked, giving her a playful smack on the ass before getting up to get dressed. She watched as he pulled on his Tommy boxers and a pair of True Religion jeans, a crisp wife-beater, and two platinum chains.

He looked back over his shoulder while stuffing his feet into Burberry Timbs. "You good, or do you need something?" Epic knew damn well that greedy ass Kendra would never keep it real, but he continued to test her just to see if she'd surprise him one day and say no. Just like the thirsty thot she'd always been, she asked for a band.

Epic didn't even blink. He just peeled off ten hundred-dollar bills and left them on the dresser after tucking his Glock 40 Cal in the small of his back.

"Act like a ho, get treated like a ho," he said, leaving the room.

Payne sat front and center stage in his second home, waiting for Epic to arrive.

Exotic Toyz wasn't just his second home; it was the place he and Epic had met two years earlier while he was checking for the bad ass redbone stripping there, and Epic had been dropping off some work for the girls there. It was still somewhat shocking to him that the two were even friends, let alone business partners, Yin and Yang from top to bottom.

For one, Payne Nevins came from money and the easy life—a two-parent home, a loving family, and the best education money could buy. But like a moth to the flame, he was drawn to the streets and the *Thug Life*, as Tupac called it. If he was Yin and the light, real darkness, a true street nigga through and through. Raised in the system until fifteen years old, he ran away from a state home to get his money in the streets by any means necessary.

Although they'd become as close as brothers, they could never pass for brothers. Payne was five feet eight, 155 pounds, and dark skinned with a shaved head, not because he couldn't grow a full head of hair, but because he felt like it made him look more street tough.

He'd been the target of bullies in high school and the bugga boo of any girl that looked his way. Shit, he'd even had to pay Kelly Smith to go to prom with him, but that had been the moment he'd learned no matter what somebody looked like, if money was involved, so were the bitches.

Epic, on the other hand, had bitches way before he ever had a dime in his pockets. No matter what it was called—game, swag, mojo, or what-the-fuck-ever—Epic had been born with it.

He was light-skinned, six-two with a naturally muscular build, light-green eyes, and a low cut with enough waves to make a seagull sick. What gave him the edge over so many others was what life had given him, and that was his *I don't give a fuck* attitude. Life or death, to Epic, was just some more bullshit life threw at him.

Payne glanced back over his shoulder as Epic entered the club like a black Adonis, and every woman inside with a heartbeat noticed his arrival.

The black lights on his skin made it seem like he was glowing, while the flashing strobe lights brought every diamond he wore to life.

"What it do, my nigga?" asked Epic by way of greeting as he slid into the seat next to Payne. Payne nodded toward the stage by way of answer as Candy, his favorite dancer at Exotic Toyz, was pussy popping on a handstand with the brass pole between her oiled ass cheeks.

"Damn, bro. You still dropping on that?"

Smiling, Payne pulled out a wad of bills, peeled off two big-face hundreds, and placed them on the stage in front of him. Candy worked her way over, rolling her hips while sucking on a red charms pop. Once in front of Payne, Candy spun, dropped into a full split, and leaned forward, making her ass clap to the beat.

"Look, dog. Don't make it sound like I'm just trying to fuck, 'cause it ain't like that. I bless her with paper because I believe in supporting single mothers," Payne replied with a straight face.

"Nigga, please. So those luscious lips, phat titties, juicy camel toe, and fuck-me eyes have nothing to do with it, huh?" asked Epic, smirking at Payne.

"Fuck yeah. I didn't say I support ugly, single mothers, just SMILTF."

Epic shook his head. "What the hell is SMILTF?'

"A SMILTF is a *single mother I'd like to fuck*, or should I say I'd love to fuck? It works either way."

15

"You got it bad, my dude, but I know you didn't hit me up just so I could watch you chase your pussy unicorn," said Epic, sipping his Grey Goose.

"Nah, never that, but a lil' eye candy never hurt."

"Then what it do?"

Payne started the same way he always did. "You trying to get paid, my nigga?" He knew full well what the answer would be.

"Only if it's lucrative," replied Epic.

"Ain't it always? Shit, I know you don't go in for petty change, seeing as how Kendra be tappin' your pockets and the cost of Asimi's tuition. We both know Yale Law School ain't cheap. Combine that with keeping yourself in the lap of luxury, you gotta stay on the grind." Payne finished while slipping another two hundred dollars from his ho fund.

Epic didn't want to criticize Payne, but he couldn't understand dumping money on a bitch you hadn't even put dick to yet. That was definitely not the mentality they shared. However, Epic had to admit that Candy was a bad ass bitch.

He listened as Payne laid it all out to him, completely ignoring the strippers who tended to gravitate around him. Payne's info was basic, at best, and his plan was less than ingenious, but if the money and merchandise were what they were supposed to be, then it would be a hell of a come-up. The best part was that it wasn't a law-abiding citizen, not that Epic really gave a fuck, but the cops worked much harder to solve those kinds of cases.

Chapter 2

Nyeama sat in the passenger seat of Kyrie's brand-new, cocaine-white Infiniti Q50, loving the feel of the soft leather on her skin. She was really trying not to be impatient while Kyrie was inside, taking care of business, but she was hungry and bored.

Nyeama was just leaning over to blow the horn when the front door opened, and Kyrie came out, carrying a black duffel bag.

As soon as he opened the driver's side door, she started in on him. "Took your sweet ass time, didn't you." It wasn't a question, but a statement.

With a deep sigh, Kyrie slid behind the wheel unapologetically. He said, "Nyeama, why do you insist on coming with me to handle business when you know that you can't come inside? I've told you a hundred times I won't rush counting my money, so quit trippin', or either stay home."

Nyeama rolled her neck with pure attitude. "First off, correct me if I'm wrong, but it was you talking about having a real ride or die bitch, so don't sit there, acting like you're not the one whining when I don't feel like rolling with you on every lick you make," she said heatedly.

"I can always drop your ass off at the crib and see you when I see you, but best believe that won't be until I'm ready."

"Boy, stop. We Bonnie and Clyde, so kill the tough guy act, and let's get something to eat."

"I got all the A-1 choice beef you can eat right here." Kyrie smiled while grabbing himself.

Nyeama returned the smile with a devilish look. "The way I feel about you right now, I can promise you, you don't wanna put that in my mouth."

Kyrie put the Q50 in drive, headed for his last stop of the night, and he really didn't give a damn if Nyeama wanted to eat right now. She'd just have to wait.

By the time he pulled up behind the side pocket pool hall, Nyeama was giving him the full silent treatment while staring out the passenger side window.

"You want me to grab you an order of hot wings?"

"Do I look like I want some greasy ass, three-day-old wings from a damn trap spot fronting as a pool hall? Fuck you, Ky. You eat 'em."

Kyrie pulled the duffel from the back seat and got out after checking both sides and the rearview mirror. Inside, J.D. led him into the back office and locked the door. One good look told him all.

"You and Nyeama fight again?"

"You already know," said a frustrated Kyrie. "If she was just a side chick, her ass would have been gone," he added, placing bricks of coke on J.D.'s desk. While JD placed twelve stacks of hundred-dollar bills beside the bag for Kyrie, he counted out another five thousand dollars beside it.

Kyrie didn't insult him by asking if it was all there. JD had never come short in the five years they'd been doing business together. Instead, Kyrie put the 125 bands inside the bag and zipped it closed, bringing the total in the bag to over three hundred thousand dollars.

On the way out, he stopped at the bar and ordered a dozen hot wings and a beer while he waited for the order.

As he sipped his beer and waited, he decided that if Nyeama started again, he was putting her ass on dick restriction for a week. That didn't mean he wouldn't be tapping some other ass. Kyrie eyed the semi-dark parking lot as he approached his Infiniti, giving a slight glance at Nyeama in the passenger seat.

He put the strap of the duffel bag over his left shoulder so he could carry the hot wings in his left hand, keeping his right hand free and close to the Smith & Wesson 9mm tucked into his waistband.

Kyrie pulled on the door handle, but his door didn't open, so he gave it two more pulls before he noticed it was locked. "Nyeama, what the fuck is wrong with you? Unlock the damn door!" he yelled.

Nyeama turned to look at him and then flipped him the bird. "Next time, you'll take the keys with you," she snarled at him.

"Nyeama, I swear, you pushing this shit too far, and I'm not in the mood to play with yo' childish ass right now, so open the fuckin' door!"

She didn't open the door. Instead, she hit the power window button, rolling the driver's side window down a small crack. Kyrie thought about punching the window out and whooping Nyeama's ass, but he'd been raised by a single mother, one who had taught him that a man should never put his hands on a woman in anger—even if she did need an ass whooping. Kyrie knew if he had to beat her, he didn't need her, and he was truly feeling like he didn't need her right then.

So caught up in his argument with Nyeama, Kyrie didn't notice that someone had crept up behind him until the cold, steel barrel of a gun was pressed to the back of his head. Instinctively, Kyrie wanted to look back, but the added pressure of the gun made him stay still.

Nyeama hadn't realized what was going down yet and kept cursing his ass out about bringing her some bullshit ass hot wings. It wasn't until Kyrie didn't respond that she looked over at him, noticing the tall, light-skinned man standing behind him.

"Who da fuck is this nigga?" she started before she saw the gun against Kyrie's head.

"Bitch, shut the fuck up before this shit goes from a robbery to a homicide!" Epic growled.

Nyeama's mind froze. She didn't know what to do as she watched the man with a gun to Kyrie's head, but it was only a split second before she came up with a plan.

Maybe, just maybe, she could distract the gunman enough for Kyrie to pull his gun, allowing her a chance to reach the .380 that Kyrie had given her, which she kept inside the armrest between the seats.

"Ease the bag over your head and off your shoulder, nigga, and this ain't TV, so don't try any dumb ass shit unless you're willing to die for this shit, 'cause I'm willing to kill for it!" said Epic with bass in his voice.

As Kyrie slowly took the strap over his head and shoulder, Nyeama slid her hand toward the armrest. Epic let the duffel bag drop to the ground without looking down at it.

Nyeama started with her distraction. "Why the fuck you trying to jack us? You a grimy ass nigga, a nigga wit' no hustle, a bitch ass coward!" As Nyeama finished her rant, Kyrie dropped the hot wings and used both hands to push off the side of the Q50 and back into Epic.

At the same time, Nyeama made a quick grab for the .380, determined to be a real ride or die chick. The only warning Epic had was a small hesitation by Kyrie, but it was enough to allow him to sidestep quickly as Kyrie pushed back.

The sidestep made two things possible. The first was that it cleared his field of vision enough to see Nyeama bringing up a chrome .380, and the second was that it gave nothing for Kyrie to ram into, therefore causing him to lose his balance and trip over the bag on the ground.

Epic pulled the trigger without a second thought, causing the driver's side window to explode as the heavy .40 Caliber slug blew through it and Nyeama's skull.

He quickly turned the gun on Kyrie lying on the ground, but the boom of his shot had galvanized him into immobility. He didn't even try for the gun in his waistband. His only thoughts were of Nyeama, and anger overrode common sense as he glared at Epic. "You killed my girl, you punk muthafucka. You a dead man."

Epic shrugged and put two rounds in his head, sending blood, brain matter, and fragments of skull across the parking lot. "We all gotta die sometime," he said while scooping up the bag and running for the fence he'd climbed to enter the parking lot.

He felt no remorse as he drove away into the night, because there was one thing he knew for sure, and that was whenever it came down to him or them, it would be them, not him, that died.

Chapter 3

Asimi hurriedly packed away her criminal law books along with her laptop, rushing from her last class that afternoon. She had twenty minutes to get back to her off-campus condo before Epic would be hitting her up for their regular Friday afternoon FaceTime.

She didn't even notice that every guy she passed stopped to look at her with lustful eyes. Many of them thought of her as stuck-up or snobby because she'd turned down their many attempts at dating her. Guys and girls had both tried to woo the beautiful twenty-four-year-old, with no success whatsoever.

The daughter of a Puerto Rican father and a Chinese mother, Asimi's features, for lack of a better word, were flawless. She had long, flowing, black hair with almond-shaped eyes, a light caramel complexion, and a body straight out of a *Go Viral* Magazine. She'd been blessed with an ass Blahgigi would envy, but her drive and determination were what first attracted Epic's attention.

She was in line, close to the door at Club Insatiable, with two of her girlfriends arguing with one of the bouncers from inside the club.

"I paid my money to get in, just like everyone else! I didn't pay to have lame ass guys groping me all night, so when I slapped the shit outta one, you gone put *me* out?"

The bouncer just stood there with his arms folded over his chest, like what she said didn't register with him at all.

She tried again. "Look. What if I had been your sister, out trying to have some fun, and some drunk ass dude started feeling her up, huh? Would you care then?"

Epic watched the drama play out when he decided to step in on her behalf. "What it do, Tank?" asked Epic, giving the bouncer dap.

"It is what it is," Tank answered, not taking his eyes off the angry young woman in front of him.

Epic then pulled out his wad of cash and removed two crisp hundred-dollar bills to give to Tank. "Check it, bro. These ladies are my guests tonight. You feel me?"

Tank looked at the bills in his hand, then back at the women. "Enjoy the rest of your night ladies," he said.

Epic turned and went into the club without a backward glance. By the time Asimi and her two friends reentered, he was nowhere to be found, although she'd checked the dance floor and the bar. She at least wanted to thank him for stepping in when he didn't have to. She was still looking around for him when the same drunk asshole she'd had to smack stepped in front of her.

"What's up, baby?" he slurred at her.

Asimi took a step back from his bad breath to get him out of her personal space. She watched as his face distorted in anger. "Bitch, you act like yo' shit don't stank, but I'ma teach your ass a lesson!" he yelled in her face while drawing back a closed fist to punch her in the face.

Asimi was in such shock that she just stood there and would have been knocked out if not for someone grabbing hold of the incoming blow right before it made contact with her left eye. The next thing she knew, the same guy she'd been looking for had punched her attacker twice in the face, laying him out cold on the edge of the dance floor.

"Are you a'ight?" he asked, and all she could do was nod. He led her and her friends to the VIP section and ordered drinks. After her first sip, he introduced himself. "Hi, I'm Epic."

23

Before she knew what she was saying, she blurted out, "Is that your hero name when you come to the rescue?"

"Nah, it's my real name," he said with a laugh.

"Oh." She then introduced her two friends. "This is Brittany and Olivia, and I'm Asimi. Thank you for saving me from that piece of shit out there and for getting us back into the club."

"Don't sweat it. I was convinced by your argument out front. You should be a lawyer," he said.

"I am. Well, not yet, but I'm in law school right now."

They'd spent the rest of that night talking and getting to know each other, and she couldn't believe he was only eighteen years old. She even made him show her his ID, and damn if his real name wasn't Epic. He was more mature than half the guys she'd dated her own age. It had been two years, and there were two loves of her life—Epic and the law, in that order.

Asimi jogged up the stairs. She set up her laptop and checked the time while pouring herself a glass of white wine. She'd just sat back when the FaceTime request icon popped up in the corner of her screen.

Just seeing his face made her heart race, and the sound of his voice sent a heatwave through her entire body.

"What it do, baby girl?"

She'd long ago become accustomed to his street slang greeting and had come to anticipate it, as was her normal answer.

"Missing you, as always," she replied.

"Say it again, baby girl, 'cause I love it when you say you missing me, but I'm missing you more," said Epic softly, showing his tender side that he only exposed to her.

"I miss you so much and wish you were here right now so I could show you how much."

Epic knew what this was leading up to and was ready to play. "It sounds like you need some computer love."

"Boy, I need some real love, but computer sexing will have to do until I can get the real thing." Asimi giggled.

"So, if I were there, what would you do to me?" he asked. "Be specific, please."

She started. "First, I'd kiss you slowly, deeply, to show you how much I truly miss you. Then I would run my hands over your muscular chest while nibbling your ear and telling you how bad I want you inside of me. Tender kisses on your neck to make you nice and hard before I dropped to my knees to unbutton your jeans, so that I could pull—"

A ding-dong interrupted her.

"Damn, is that your doorbell?" questioned Epic.

"I'm not going to answer. I'm not about to ruin my freak-nasty mood."

The doorbell sounded again.

"Yo, who da fuck is ringing your doorbell like that? If it's some other nigga you got on the side, I'ma drive to New Haven tonight and catch a body!" Epic growled.

"Boy, stop. Don't even question my love or loyalty," Asimi popped back with attitude.

The doorbell rang again.

"Hold on, bae. I'll be right back after I'm done cussing somebody's ass out."

"Do I need to come set it off at Yale and deal with some wannabe stalker?" Epic yelled as Asimi left his view to answer the door.

Asimi was in flip mode as she went to the door. She didn't give a damn who it was. She was about to blank on them. Asimi snatched the door open. "Why the hell are you ringing my—" The rest of her words turned into a deafening scream.

"Surprise!" Epic barely got the words out before Asimi jumped into his open arms, almost making him drop his laptop. Asimi couldn't believe it. He was there! Epic had come to surprise her at school, and damn, his physique was even better than she remembered.

Epic carried Asimi back inside the condo from the front stoop, her raining kisses all over his face, her arms and legs wrapped tightly around him.

"I was in the neighborhood and thought I'd stop by to see my baby," Epic lied smoothly.

Asimi knew it wasn't the truth but didn't care. Her man was there, and damn the internet sex. She was about to get the real thing.

Epic kissed Asimi deeply, trying to convey every emotion he couldn't describe with words in that kiss. "I love you, Simi, more than life itself."

Asimi gazed into Epic's eyes and knew every word he'd spoken was true.

Epic stepped back after slowly undressing Asimi down to the matching Victoria's Secret bra and thong. The light-blue silk with white lace made her skin seem to glow. He shook his head in disbelief. "If God ever made anything more beautiful, he kept it for himself."

"Don't bring God into this. I'm planning on being so bad right now." Asimi smiled while running her hands down her inner thigh.

Epic removed the rest of his clothes, allowing Asimi to feast her eyes on every inch of him as she lay back on the bed.

He went down on his knees between her spread legs and breathed deeply, taking in her feminine scent as he ran his tongue from her inner thigh to place a soft kiss on her silk-covered lower lips. She moaned as he slid the silk panties down the length of her toned legs, his tongue driving all thoughts from her mind as he used it to circle and tease her clitoris.

Asimi raised both legs and placed them on Epic's strong shoulders to grant his tongue deeper access to her velvet tunnel. She could feel the waves of her first climax building deep within her core, and each time the tip of his tongue flicked across her clit, she drew closer to the edge.

While still going down on her, Epic reached both hands up to push the silky material away from her perfect breasts, exposing her sensitive nipples to the chilled air of the room. His thumbs played over her tight, budded peaks. The thrust of his tongue inside her made Asimi arch her back and explode through her first orgasm, but he didn't stop there. He continued to suck, nibble, and slurp, working to bring her to another orgasm. It was yet another thing she loved about Epic. He didn't just eat and run; he made love to the kitty.

As she came on his face a second time, he began to kiss way up her body, sucking first one nipple then the other, but before he could do more, Asimi reached down between them to grab his hard, throbbing dick. She could feel the pearly white drop of precum on the fleshy head of his meat steel rod. As bad as she wanted it inside her, Asimi wanted to taste it more.

She loved the vulnerability only she could draw from him and rarely failed to have him moaning her name when she applied herself to the task. Asimi took hold of him possessively, stroking him slowly while confidently swirling her tongue around the head of his enlarged penis. The beauty and perfection of it motivated her to take it deep into her mouth.

Epic hissed as she raked her teeth lightly up his shaft before nibbling the sensitive head, bringing him close to ejaculation. Asimi followed this up with some serious suction, knowing he was close, but would not stop. She'd had too many fantasies of making him tap out.

She stood while still stroking his saliva-covered dick, and with one swift move, sat down on his skyward pointing rod, sinking it balls deep in her wet, hot tunnel.

Their orgasms were animalistic in nature as they both cried out with deserved pleasure. Asimi started to rock back and forth on his still hard dick, using the mixture of their combined juices as a super lubricant. She rose to the top of him before slamming back down to his lap, taking every hard inch of him excruciatingly deep, so deep that the pain it caused even gave her pleasure.

She allowed herself to be rolled onto her back so that he could plunge deeper, and she surrendered to each stroke and thrust. Epic kissed her through the next wave of her climax as she shook with the intensity of her release. Her recognition that he was reaching his second orgasm had her wrapping her legs around his waist and clenching her pussy walls to tighten even more on his thick rod.

With one last, deep thrust, Epic exploded in her depths, panting and sweat-covered. The two smiled in mutual satisfaction as they drifted off to sleep. Epic woke to the smell of bacon, eggs, grits, and a side of toast with strawberry jam that sat on a bed serving tray. The breakfast looked great, but not as great as Asimi in a double XL Yale T-shirt and nothing else.

"Morning, babe. I figured you'd need to fuel up after you put it down like that last night," said a smiling Asimi.

She took a crisp strip of bacon off the plate to feed him as he lay back on the pillows. "Damn, if I knew you would spoil me like this, I'd come up here every weekend—for the food that is," he finished jokingly, lifting the front of her shirt to peek at the freshly waxed kitty kat.

"You keep that up, and you won't be getting any more of this," she returned, patting her smooth mound.

"A'ight, peace, and since you spoiled me last night and this morning, I guess I'll spoil you by taking you shopping and to dinner."

Asimi's eyes lit up at the thought of shopping and dinner with Epic. Maybe, just maybe, seeing her out with her man would put some of the rumors around campus to rest.

Another surprise Epic had waiting for Asimi was the Brandywine-colored Bentley Continental GT with a pearl-white leather interior—classy, not flashy.

Asimi loved the car at first sight and knew better than to ask if he could afford it because one thing she'd learned was

28

her man didn't believe in the 'fake it 'til you make it' frame of mind.

Epic explained that he'd traded in his year-old BMW 7 series and a good bit of cash for his new whip because there was no way he was flossing around Yale with the baddest bitch in town, pushing an everyday BMW.

Southgate Mall held every up-to-date store and all the more expensive, over-the-top shops. Those were the only ones Asimi loved to shop in—Gucci, Prada, Fendi, Coach, and more. Epic knew he'd be dropping at least thirty bands in the Chanel store, but when it came to Asimi, money wasn't a thing.

Asimi was treated like a queen by the saleswoman in the Chanel store. She was sure to get a large commission or bonus on such a large sale. Unlike most men, Epic didn't mind going store to store and waiting while Asimi tried on every outfit in the place. The fact that she never had to look at price tags made every woman in the store sweat Epic.

The next store they hit was more for him than it was for her. Even though she loved the way Victoria's Secret silk underwear felt on her skin, she loved even more the way it drove Epic crazy.

Epic sat in the waiting area as Asimi went into the dressing room with ten sets of bras and panties, plus six or seven see-through camisoles, and some very sexy bootie shorts for sleeping. He'd only been sitting there a few seconds when the tall blonde working the sales floor walked by, headed toward the dressing rooms, giving him a mischievous look that said she was ready to more than misbehave.

He watched as she stepped into the back dressing room, leaving the door open so he could see her in the full-length mirror. He locked eyes with her reflection in the mirror as she dropped her skirt to the floor and stepped out of it, and his dick jumped in his suddenly too-tight jeans. Her top and blazer followed the skirt as she slowly popped the front clasp on her bra, freeing two perfectly pink-tipped, firm, tan-lined titties.

Epic's dick was so hard that he could feel his heartbeat in his enlarged bell head. She licked her lips as she sat back on the dressing room bench and spread her long, tan legs wide. Epic checked over his left shoulder to make sure no one else was wise to what was going down. When he saw the coast was clear, he returned to his dressing room peep show. The beautiful, blonde Barbie had one leg cocked up on the other bench with her thongs pulled to the side, two fingers sunk deep into her clean-shaven pussy.

Epic damn near came in his Tommy boxers as she took the two wet fingers from her dripping pink slot and put them in her mouth. She bit down on her bottom lip as she made circular motions on her sensitive clit. He imagined sinking his thick, black dick deep in her sweet, tight pussy. Just the thought of those shaved, white pussy lips glistening wet around his chocolate root had precum leaking from his tip.

She stood and started to dress, the door still open, while he watched, never breaking eye contact with him.

Epic stood as the blonde came out of the dressing room, walking past him with a wink when she saw the huge dick print in his jeans. He was about to say something to her when Asimi's dressing room opened, and Asimi came out with an arm filled with some of Vicky's best secrets.

"Sorry it took so long." Asimi smiled, stopping long enough to give him a peck on the cheek as she headed for the register and the same Barbie from the peep show.

"Are you ready to check out?" asked Barbie in a sweet-as-sugar tone of voice, smiling at Asimi and paying him no mind whatsoever.

"Kinda," said Asimi, placing all of the items on the countertop by the register.

"I can't decide which ones to get. I like them all." Asimi gushed, looking at a silk, white bra and thong set.

"Which ones do you like most, bae?" asked Asimi.

Epic looked down at all the sexy underwear and noticed a black garter belt and ran his hand over it. He cut his eyes to see a small smile play across Barbie's face. Epic smirked as he told her, "I like them all, especially this." He held up the black, lacey garter belt. "I want you to get this also in white."

"Okay, bae. I'll be right back." She was only a few steps away when Barbie picked up Epic's iPhone X and tapped it to hers, transferring her number to his without saying a word—just another sexy wink, which stiffened up his dick again.

Asimi came back with not only the white garter belt, but also a blue and red one.

"Which one do you like best of all, bae?"

"On you, I'll like them all, so get them all," he said.

Barbie finished scanning the last items, then hit the total button, watching to see if Epic would flinch when he saw the total amount of the sexy underwear.

The glowing, green screen had a total of $2648.84. "Cash or Credit?" Barbie asked Asimi.

"Cash," replied Epic, pulling a thick wad of bills from his pocket and counting out three thousand in big-faced, hundred-dollar bills without flinching.

Barbie took the money and gave Epic his change, which he set on the counter as Barbie bagged the items and added tissue paper smelling of roses in it.

As they turned to leave, Barbie sweetly called behind them, "Thank you for shopping at Victoria's Secret! Please come again soon!" Epic knew that was a shout-out at him and gave Barbie a wink of his own.

An hour later, Epic sat across from Asimi, smiling at her Yale school days stories while he encouraged her to get her drink on and unwind.

The food at Sinful was always great and always expensive, a place whose motto was, *If you have to ask the price of a dish, then you can't afford it.*

Asimi finished her third Long Island Iced Tea by the time their waitress returned to offer dessert, but Asimi was past a good buzz; she was hammered. Epic passed on dessert and paid the bill, leaving a very nice tip for the less-than-cute waitress.

Back at the condo, Epic carried a passed-out Asimi up to her bedroom, undressed her, and put her to bed, knowing she wouldn't get up before sunup. Epic scrolled through the contact information in his phone until he found the contact information for Barbie. He was sure it was hers because he didn't know anyone named Sarah.

He pushed the send button, thinking of Barbie's, or rather Sarah's, pretty, shaven pussy.

She answered on the second ring. "Hello."

"Yo, Sarah, what it do?" asked Epic.

"Wait. Is this the really sexy guy from the store today?" she all but yelled into the phone.

"Yeah, shawty. It's Epic, by the way."

"Epic? As in like, an epic event or something? Is it a nickname or your real name?"

Epic was shocked by the rapid-fire questions but answered them anyway.

"I was really hoping that you'd call. Oh, my God, I can't believe I did that today."

"Then why did you?" he asked, really wanting to know.

"Well, when I saw you, I wanted you and didn't know what to say because you were with your girlfriend. I swear to you, I wasn't planning on giving you a sex show, but just seeing you made me so wet that I had to do something about it right then and there. It was only fair that you should get to watch it since it was you who made it happen."

"Oh, so I'm special, huh? Tell me how.'

"In more than one way," she replied. "Well, first off, that's the only time I've ever done anything like that before, and second, you're going to be the first black guy I've ever slept with."

Epic's dick jumped to a full hard-on at the thought of being the first black dick to sink into that pink paradise. "Check it. Where you at now?"

"Out with two friends from work, having drinks," answered Sarah. "Do you know where Dunn's Pub is, off Lanteren Drive?"

"No doubt. I'll be there in ten minutes," replied Epic.

"Okay, see you in ten. I'll be out front."

"That's what it do," finished Epic, ending the call.

Epic pulled up in front of Dunn's Pub twenty minutes later, not that he couldn't have made it in ten, but he didn't want Sarah to think he was thirsty.

Sarah saw the Brandywine-colored Bentley Continental GT pull up and stop right in front of her and was more than thrilled to see Epic sitting behind the wheel.

"What if do, yo?" called Epic, lowering the passenger window.

"Whatever you want it to," returned Sarah with a lustful smile. The automatic lock on the door clicked so she could get in.

Epic pulled off once she'd settled back into the leather seat, heading for the Adams Mark Hotel.

"So, not to be nosey, but where's your girl?"

"Yo, that's what we not going to do, so don't go there," spat Epic, getting heated at the question.

This outburst didn't bother Sarah at all as she went on. "I was just asking because you seemed booed up at the store earlier."

Epic laughed at her attempt at hood slang, starting to truly believe that he really might be the first nigga to tap her prim and proper ass.

"I asked because I don't want any drama or problems with her, and I'm sure you're not looking to trade out what you have, so let's just say we can be friends with benefits," said Sarah, running her hand up his thigh to squeeze his throbbing dick.

"Say no more. I can do the fuck-buddy thang, but I don't want you to get dicked down and cause no shit. A'ight?"

"Wanna pinky swear?" Sarah laughed.

Inside the room, Epic pinned Sarah to the wall and began tonguing her down with that thug passion while he pulled down her skirt and raised her blouse over her head. He then stepped back to look at her and damn near came on himself at the sight of the black, silk garter belt clipped to the thigh nylons, then down to the six-inch, black, fuck-me heels.

"I bought this for you after seeing how much you liked it, with the hope you'd get to see me in it." Sarah smiled while stepping out of her damp thong.

The deep tan lines made all the parts Epic wanted to see and touch seem highlighted by the pale skin, untouched by the UV lights of the tanning bed.

Her rose-pink nipples nicely capped the perfect twin mounds sitting perky over a flat stomach and a shaved pussy with lips that looked like they were pouting.

"You like what you see?" Sarah asked while running her middle finger between her lower lips. In answer to her question, Epic unbuttoned his jeans and pushed them, along with his boxers, to the top of his Timberland boots, giving freedom to his straining dick. Sarah licked her lips at the sight of his thick dick sticking out with a slight curve to the right.

"Whatchu gonna do with that?" inquired Epic.

Sarah took hold of his flesh-covered rod, unable to make her fingers wrap completely around the thick shaft, more excited than she'd ever been in her life. She raked her manicured nails down his six-pack abs, on the way to her knees.

Epic's whole body tensed as her warm, wet mouth covered his blood-swollen bell head. He could see the same passion burning in her sea-green eyes. The sight of her lips covering his dick caused him to grow even harder and made Sarah's eyes widen in surprise. Sarah knew she could never swallow his massive, ten-inch dick, but she still had a few tricks in her fuck box, and she intended to use them all.

Sarah swirled her tongue under the crown of his dick head while applying suction, then popped the head from her wet mouth to rub all over her lips and face. Epic was loving to see his dick being worked by the snow bunny on her knees in front of him. Sarah began to suck his dick like gold would come out the end if she stroked and pulled enough.

Epic was fighting a futile battle, trying not to cum, but damn if that wasn't the best head he'd ever had in his life. He would have sworn no one could suck his dick better than Asimi.

He started to pump his hips, feeding her more of his thug meat, causing Sarah to gag, but she surprised him by shoving even more dick down her throat. She moaned with pleasure as she stroked up and down his shaft, wanting what she'd worked so hard for, and she could feel the first small jerks of his orgasm.

Epic looked down to make eye contact with her as the first hot jet of his cum shot into the back of her throat. He took two handfuls of blonde hair and fucked her beautiful face as spurt after spurt coated her tonsils. Sarah swallowed every drop of his seed and continued to suck, making sure his dick stayed hard enough to punish her soaking wet pussy.

Sarah stood and grabbed Epic by the dick and pulled him toward the California-king-sized bed. "I'm submissive, so dominate me, Epic," she cooed.

Epic spun her around so that her tone, firm ass cheeks made a fat ass hot dog out of his hard dick. Her blonde hair smelled of apricot shampoo as he kissed her neck while tweaking her sensitive nipples.

"I want you deep inside me." She moaned. "Fuck me hard, daddy."

Epic pushed her doggy style onto the edge of the bed while still slowly stroking his throbbing dick. It was all he could do not to rain balls deep into her pink, wet oasis.

"You want this dick, then you have to beg for it." He finished by slapping his hard dick against her clit and pussy lips.

"Ohhh, yeah, daddy. Please, fuck me with that big, black dick." Sarah moaned while using two fingers to fuck herself.

Epic smiled, placing the tip of his dick at her slick, wet entrance, feeling her hot juices coat the tip. Sarah used her same two wet fingers to spread open her pouty pussy lips so he could see her creamy, tight, pink opening. Epic was going to tease her more, but the sight of her dripping pussy provoked him to thrust more than half of his thick dick into her tight passage. Her scream was muffled as she bit down into the pillow and arched her back more, allowing Epic a down thrust angle.

After two more shallow strokes, he couldn't refrain from grabbing her by the hips and slamming the full length deep into her over-stretched pussy. Sarah thought she was ready for all of him until he'd impaled her with enough dick to feel it ram against her uterus. She squirmed, trying to run from the dick, but Epic held her by the hips so she couldn't get away or lie out flat to avoid the dick.

Her narrow tunnel squeezed down snug on his enlarged member, yet he didn't thrust or pull out. He waited for the pain to turn into pleasure. Using his thumb, he removed some of the creamy, white pussy juice at the base of his dick, lubing his thumb well before circling her pretty, puckered asshole.

Sarah shook with anticipation. Epic slowly pushed his thumb into her resistant, risen bud, drawing a moan from deep in her core as he slid his dick back at the same time. As he began to fuck her creamy pussy with a slow rhythm, Sarah wanted more and began thrusting her ass back to meet his deep strokes. The thought of having her asshole violated slammed her head long into her first orgasm of the night.

"Oh my God! Fuck me! Yes, fuck me!" she wailed. "Oh, shit, I'm going to cum, baby! I'm going to cum!"

Epic picked up the pace as he pumped deep into the now stretched and swollen pussy, driving Sarah crazy with lust. Epic spread her ass cheeks so he could watch his dick sink balls deep. Sarah slammed back against the dick as wave after wave of her orgasm tore through her, and she continued humming as Epic reached around to play with her ultra-sensitive clip.

Sarah was ass up, faced down, and loving each and every stroke of thick, black dick, but there was still something she wanted to try with him.

"You wanna fuck my tight, white asshole, don't you, baby?" asked Sarah, looking back over her right shoulder.

Epic almost came at that question. "Hell yeah, that's what it do," Epic replied.

"I want you to so bad, but you have to beg to fuck my tight, virgin ass. Will you beg to ass fuck me, Epic?" She moaned, turning the tables on him.

Epic was a real nigga, and he'd be damned if he begged a bitch. Before he knew what he was saying, it came out. "Please, baby, let me ass fuck you."

"Yes, baby, you can ass fuck me, but I wanna change positions."

"Naw, ma. I wanna hit it from the back." Epic growled.

"I have a better way. Trust me. And it will allow me to warm up to the monster."

Epic lay back on the bed as Sarah stood over him on the bed. He watched as she slowly lowered herself onto his ramrod dick, using one of her hands around the shaft as a buffer to keep it from going too deep too soon. His bell head popped past her tight sphincter, astonishing her that it would fit. The pain was blissful as she allowed a few more inches to slip in.

God, he was stretching her to the max, and she loved it. She began to bounce on the big, black dick in her asshole, and on impulse, she slammed her ass cheeks all the way down to his thighs. Sarah would have screamed, but all that dick knocked the wind out of her lungs, forcing her to sit impaled on his black stake.

Epic couldn't have imagined her asshole would feel so great on his dick, but every inch of her rectum embraced his shaft, milking him as she began to grind and tweak on his dick.

"Oh, fuck. Bae, ride that dick. Take it all."

"I'm cumming!" she cried out, leaning back on his dick to give him a perfect view of her swollen pussy and the meeting of black and white. Epic could feel the nut building, ready to explode deep in her ass.

Sarah threw her head back, screaming his name as her pussy started to squirt creamy, white pussy juice on his public hair and washboard abs. As her female ejaculation splashed his stomach, Epic dumped his seed deep in her bowels, each shot of cum draining him more.

Sarah came endlessly as Epic filled her ass with his seed. It was incomparably the best sex she'd ever had in her life, and for a brief moment, she was super jealous of Asimi getting this all the time. Epic lay sweating and panting, and though he'd told Sarah that they couldn't be more than fuck buddies, he knew now that he'd lied to himself.

Barbie had turned him out.

Sarah was more than happy to become Epic's side chick, but she had her mind made up to become number one, and only if Asimi had slack.

Chapter 4

Asimi awoke to the smell of coffee with a hell of a hangover and an upset stomach.

Epic came in with a glass of water and a bottle of Aspirin, knowing that she was going to have a mean ass hangover after the strong Long Island Iced Tea she'd drunk at dinner last night.

"Thank you, bae," she said, taking the water and Aspirin from him. "Sorry about last night, but school has been hectic, and I wanted to let loose, but I think I overdid it." Asimi winced.

"You good, baby, and don't apologize. It was funny to see Miss Prim and Proper wild out."

"Prim and proper? Don't play. You know I'm still hood," said Asimi, giving him her best mean mug.

"A'ight, peace, boo. I'm not trying to leave on a bad note. I was just joking with you. Damn, you're a mean drunk." Epic laughed.

Asimi softened up immediately. "Do you have to leave so soon?"

"Yeah, I've got to get back to the land before niggas start thinking shit sweet," said Epic, only half kidding.

"When will you be back, bae?"

"Shit, you never know, so don't try sneaking none of these lame ass frat boys up in dis piece."

"There's no one gettin' up in this place but you," said Asimi, patting the kitty cat.

"That's what it do, ma. Now, get some sleep. I'll call you later," he said with a final kiss before leaving.

Sarah answered the phone, anxious to talk to Epic. Every step she took was a sweet, painful reminder of last night. "Well, hello there, sexy," said Sarah with a voice full of desire.

"Sup, ma? What it do?"

"Just thinking about you," she replied.

"That's what's up, but check it. I'm on my way out, and I won't be back this way for at least two weeks. You feel me?"

"Two weeks? So I have to go without you for two weeks?" she questioned.

"Yeah, ma, unless you're planning on coming to Cleveland for a weekend," said Epic jokingly.

"Sure, if you're okay with that! I wouldn't wanna seem—what do you call it?—thirsty."

Epic laughed. "Are you thirsty? Because if you are, so am I, 'cause I wasn't planning on coming back that soon."

"I'm glad to have given you a reason to come back so soon, but I'll definitely be in Cleveland this weekend coming up."

"That's what it do, and bring that sexy ass garter belt with you and anything else sexy."

"Yes, daddy," she said, gassing up Epic's ego.

Epic called Payne once he jumped on the highway. "What up, dog? What it do?"

"Shit, my nigga, you got ghost, didn't you?"

"Yeah, brah. I bounced outta town to visit Asimi and to lay low for the weekend, but shit. What's poppin'?"

"Same ol', same ol', just got some info on a nice move, a move that will allow us both to sit back for a while. You feel me?"

"What it be like?" enquired Epic.

"I can't put it down right now, but I'll hit you with some clarity when you touch down, so pull up on me, a'ight?"

"It's on," Epic said, ending the call.

The next morning, Epic pulled into his parking space in front of his and Payne's business, Epic Investments. He noticed that Payne's Range River was parked two spaces down from his own.

Payne was at his desk, talking on the phone, when Epic walked in. "Yes, Mr. Hartfield, with a minimal investment of a hundred thousand dollars, you can buy into Kline Storman Bio Tech with an expectation of a two-hundred percent return in twelve months." After listening for a minute, Payne replied, "Thank you, and I'll have a carrier bring by the paperwork for you to sign, alright? Goodbye."

Payne typed in a few notes on his computer. "So how is Asimi, brah?" he asked Epic.

"Baby girl good. How you? "

"Shit, you heard. Gettin' that paper by pen or pistol, but mostly by pen right now to make sure we both have accountable income, Mr. Bentley," Payne finished, smiling.

Epic let the shot slide. "If this lick you talking about is all that, then you're going to have to do a lot more than just cook the books, my nigga."

"This some real shit, my nigga. I'm talking about life-changing shit, and I'm not cappin'."

If only Epic had known how prophetic Payne's words would turn out to be.

"So, what it do? Clean or dirty?" questioned Epic, anxious to get the four-one-one on who had to lose so he could win.

"Dude been getting money forever, on some true incognito shit. From the outside, looking in, he legit—squeaky clean. That is, until you peel away the top layers and get to the real meat. His legit holdings are a hundred, but this muthafucka counterfeit brand and his dirty money is the money we gonna get at. It's not like he can call the police on illicit gains."

Epic said nothing, so Payne continued. "Back in the day, this nigga had his hands in everything that jumped off in the

41

city. I'm talking dope, pussy selling, extortion, hits, money laundering—shit, you name it, he did it."

"Wait. If this nigga like that, then why we didn't know 'bout him sooner, or is he just a has-been?" Epic wanted to know. "The streets be talking, yet you saying this nigga been flying under the radar all this time? Ain't no way, my nigga," said Epic.

"I don't know why he pulled a Houdini back in the day, but he's back in effect now, and it's our time to make his ass disappear again. All I know is that this muthafucka got Vegas money, and most niggas scared to take it, so where your heart at, my nigga?"

"You got me fucked up, my nigga!" Epic spat at Payne. "It's two thangs you can never question about me, nigga, and that's my heart and loyalty. Nigga, act like I ain't T.T.G.!" Epic growled, upset.

Payne raised both hands, palms up. "Damn, chill, my nigga. You know I know you Trained to Go. Shit, the streets don't know your name, but they do know there's an official nigga in the land, puttin' in work."

"Look. Just give me the rundown on the Mr. Incognito so I can pull up on ol' boy and get this money," said Epic, trying to regain his composure. Epic took the information that Payne had given him and another three days to do some of his own reconnaissance on Mr. Incognito.

The first thing he learned was that Payne was right about this nigga having mad loot. The gated home in Shaker Heights was worth at least three million, with another two million in whips sitting in the driveway and a four-car garage.

Something they'd been wrong about was that Mr. Incognito wasn't a nigga at all, but an older white man in his mid-fifties, salt and pepper hair, tall and lean, in shape for his age, and he also had a security team on the premises with video cameras. Top that off with two 120-pound Warlock Doberman Pinschers, getting at this muthafucka at home was definitely out of the question. He knew, though, where there was a will, there was a way.

The harder the objective, the more motivated Epic became, and Mr. Incognito had him motivated as a muthafucka.

Cal Bower sat across the table from the only man he'd ever feared in his entire life—a stone-cold killer with the emotionless eyes of a great white shark and a hundred times more deadly.

"So, I take it all went well in Detroit. That there's no longer a problem with the union." Cal stated more than he asked.

"Their union leader couldn't be persuaded to see things your way, but I can guarantee you'll have no more work stoppages."

"Thank you for all these years you've been with our family, and I know the loyalty you had for my father—may God rest his soul—has been transferred to me. It's not your fault my father made mistakes; it was his failure to guard against what happened, just as it was the right of the cartel to end his life for those mistakes. It was a high cost to pay, a cost that was passed on to me, because, even in death, the cartel does not forgive debt unpaid."

Cal Bower expected nothing and got nothing from this emotionless killer, but he'd watched his father stroke the ego of his trained killer as one might stroke his favorite pet.

Chapter 5

Epic owned property just outside of Cleveland, in Westlake, where he'd bought land to build his house, but instead, he bought two identical modular homes, which he'd had built side by side, connected by a glass-enclosed walkway.

Altogether, it was a ten-bedroom, four-bath, two-kitchen, and a six-car garage with a custom oasis pool in the backyard. The entire property was also fenced in by a seven-foot, steel, rebar-enforced brick wall with black, steel twin gates crowned with the silhouette of a black rhino and the name 'Rhino Estate' above it.

Epic didn't miss the fact his name was very similar to Mr. Incognito's setup, minus the security team and two big ass, man-eating Doberman Pinschers. He knew it was a lot more space than he needed for himself, but he hoped to one day live there with Asimi and raise a family of his own.

Epic punched in his security code as he entered, thinking of Asimi, when his phone started to vibrate. He looked down, expecting it to be Asimi or Payne.

It was neither. The screen read Sarah, and smiling, he answered. "What it do?"

"Hey, sexy! Just thought I'd call to see if it was still okay for me to visit you tomorrow?'

"Yo, so you really coming to Cleveland?" asked Epic, kind of shocked that she was really going to make the trip.

"Yes, I'm still coming, and I have a big surprise for you!" Sarah gushed.

"That's what it do. I like surprises as long as there's no bullshit in the mix."

"Never that. I wouldn't chance messing up the great time we had. I just think I can improve on what we did last time—unless you don't want me to!"

'Improve?' Epic thought. He didn't know how she could improve on their last fuck session, but he was willing to find out. "A'ight, surprise me then," he said, sitting down on the corner of his pearly white with blue felt Catalina pool table, wishing he could fuck Sarah from behind on the luxury table.

"I've booked a suite at the Hyatt in downtown, near the Flats, with a king-sized bed and a jacuzzi, "Sarah told him, already feeling the moisture between her thighs.

"I'm wit' dat," Epic replied. "Text me when you touchdown with the room number, a'ight?"

"Okay, see you then. Bye-bye."

"'Til then, shawty. It's on," finished Epic, ending the call.

He had just set his phone down when there was a quick, three-beep tone indicating he had a picture text.

Epic opened the text to find a nice shot of Sarah's pretty, shaved pussy with the following words: Fill soon please.

His dick hardened immediately, and he wished he could fill it right then.

The next morning, Epic met Payne at Hardbodies Gym off Broadway for a quick workout to start his day, just to hear Payne ask the same old question he always did.

"Brah, why do you come to the gym here when you've got a state-of-the-art home gym at the crib?"

Epic didn't answer as he watched a bad ass red bone in yoga pants and a sports bra walk by. Payne followed his line of sight as Epic said, "For the view, dog. For the beautiful view."

"No doubt about that. So how are things looking on the lick, my nigga?" asked Payne as he curled a set of forty-pound dumbbells.

Epic waited until he'd locked the 325 pounds he was benching. "Harder to knock off than we first thought, and he's not a nigga, brah. He's a funky, old, white dude with mad security and firepower."

"So what you sayin'? It can't be done?'"

"Naw, what I'm sayin' is that dude's official, so it's got to be my A-game. This muthafucka ain't some kilo-moving, street-level dope boy," Epic mumbled, wiping sweat with a towel.

"Well, I'll let you do what you do on that. I've got to be somewhere in an hour, and I can't be late," Payne stated vaguely.

Smirking, Epic said, "Tell Candy I said what it do?"

Payne stopped mid-step, shocked into immobility by Epic's words. "Aye, my nigga, how the fuck you know I'm bouncing to see Candy?" Payne questioned.

"That's what I do. Now take yo' pussy-whipped ass on before some other nigga be layin' up in ol' girl."

Payne knocked on the apartment door while reading the number to himself. '23F—F for fuck,' he thought, smiling, which he was still doing when Candy opened the door, wearing only a housecoat. The cleavage was enough to wipe the smile from Payne's face.

"Hey, daddy," Candy said with a moan in a voice that gave Payne instant wood.

"Damn," was all Payne could say. He loved hood bitches, and Candy's ass was as hood as it got.

"So you gonna just stand there, or are you gonna come in here and throw that dick in my mouth?" Candy wanted to know, licking her luscious, thick lips.

Payne was pushed against the door as soon as it closed, and Candy pulled his fat, short dick out of his pants.

Candy couldn't believe she was about to suck this chubby ass nigga's little, stubby dick, but it was worth having her rent paid, car note paid, and hair done. Shit, it wasn't even a mouthful. She'd nicknamed him baby dick 'cause sucking his shit was like having a binky in her mouth.

Payne watched as Candy's lips wrapped around his meat, causing his knees to shake. He could already feel his nuts tightening up. Candy was rubbing her clit while she sucked, pulling and nibbling Payne's dick while wishing it were his friend Epic's. Payne's dick popped out of Candy's mouth with a loud smack.

"Yo, ma, I'm 'bout to punish that pussy. You think you can handle this big dick?"

Candy rolled her eyes as she crawled on the bed doggy style, knowing she'd have to fake another orgasm because this lil' dick nigga couldn't get anywhere near her deep g-spot. She wasn't even sure he was inside her until his stomach started to bump into her juicy ass, pushing her forward onto the bed.

"Whose pussy is this?" asked Payne, fucking her for all he was worth.

Candy couldn't believe this nigga had the audacity to even ask some shit like that, and when she didn't answer, he asked again.

"Bitch, whose pussy is this?" Payne asked, shoving his thumb into her spread-open asshole.

"Ohhh!" Candy moaned, liking the exploration of his thumb in her ass.

"Fuck that hot ass, daddy. Make it yours like this pussy," cooed Candy, hoping to get some excitement out of this fuck session.

Payne slipped his dick out of Candy's wet pussy and into her asshole. He didn't even have to lube it up, as he sank balls deep through her back door.

Candy reached under her pillow and pulled out her eight-inch vibrator to slide into her wanting pussy as Payne pounded her asshole. She was amazed at how good it felt to have both of her holes filled, and although Payne's dick did nothing for her pussy, it was working wonders in her asshole.

Payne was fucking the shit out of her raunchy ass and feeling like the man as Candy started to scream.

"Oh, Payne, fuck me! I'm cumming! Oh, make me cum, Payne!" Candy moaned. "That's your asshole, baby!"

Shit, she had him feeling like the man as he shot his seed in her asshole as she came with the vibrator deep in her pussy. Payne was sure he'd found himself a new baby mama, maybe even a potential wifey.

Chapter 6

Epic watched as a hunter-green Honda Accord pulled out of the driveway of Mr. Incognito's house, driven by an older black woman dressed in a housekeeper's uniform. He waited until she was a block ahead of him before he started the rented Chevrolet Impala and began to follow her, thinking of a way that he could use this new piece of information to his advantage.

The housekeeper pulled into the BP gas station on the corner of Miles and Lee Road, stopping at the last pump on the left. She turned her car off, then began to rummage in her purse. As Epic rolled to a stop, he noticed a shabbily dressed man headed toward the driver's side window. A dark shadow fell over her, blocking the light from the gas station's awning. She looked up to find a scruffily, unwashed man tapping on her window with a gun.

She was gripped by panic at the sight of the gun, frozen like a deer in headlights, so it took her brain a few seconds too long to realize her door was unlocked, and the man opened it and was dragging her from the car. She cried out as she skinned her knee when he threw her to the concrete.

"Give me yo' pocketbook, bitch, 'fore I blow yo' damn head off!" yelled the piss-smelling robber.

Pure terror made her curl into the fetal position, not willing to see the shot that would take her life, but instead of the sound of a gunshot, there was the sound of flesh striking flesh.

Epic let loose a devastating right, knocking the drunk robber into the open car door. He then slammed a mean blow into his left kidney. A new kind of rage consumed him as he kicked the downed man over and over again in the ribs. He was still kicking him as the woman screamed for him to stop.

It wasn't her screams that stopped him, but what she said. "Epic, stop! Don't be like your father was!" She sobbed. In one lightning-quick move, Epic spun while pulling his Glock 40 Caliber, pointing it at the woman who'd just called his name.

"How the fuck do you know my name, old lady?" he barked. She looked up into his eyes, eyes she knew so well, but before she could answer, they could both hear sirens in the distance.

Epic was torn between staying to find out answers or fleeing before the cops showed up, but she made up his mind for him. "You have to go, but listen. If you want to know how I know your name, then remember this number. 216-748-2209. We need to talk. There's a lot I can explain," she finished hurriedly.

With one final look at her, Epic tucked his Glock and took off across the street where he'd parked the Impala. Epic's head was spinning as he sped away. How the fuck did she know his name, and what the fuck was Payne playing at with this shit? He was about to call Payne but decided against it, not willing to let Payne know he was hip to his shit if Payne was, indeed, on some left-hand shit.

The reason he'd played *Rescue Roger* was thinking he'd be able to use the good deed to get an inside track on Mr. Incognito, or at least get some info. He drove back to Avis Rental Car to return the rental in case the cops were looking for a silver Chevy Impala. Epic pondered his next move while smoking a blunt of O.G. Kush, listening to some old-school Tupac.

The incoming call had the Bentley automatically mute the volume on 'All Eyez on Me'. Looking down at the screen,

Epic couldn't believe he'd forgotten all about Sarah hitting him up tonight. He was tempted to let the call go to voicemail, but he thought beating Barbie's back out might've been just the thing he needed to clear his mind and help him think straight.

"What it do, gorgeous?" he answered.

"Nothing yet, but I'm missing you. I hope that we can fix both of those problems soon!"

"Best believe it," he said in a less-than-enthusiastic tone.

Sarah noticed at once that he didn't sound as excited as he had earlier, so she asked what was wrong.

"It's all good, ma, just some work shit got a nigga stressed out a little," he replied.

"Would you like me to come put the smack down on someone?"

Epic couldn't help but laugh. "Naw, yo. I got it. So, you 'bout that life now, huh?"

"I'm not black, but later, I'm going to have some black in me, right?"

"Best believe me, you're going to have a lot of black in you, on you, all over you," he said, setting his intent.

"Well, I'm at the Hyatt in downtown Cleveland, Suite 1216, wet, ready, and horny as hell," Sarah said seductively.

"Check it. I'll be there in twenty minutes."

"Okay, I'll be waiting with your surprise, and tonight, I hope you've got a lot of stamina."

"I got all you can handle and then some," he growled.

"See you in twenty."

"It's on," he said, ending the call. Fifteen minutes later, Epic pulled up to the valet parking at the Hyatt Hotel, a little more relaxed and a lot more excited than he had been. Epic rode the elevator up to the twelfth floor, visualizing how he planned to gorilla fuck the shit out of Sarah that night. He turned left as he got off the elevator, following the arrow on the wall that pointed to the room numbers.

Epic stopped in front of suite 1216 and checked his gear before knocking. He was rocking new Burberry Timberlands, Red Monkey jeans, with a limited-edition Red Monkey mock bulletproof vest, and a twenty-six-inch platinum chain weighed down by a three-inch capital letter E filled with crushed diamonds. He sported two karats in each ear with a completely iced-out Christophe Claret Soprano watch, custom-made, with an 'E' at the twelve and an 'A' at the six positions.

Epic knocked and waited a few heartbeats for Sarah to open the door, and she smiled ear to ear in a Hyatt furnace housecoat, six-inch Jimmy Choo heels, thigh-high stockings, and a garter belt.

Epic felt his dick jump to attention in his pants just at the sight of the blonde goddess standing before him. She stepped to the side to invite him in. After a very passionate kiss, she took his hand, leading him toward the bedroom.

At the door, Sarah pulled out a silk blindfold for him to put over his eyes. Epic stood for a moment, holding the silk, looking deep into her green eyes without putting it on.

"Trust me, it's for your surprise," she said, leaning forward to nibble his bottom lip.

Epic slipped the blindfold over his eyes but was ready for anything, feeling like nothing could surprise him more than the old lady had earlier tonight. He wasn't wrong, but he was close.

When Sarah opened the bedroom door, the entire room was aglow with candlelight. Epic allowed himself to be led inside and over to a plush armchair that had been pulled in front of the king-size bed.

Once seated, Sarah told him to remove his blindfold and enjoy. Epic removed his blindfold to see Sarah walking toward another blonde goddess dressed identically in a white garter belt, thigh-highs, and heels. His dick reached a new level of hardness.

"Epic, allow me to introduce you to your surprise—my best friend, Mason, who came from me just telling her how good you fucked me and how big your dick is. She begged me to come along with me to see if it was really true, so tonight, if you can handle it, you get to have your cake and eat it too!"

Mason was almost a carbon copy of Sarah with the exception of a beautiful set of double D's with deep, rosy, red-colored nipples. Epic watched as the twin goddesses tongued while rubbing each other's wet pussies. Epic started to remove his clothes as Sarah and Mason got into a sixty-nine position. Mason's pretty, shaved pussy was facing Epic, spread wide with Sarah's tongue buried deep as she used her middle finger on Mason's tight asshole.

He continued to watch as their tempo built until both women were moaning and squirming, their urgent need to cum making them both wild. Mason lowered her perfectly sculpted ass down farther on Sarah's face, allowing her tongue deeper penetration, and she began to pump her pussy, fucking Sarah's face.

Desperation to cum drove them to an animalistic degree of desire, pleasure totally consuming them both as their first orgasms tore through them. As Mason shook through her orgasm, Sarah continued to suck and lick her clit. On impulse, Epic stepped behind her and drove the full length of his swollen dick deep into her red, hot, soaking pussy, causing her to cum a second time as he filled her.

His big dick stretched her pussy to the point of painfulness. The sensation of tongue and dick had her trembling as spasms shot through her with every pounding thrust. Sarah pulled Epic's thick, hard dick from Mason's scolding wet pussy and took him deep into her throat while fondling his balls. Epic could feel his nut explode down Sarah's greedy throat as she swallowed every drop and continued to suck. When she'd had her fill, she placed his still hard dick into Mason's lava-hot pussy.

Her tight pussy rejuvenated his dick even more as Sarah slid from beneath Mason. "Oh, daddy, that's it. Fuck her tight, white pussy. Make her cum all over that big, black dick." Sarah moaned.

Epic pulled out and flipped Mason onto her back while Sarah climbed on top of her, raising both of Mason's legs onto her shoulders in the buck position. Mason's flexibility had hers and Sarah's pussies lined up evenly as they tongued and sucked each other's titties, leaving Epic with two hot, shaved pussies to choose from.

Epic embedded every inch of his dick into Sarah's wet hole, quenching the thirst for dick she was suffering from.

"Oh, shit, daddy. You're too deep!" Sarah screamed as Epic exploded her depths without sympathy.

Mason used both hands to spread Sarah's ass cheeks apart while saying, "Yes, that's it. Take that big dick. Take that magnificent dick. Fuck that tight box. Make her cum 'til she squirts for you, baby."

Mason's encouragement had Epic pumping like a piston in Sarah's well-lubed pussy. Sarah shivered as Mason slipped her middle finger deep in her asshole. It was absolutely taboo, and she loved it.

"Oh, my God! This is so much better than my fantasies. Fuck me, daddy! Fuck me!" Sarah moaned.

Epic watched his glistening dick slide in and out of her red, swollen lips. The only word he could think of was captivating. He increased his rhythm and started to make circular motions so he could hit every wall.

The heat building in her internal core was overwhelming and could no longer be held back as a world-shattering orgasm ripped through her.

"Ah, oh, shit! I'm cumming!" screamed Sarah, bucking back on his dick and punishing her own uterus as stream after stream of feminine cum squirted all over Epic's thighs. Sarah was panting as she collapsed on her stomach, allowing

Mason to mount her, making a double stack of pussies and assholes.

With a devilish look back over her shoulder, Mason said, "Fuck our asses with that hard, black dick. I wanna squirt all over you too!" She leaned forward, tooting her ass up to better expose her pretty, little, puckered hole. Epic pushed the head of his cum-lubed dick against Mason's tight backdoor, feeling the resistance as they merged. Her sphincter opened to accommodate his long, hard intruder.

"Oh, fuck," Mason said, trying to get away from the piercing pain of her tight tunnel being stretched to its limits.

After a moment of pain, streak after streak of pleasure, maximized by Epic's finger on her hypersensitive clit, had her speaking in tongues. Epic deepened his strokes, raising the volume of moans coming from Mason. Her ass absorbed every thrust. Just as he was about to drive her crazy, he pulled out of her possessive asshole and, in one nonstop motion, shoved his massive tool into Sarah's strawberry-puckered asshole.

Two miracles happened at once. The first one was that he entered her unyieldingly. The second was that she didn't pass out cold. The squeeze of her tight asshole was intoxicating. Grabbing the base of his dick, he pulled it out only to slam it home again.

Her lower region was electrified, the pain and pleasure, an enigma her body was more than willing to endure. A few more strokes had him abandoning all pretense of control as he began to pound the full length of his dick into her anal shaft mercilessly.

Sarah was unable to speak, so without warning, she started to cum, shooting jet after jet of female cum on the bed, her orgasm so strong she saw spots. Epic's dick exploitation of Mason's asshole certainly left no doubt that he planned on giving her the fierce fucking he felt it deserved.

She squirmed, trying to run from the dick, but only succeeded in helping his dick sink balls deep in her ass. Repeat strokes pushed her over the edge as she squirted her sticky, slick cum over Sarah's back and ass.

The tightening of Mason's anal passageway devastated him, and Epic's last hope of holding back his climax as Mason's cum cascaded over Sarah's ass. Epic spew spurts of his sperm into her clenching asshole, exploding until his dick gave only little jerks. The three of them lay panting and in mutual satisfaction, intertwined, unable to move after the chaotic fuckathon.

Evidently, it was going to be a long, cum-filled weekend.

Chapter 7

Payne wiped away the lipstick smudge on his cheek as he drove away from dropping Candy off at work. He had a lucrative opportunity set up, and he wasn't about to be late or let a little thing like being pussy-whipped tarnish his business reputation.

Epic had been pretty much unreachable for the second weekend in a row, but it didn't really bother him that much, as long as he was taking care of that Mr. Incognito business.

Payne was seated at a table near the back of the restaurant for twenty minutes and was becoming more than irate after rushing to be on time, only to not be shown the same level of respect. Ten minutes later, he stood to leave when two of the most beautiful women he'd ever seen walked in, escorted by four aggressive men in suits. He watched as they made their way to his table and stopped in front of him.

"Sit. There are things that we need to discuss with you," said one of the supermodel-worthy women.

Payne put on one of his cocky, hood smirks before he replied, "Evidently, you've mistaken me with someone else. I have a meeting with Ari Acousta, so if you will, excuse yourselves."

Two of the large men pushed Payne back into the chair, forcing him to sit down, while the others pulled out chairs for both women to sit. Payne was already pissed that Ari Acousta hadn't shown up or had the decency to call and reschedule, and now these muthafuckas were laying hands on him.

Looking up at both men standing beside him, he said, "Yo, don't let this suit and tie fool y'all, 'cause this shit is just a smokescreen. I'm 'bout that life, so ease the fuck back before I make it happen in here and ruin everybody's dinner in this bitch." His threat may have carried a little more weight had he not been perspiring under the glare of the two silent women.

The silence stretched on for another minute or two before the woman to his left spoke. "You feel that we've mistaken who you are, but in truth, you have mistaken who we are. You are here to meet with Ari Acousta, who you've met in person, yet your greed has kept you waiting for over half an hour in the hopes of financial gain. Here, again, you are mistaken. You are here to right a wrong of your own making, a wrong that cost me over three hundred thousand dollars and a very loyal, trustworthy associate.'

"Fuck is you talkin' 'bout, bit—" he started to say, but couldn't finish, as the man on his right backhanded the shit out of him, basically slapping the insult back down his throat.

She continued. "As I was saying, you find yourself in this predicament because you're not as smart as you think you are and have overestimated your own ability to keep your inquiries secret from those you've stolen from."

"I've never stole anything from anyone, especially Mr. Acousta, so it's you who are mistaken," Payne replied, trying to stay calm.

He watched as the woman he'd been speaking with cocked her head in amusement. "Mr. Nevins, allow me to introduce myself. I am Ariella Acousta—Ari for short. So, you see now that you are wrong on both counts. I'm not a man, and you have stolen from me, the Head of the Acousta Cartel, the most powerful of the Dominican Cartels."

Moisture trickled down his spine, along with the realization that this was perhaps his last meal.

"I can see by the look on your face that you are wondering why you are still alive. The answer to that is quite simple. Dead men can't pay their debts. A debt, in itself, is small to me, yet you had the audacity to touch those who fall under my protection. Now, I admire your setup, but there are only three things keeping you alive right now."

Payne was stunned in silence.

"First, you will use your Investment Company to launder cartel money. Second, you have five days to pay back the money you stole, plus pain and suffering, which brings it to a total of one point five million dollars. Last but not least, you will give us the name of the man who pulled the trigger that killed my worker. If you fail at any one of these things, you will be killed at once," she finished with a nod before standing.

He opened his mouth to speak, but no words came out. The coppery taste of blood was heavy on his tongue. She stopped as she turned to leave.

"The first shipment of cash to be laundered will arrive in two days. By then, I expect the name of the shooter, and three days after that, you will pay your debt in full—one way or the other."

Chapter 8

Epic ended his FaceTime chat with Asimi, feeling a little guilty about dicking down not one but two women all weekend long, but not guilty enough to confess it to Asimi. He hesitated as he strolled through the phone numbers programmed in his phone. He could have just dialed the number, a number he had memorized.

The number of the woman who said she could answer his questions, but if he was being honest with himself, was he strong enough to hear those answers? If the old lady was telling the truth, did he want to have confirmation that he was the product of a dysfunctional father and a loveless mother? Would any answers she gave him change everything? Would he be satisfied with them? Could they make a lifetime of feeling inadequate dissipation?

Whether or not, it was something he had to do. Life had more than taught him to face his fears head-on, and he was going to do that now. Looking at the number, he pushed send. His anxiety built with each ring, and he was about to hang up when the sophisticated voice of the old lady answered.

"Hello? Hello?'

Epic released the breath he'd been holding. "You told me to call this number if I wanted answers, so I'm calling."

"Oh my God, Epic. You called," she said, surprised. "How are you? Is everything okay? I wasn't sure you'd call."

"How do you know my name, and what did you mean by, don't be like your father?" he questioned. The line was quiet. "I should have known you were bullshittin'. You don't know shit about me but my name, and I'll find out how you know that much!" Epic snapped, ready to end the call.

"No, no. I do know the answers you want to know. I was just collecting my thoughts," she said hurriedly.

"Then spit that shit out!"

"You need to watch your mouth, Epic Anders. I will not stand for that kind of language from you or anyone else, but especially not you."

"Yo, what the fuck ever, and if I'm correct, you're too damned old to be my mother, so kill that shit," he said heatedly.

"I'm sorry. Please allow me to start over. My name is Erica Bates, and I know your name and more because you are my grandson." The quiet answered her. "I can't even imagine how this news must affect you. You are right. I'm not your mother, but I was her mother," she said, still, into the quiet.

Epic's mind couldn't lock onto the words bouncing around in his head. The one thing he kept repeating was, 'I was her mother,' as in the past tense. The only conclusion he could draw from that was that his mother was dead. What he wasn't prepared for was the wash of emotions that came with that knowledge. Had he not been abandoned after all?

"Epic, I understand this is a lot, and there's so much more, but we need to sit down and talk. Please, will you sit down and talk with me? When we're done, if you never wanna see nor speak to me again, I'll understand and respect that."

After a minute, Epic agreed to meet her for coffee the next morning at Starbucks downtown.

Chapter 9

Payne lay back as Candy's head bobbed up and down on his semi-hard dick. It wasn't that the neck game wasn't good; the problem was that he was stuck like Chuck. For a minute, he'd thought about running or setting up a meeting and killing the bitches, but common sense had overridden that stupidity.

Candy increased her suction, trying to bring him to a full erection, not really getting any better results, so she stopped to ask, "Why the fuck am I sucking your dick if it won't get hard, Payne?"

"I'm sorry, baby. I just got a lot on my mind right now."

"What? Some other bitch got yo' mind fucked up?" she asked, getting hostile. Leave it to a bitch to think every problem with a nigga had to do with pussy.

Payne shook his head. "Don't trip, a'ight? You the only one, baby girl. This some work shit I'm dealing wit'."

Candy turned and put her naked ass in his face, then bent forward, grabbing both ankles, causing her pussy to spread out wide.

The sight of her wet pink did the trick better than any aphrodisiac known to man could have. He decided he'd worry about Ari Acousta later, but right now, his dick was about to get reacquainted with Candy's pussy.

Epic, needing someone he could trust to talk to, called Asimi.

"Hey, babe."

"What it do, ma?"

The slower cadence of his voice told her that something was wrong. "What's wrong? Are you okay? You sound funny right now," Asimi said.

With a deep sigh, Epic told Asimi about the whole conversation with the woman claiming to be his grandmother, a thought he honestly believed now. Remarkably enough, Asimi asked all the right questions, even some he hadn't thought of, and the fact that she was there for him a hundred percent was what made Asimi a true ride or die chick.

"Bae, you know I gotchu through thick and thin, right? I don't know if I tell you enough how much I appreciate you and all that you do. I love you, Epic Anders, and no matter what she tells you tomorrow, please remember how much you are loved by me," Asimi said with her voice trembling, on the verge of tears.

With Asimi by his side, Epic knew he could face whatever life threw at him. He understood that life owed no one anything, but he was well aware that the shit one never saw coming could destroy a person.

"Yo, baby girl, I'm still coming up this weekend, no matter how tomorrow goes. There's a few other things I need to chop it up with you about."

A note of worry entered Asimi's voice. "Like what, bae?"

"Naw, not over the phone, ma. This some real face-to-face type shit. I feel I owe you that much."

"A'ight, bae, but remember, I love you, no matter what. 'Kay."

"Love you too!"

Epic drove through the 30th Projects just to feel the vibe of the streets he lived on, watching the D-Boyz slang, the hood rats fish for their next baby daddy, and the everyday struggles that defeated the strong and weak alike. He rolled past Kendra on her front stoop with two fake ass goon niggas smoking a blunt. He thought about the last time he'd seen her and couldn't care less someone else was beating her trifling ass back out. That was one less problem he had to deal with. The last thing he needed now was a conniving hood rat's extra ass bringing more drama.

His Bentley stood out like a diamond in a pile of shit, surrounded by the run-down apartment building and the ever-observant D-Boyz.

He left the dirty 30 and headed for Exotic Toyz to see Payne and get a feel of where they stood because he was still unsure if Payne was on some left-hand shit or not. He could have called, but he needed to see Payne's face when he asked his question.

As he pulled into the parking lot of Exotic Toyz strip club, he noticed that Payne's Range Rover wasn't up front as usual, so it was more than likely that he wasn't there.

He parked up front and went inside to have a drink while waiting to see if Payne showed up. Center stage, the thick ass German Chic Skky was pussy poppin' to 'Let Me Cater to You' by KeKe Boyd, and for the first time, he realized how damn thick she was for a white chick. The more he watched, the badder she got, but she couldn't fuck with Sarah or her girl Mason.

Epic sat there, thinking about his situation concerning Sarah, when Candy sat down across from him in a see-through bra and thong set. He was caught off guard and irritated at being interrupted when deep in thought.

"Hey, Epic. You looking for Payne?" she asked, cocking her legs so he could see her pussy lips through the thin material.

"Yeah. You seen him tonight?" Epic asked, keeping his eyes on hers.

She noticed where his attention was. "What? You don't like my outfit, or are you afraid it's more than you can handle?"

"'Sup with that shit? 'Cause last time I checked, you and bruh was booed up," snarled Epic.

"True. We kickin' it, but do you see a ring on it? Don't the two of you share everything, and if not, what he don't know won't hurt him."

'Damn, this bitch's stage name should be Mayhem,' Epic thought. "That's some trifling ass shit right there, yo, and you don't deserve to be down with my nigga, pulling this stank, hoe shit. What you fail to see in me is a real ass nigga, and loyalty is what it be, so you need to tell bruh how you made a play with me, or I will. You feel me?"

"Nigga, stop trippin'. You need to pause for the cause. It's my word against yours, and when we intimate, this pussy can make that nigga do whatever I want him to," she said, running her hand between her thighs.

For Epic, that wasn't a turn on but a last straw.

He shot to his feet and grabbed a handful of Candy's hair while leaning in close to her face. "Bitch, you think it's a game, huh? You think yo' ass won't be on the side of a milk carton or in Lake Erie? The best thing for you to do is play yo' roll until my nigga drop yo' slut ass, a'ight?" Epic growled.

Candy watched as Payne walked in. She then wrapped both her legs around Epic's waist and pulled his lips to hers. Payne had seen Epic's Bentley parked out front and was about to come in and give his partner in crime the lowdown with Ariella Acousta when he caught sight of his main man damn near balls deep in his bitch. That was a bitch he was close to making wifey, and that shit tore through him worse than any bullet the Acousta Cartel could fire at him. In the end, he just turned around and walked out. He had some serious thinking to do.

Candy's quick move took Epic by surprise, but only for a second. He pulled back and commenced to choke the shit out of her ratchet ass until the bouncer pulled him off of her before he could finish the job.

"Yo, Epic! Chill, my nigga!" Dizzy, the bouncer, roared at him.

In the blink of an eye, Epic had his Sig 40 Caliber pointed between Dizzy's eyes with the safety off.

"Damn, my nigga! You gonna up pipe on me for doing my job?" asked Dizzy, holding both hands up chest high.

"What you think, nigga?" spat Epic.

"You got a winner, my nigga," said Dizzy, stepping back.

Epic moved back toward the exit while keeping the room covered, but he realized not many people even noticed the near-death confrontation. Epic peeled out of the parking lot at the same time he speed-dialed Payne's number. He wasn't worried about Fatal, the owner of the club, calling the police.

Fatal was a real street nigga that had been a D-Boy back in the day before he opened Exotic Toyz, but he would definitely want to have a few words with him. Fuck it. It was what it was. Payne's phone went straight to voicemail, so Epic sent a text.

What it do brah? Check it brah, ya' girl is foul ass a muthafucka brah. Bitch came at me tonight at the spot. Get at me.

Epic flipped through his old-school CD booklet and picked out a classic, Eric B and Rakim, and began to rap along with the music. "I ain't no joke. I used to make the mic smoke. Now I slam it down when I'm done and make sure it's broke," he spat, feeling the track. The music started to relax him. His mind was preoccupied with meeting Erica Bates his grandmother, in the morning.

When he walked through the doors of Starbucks the next day, twenty minutes early, he was surprised to see Mrs. Bates sitting at a table off to the left side. He went to the counter and ordered a Grande iced latte with cinnamon and waited until it was made before he approached the immaculately dressed older woman. He sat without being asked.

"Hello, Epic. I wasn't sure you would come, but I wanted to be here early to gather my thoughts," she said, looking even more nervous than him.

Epic sipped his latte without answering.

She continued with a sigh. "Well, first off, my name is Erica Bates, and as I told you, I'm your grandmother. In fact, you're the only grandchild I have. Your mother's name was Imani Williams Anders. She met and married your father, Devon Anders, when she was barely twenty years old. We were not on speaking terms, because I didn't approve of their relationship. I think back now on how foolish I was to allow something I didn't care for to ruin the time I could have been sharing with my only child. I could never come between them and the love they had for each other, but I allowed it to come between us," she said, rubbing at moist eyes.

"If my mother is dead, where is my father?"

"Oh, God, help me. Are you sure you're ready to hear this story?" she asked Epic, silently praying he'd say no.

"That's what I came for, if there really is a story."

She reached into her purse and removed an old, worn manila folder, and placed it on the table. From it, she put pictures of a very young, beautiful girl on the table in front of him. He couldn't stop himself from picking one of the pictures up. It was a shot of the girl who would later in life give birth to him and then give him away. She had the same eyes as her mother, the same eyes shared by her son. Looking at the picture removed the last trace of doubt from his mind.

"So what happened to her, and why'd you say 'don't be like your father,' and if you knew I was your grandson, why didn't you take me in and raise me?" he questioned.

"Back then, I was a bitter woman, mad at the fact that I couldn't control my daughter and keep her away from the street thug she chose to marry. I felt that she chose him over me—her mother. But what I couldn't understand at that time was that true love bound hearts, minds, and souls together. I never had that with your grandfather, God rest his soul, but Imani found that with your father. Their love was a love the newspapers called a new-age version of Bonnie and Clyde. They died from gunfire the same day." She went on to tell the story she knew, and what the papers said, and what she could learn from the detective in charge of the case.

He sat silently, watching the agony play over her face, seeing that all these years had only dulled the pain enough for her to only go through the motions of going on with her life. There were many questions he wanted to ask, but only one stood out from the rest, so boldly that he blurted it out.

"Why didn't you take me?"

She took a deep breath as she removed another picture from the folder. "You look just like your father and have since the day you were born. The hatred I felt for him, I wrongly placed on you, so I refused to take you. I've made plenty of mistakes in my life, but that was the worst one ever. Epic, I can't expect you to forgive me. Hell, I can't forgive myself, but maybe we can get to know each other a little." She finished, looking down at her clasped hands.

Epic wanted to offer comfort, but another question popped into his mind. "You dress well for a maid. Does your job pay enough for you to have Coach bags?" He watched as sorrow so deeply consumed her. He forgot his anger and reached his hand across the table to cover hers.

The contact seemed to steady her as she spoke. "The detective believed that Imani and your father were killed for something they stole from a very dangerous man—a man connected to a powerful drug cartel or the mob. I convinced him to give me the man's name, and when he did, I died myself because I realized that I was the reason my daughter was dead."

"Wait. I don't understand." Epic was clearly shocked.

"One of the last times that I spoke with your mother, I was complaining about how someone with so much money could be so careless with it."

It suddenly clicked into place for Epic. His grandmother had spoken of the amount of money the man she worked for had and how easy it would be for someone to rob him, and his mother and father had tried to. Damn, how fucked up was that? His thoughts were interrupted as she continued.

"The police could prove nothing, but I knew—I knew by the tension within the house. The fear of Mr. Bower when phone calls started, then the sending of his only son away, the absence of his head of security... Mr. Bower sent me home early the day whoever he owed came for him. In truth, he probably saved my life by doing so, but I needed to know if that psychopath he used for a head of security had anything to do with the murder of my daughter. So, I came back to work for his son, who still uses the same head of security as his father did. I know this may sound silly to you, but I want justice for my daughter. She deserves that much, at least." She then hit Epic with a question of her own. "How did you happen to be there to save me that night at the gas station?'

It was Epic's time to squirm a little under her teary-eyed gaze. "Yo, I was driving by and seen what was going down and decided to do a good deed," he said.

She didn't believe a word of it but didn't call him on the lie, not wanting to upset him. "God works in mysterious ways, or the world has become so small that we were destined to meet".

Epic didn't reply. He was still sorting through all he had learned in the last hour.

She next removed a gold cross on a herringbone chain and slid it on the table to him, then a flash drive. "These were your mother's personal effects that she had on her at the hospital. They gave them to me, and I kept them for you, should we ever meet."

Epic ran his hand over the smooth, cold golden cross, hit hard by the fact that this very cross belonged to his mother.

"I would like to get to know you now. If you could find time for me in your life, but I won't push you. Just call whenever you'd like, if you would like to," she said, getting to her feet. She started to leave and stopped. "Epic, I'm sorry for being a stubborn fool. I see your father when I look at you, but I also see my daughter in your eyes." Without another word, she walked away.

Chapter 10

Epic called Payne's iPhone since Payne hadn't hit him back up after he'd left a voicemail and text about Candy's ratchet ass. Next, he called the office, only to be told Payne had taken the day off by Payne's secretary, Erin.

"Well, if he check in for messages, tell him to get at me ASAP," Epic said.

Epic hoped Payne wasn't trippin' about that conniving ass bitch he was shacking up with, but he'd always known Payne was a sucker-for-love ass nigga.

'Fuck it. It is what it is,' he thought as he headed for home. Payne looked down at his iPhone screen, then turned the power off. He didn't need to hear shit from Epic, because he knew what he'd seen with his own eyes.

"Thank you," he said as the bank's branch manager finished counting out the last two hundred thousand dollars to make up the $1.5 million he had to pay Ariella Acousta.

The money was a mean chunk out of the savings he'd been skimming from the business as a safety net. He just didn't think he'd need it so soon, but that was only part of his problem solved. He couldn't believe he was thinking about giving Epic up to that cartel bitch, but he'd also believed his main man, his brother, would never go behind his back and fuck his bitch.

Payne called the office and listened to the messages Erin had for him. He then told her to close up and take the rest of the day off with full pay. He didn't want anyone around when the Acousta's showed up with their cash that he had to clean.

70

Plus, he didn't need Erin to see anything she could tell Epic. This situation was volatile enough already.

He was sitting at his desk when the Acousta's arrived in a white-paneled van and two Humvees, all blacked out. If this shit wasn't a drug-cartel stereotype, Payne didn't know what it was, and the armed guards didn't help either.

Ariella Acousta led the rest of her entourage into the lobby of Epic Investments, where she found the front desk empty as well as the lobby. She was about to send one of her bodyguards to fetch Payne when he stepped into the lobby from his office. He carried two black, leather briefcases, which he placed on Erin's empty desk and popped the tops to display the bands of hundred-dollar bills.

Without taking her eyes off him, she spoke. "Yasmeen, collect the money."

The second beautiful woman came forward, closed both lids, took the two cases, and returned to where she stood behind Ariella.

"You're not going to count it?' Payne asked.

"Would you really be fool enough to attempt to short me and piss me off a second time?" she replied, the threat unspoken. They just stared at one another for a few seconds, and then, at some unseen signal, the sliding side door on the paneled van opened, and men with black duffel bags began to get out, bringing the money inside the lobby.

Ari said, "Each bag contains five million dollars."

Payne quickly did the math in his head—four men, two bags each, for a total of forty million dollars.

"You will receive ten percent of everything you clean. This first forty is to assure me that you can handle it and more," Ariella said, eyeing him. "But know that if you fail, you die. If you're short, you die. If you get caught, you die. Do we understand each other?"

"Yes. Yes, we do. Anything less than perfect business, and I die," said Payne, already spending his ten percent.

"Now that we've handled that business, give me the name of the man who is going to die tonight."

Payne was sure he was going to lie about who pulled the trigger on Kyrie's bitch ass, but then the image of Epic kissing Candy and then fucking her had him pissed all over again.

Without pause, he said, "Epic Anders is his name, my partner in this business. That's who killed your worker."

Ari cocked her head a little to the side to look at him and judge whether he was lying or not.

Payne stood there, trying to convince himself that he'd been betrayed first, that neither the money nor the threat to his life had anything to do with him giving Epic up. Deep down, he knew the truth. Greed and jealousy had won out over loyalty. He'd just sold out his brother and roll dog, over a piece of pussy and some money. Could he live with his decision? He'd have to because now, there was no going back.

Ari's voice broke through his thoughts. "You will set up a meeting with this Mr. Epic Anders, and we will take care of it from there. If you try to help him or warn him in any way, you will join him in the afterlife," she said with a gleam in her eyes, hoping he *would* try something like that.

"So be it," Payne said.

Epic sat, eating Oreo's while watching an MMA fight on his custom, eighty-five-inch widescreen. He was high off a blunt of Sky Walker dipped in gorilla piss. He didn't usually fuck with the wet, but he was uptight and needed to unwind and clear his head of all the shit he'd learned from his grandmother.

He picked up his phone as it began to vibrate and checked the caller ID to see who was texting him.

Whats up brah? Sorry I didn't hit you back up sooner, but I was dealing with Candys stank ass. Good looking on puttin' me down on her dirty ass. We need to get together and celebrate tonight at The Memosa Grill. You in?

Epic texted back.

What it do bro'? Shit you better leaving that bitch on the side of the road, glad you didn't listen to that lying ho. Memosa Grill at about 8:00 pm, that's whats up.

He needed to fill Payne in on the shit with the Bower family and who they were, and the fact old man Bower had more than likely had his mother and father killed. He didn't give a damn about the money now, but he couldn't let that shit ride no matter what.

Epic showered and got dressed in a pair of Diesel jeans, a Diesel wife-beater with a mock bulletproof vest, and Timberland boots. He started to rock his platinum chain, but changed his mind and put on the gold cross that belonged to his mother when she died.

As far as he was concerned, the Bower family would get what they deserved. They had created this monster. The Memosa Bar and Grill was located off the lobby of the Cleveland Ritz Carlton Hotel. It was as classy a place as the Ritz Carlton itself, with chrome-edged tables and mirrored glass walls, with a bar and grill that ran the length of the interior.

When Epic entered, he found Payne sitting at the bar, sipping on a Hangover. It was a drink he and Payne had come up with, consisting of Grey Goose, a shot of Everclear, a dash of Sprite, then topped off with Tropicana Orange juice.

By way of greeting, Epic said, "Damn, brah breaking up with Candy hit you that hard, my nigga?"

Smirking, Payne replied, "Naw, brah, but I hit her ass that hard for tryin' that left-hand shit with you, my nigga. Bitch was begging and cryin' when I told her ass to get to steppin."

Epic was still laughing when the bartender asked what he'd like to drink. He was about to order a Red Bull when Payne cut him off. "Excuse me, but could you bring us a bottle of Dom Perignon Champagne, please?"

At Epic's questioning look, he said, "To celebrate getting rid of Candy's nasty ass, and to friendship and loyalty."

"Naw, my nigga. Fuck that friendship shit. Brah, this shit is a toast to family!" Epic growled, glad that Payne wasn't tight about that Candy shit.

"Yeah, to family," Payne said, but Epic thought he sensed some aggression in his tone.

They had just popped their bottle when a beautiful, dark-haired Spanish or Costa Rican chick came up to the bar beside Epic. She was wearing some type of designer perfume that seemed to wrap itself around him. He turned to get a full look at her silky, black hair, caramel-tanned skin with nice, firm tits, and a phat ass. She wore a sheer white dress by Ralph & Russo that left very little to the imagination but made someone want to take it off to know if one was right. She had the body every woman wanted and every man wanted to possess, and they were both well aware that she knew it.

She shocked Epic with her order by asking for a Macallan Rare Cask Single Malt Scotch Whiskey on the rocks, which also earned an approving nod from the bartender. Epic couldn't quite pinpoint her accent, but was still taken by its broken cadence. When he glanced back at Payne, he noticed that his mouth was hanging open, and his eyes had glazed over like he would pass out.

"Should I start a tab?" questioned the bartender.

Epic cut in before she could answer. "No need. Please, put all of the young lady's drinks on my tab."

"That's very nice of you, but completely unnecessary," she said with a seductive smile.

Without trying to sound arrogant, he replied, "It would be my pleasure to treat such a beautiful woman tonight."

"Sorry, but I can't let you pay a hundred dollars a drink for me. It's far too expensive a habit to push off on someone else."

"Don't worry. I got you. Drink all you like. Take the bottle if you want to."

"But it's a hundred dollars a drink!" she exclaimed.

REMEMBER EVERYBODY AIN'T LOYAL | KEESE

"Yeah, I heard you, and did I blink?" Epic asked.

"Okay, on one condition. You have to come drink it with me," she said, and Epic looked back at Payne again, who he was sure had stopped breathing. "That is, if your friend doesn't mind," she said, glancing at Payne.

"Naw, he don't mind. Do you, brah?"

Payne came out of his daze. "Hell naw. Go ahead. We can talk later," said Payne hurriedly.

"Excuse me, but I hope you don't mind me asking the name of the perfume you're wearing," said Epic.

"Not at all," she answered, smiling. "It's called *Man Killer* by Trinity. Do you like it?"

"Naw, I love it," he said, picking up the bottle of Macallan Single Malt Whisky and following her to a corner table.

"Forgive me for being rude. My name is Yasmeen Acousta," she said, holding out a hand for him to shake.

"No, please. Forgive me. My name is Epic Anders, and I'm pleased to meet you."

"So, what do you do for a living, Mr. Anders, that you can afford a two-thousand-dollar bottle of Macallans without blinking?" she inquired by way of small talk.

"Well, I'm part owner of an Investment Company here in Cleveland, and what is it that you do that you can afford to be such a connoisseur of rare, single malt scotch?" he asked.

She answered as she ran a single fire-engine-red fingernail around the rim of her glass. "I'm somewhat of a problem solver, or a trouble shooter, if you will, for a large pharmaceutical company." She smiled her seductive smile again. "And it pays quite well."

"I can resist a successful woman with her own money, drive, and determination".

They continued to chat and drink more of the single malt while the conversation turned more intimate as the night went on. At 10:20, she checked her watch, which he noticed and asked, "Do you need to get to bed?"

"I was just wondering how much longer I should wait before I invite you up to my room." Her voice was sexier than ever.

Epic felt his dick stiffen in his jeans. "Preferably right now would be a great time if you ask me."

Without another word, she took his hand and led him to the hotel's bank of elevators. Inside, she pressed the button for the penthouse. She was in his arms as soon as the door closed. They locked into an intense kiss, which allowed him to feel her very excited and erect nipples on his chest. He pressed his hard dick into her thigh, causing her to moan in his ear like a lioness purring.

Epic made sure to keep her hands away from the small of his back, where he had a Smith & Wesson M & P .40 Cal pistol tucked away in a paddle holster. Doors opened just as she ran one hand over his physique, and the other fire-engine-red-nailed hand over the dick print in his jeans. Yasmeen broke away from him and walked into the living room, allowing her dress to fall to the floor, pooling around her six-inch stilettos. She stood nude before she looked back over her shoulder at him.

"Come. Show me what it is that you really want."

Epic started to undress on the way to the bedroom, making sure that he timed it just right so he could get away without her seeing his gun. As they began to kiss again, his rock-hard dick smacked her flat stomach. Her sensitive nipples poked him in the chest, while her nails raked his dick.

Yasmeen was turned on and burning with lust as she placed both her hands around his neck, then both his shoulders, and began to push him down to his knees. She gasped when his lips closed over her right nipple, which sent an electric shock straight to her hypersensitive clit. His warm tongue slipped over her belly button, and he paused as if he was going to stop, causing her to apply more pressure to his shoulders, forcing him the rest of the way down to the promise land.

She then used two fingers to spread her Moca brown pussy lips to expose an excited clit. Yasmeen shook as his tongue made contact with her clit, and she felt him slide a finger deep between her wet folds.

She started to grind her wet pussy on his swirling tongue while pulling his face deep in between her legs. She leaned all the way back against the dresser, resting her ass on the edge, then spread both her legs wide so he could make love to her soaking wet pussy with his mouth.

He skillfully resumed his attack on her lower region, drawing louder and louder moans from her lips as she went crashing and shaking through a full-body orgasm. Epic twirled his tongue around her clit as another feverish climax built deep within her core, his thumb lingering at the entrance of her wet well.

She used two of her fingers to spread her swollen lips like the petals of a blooming flower to reveal the creamy, pink, inviting tunnel waiting to be filled by him. He pushed two fingers deep inside her tight, wet sheath while simultaneously nibbling her clit and sending shockwaves of pleasure from the soles of her feet to the top of her head. Her second orgasm was a devastating release of pent-up, intense pressure that had her screaming his name.

"Oh my God, Epic! I'm cumming!" she yelled as black spots danced across her vision. Just the sound of her screaming his name raised her to a new level of fuckability that almost made him bust a nut before he put dick to pussy.

Yasmeen pushed his torturous mouth away from her dripping pussy. His talented tongue had her all but begging for every inch of him inside her. She repositioned herself, slowly turning around, facing the mirror, and bending forward so he could take her from behind while she watched him in the mirror.

A thrill shot through her as Epic placed a hand in the center of her back, forcing her even further down on the dresser, and when she tried to rise, he added more pressure to hold her still. Yasmeen was used to being in charge of men, so to have one dominate her turned her pussy into a raging inferno that seemed capable of turning her own body into ash.

Their eyes met in the mirror as the head of his throbbing dick stretched her well-lubed pussy to its limits and then some. With only half his dick finding a very snug home in her tight passageway, Epic had to wonder if he could get the rest in before she tapped out.

Surprisingly, she pushed back, tentatively sliding a few more inches in. Epic drew back slowly, then began to softly stroke her, purposefully not going very deep. He could feel the tight walls of her pussy squeezing tighter as she started to cum again for him. As she started to quiver with an orgasm, he callously slammed every inch of his dick deep in her twitching pussy while at the same time grabbing both her hips to hold her still.

Yasmeen was one hundred percent sure that the head of his dick was exploring the very depths of her stomach, and before she could get her breath back, he started a long, steady stroke, which built his momentum until he was pounding his big dick into the tightest pussy he'd ever fucked. Yasmeen's screams and moans echoed around the room, and for the first time in her life, she was willing to fully accept a man's authority and obey.

Epic's heavy balls slammed against her clit as he slayed the pussy. Sensation after sensation flooded her body as she bent to his will and endured the incredible fucking Epic was putting down on her.

"Don't stop! Oh, please, don't stop! Make me cum, Epic. Cum deep in me." She moaned and begged like she'd never begged any man. That was his undoing as they came in unison, and he shot spurt after spurt of hot cum into the tightest pussy he'd experienced in his life. Epic collapsed on her back as the last of his seed sprayed into her Honeywell, and again, their eyes met in the mirror. He pulled his semi-hard dick from her well-fucked pussy, picked her up in his arms, and carried her to bed as if she were a precious gem.

Later that night, as Epic lay asleep, Yasmeen stood beside the bed, pointing a silenced Glock 17 at the back of his head. She had never before hesitated to follow a single order or wish that Ariella had given her, but now—now she found, as delusional as it was, he made her feel innocent, something she could now never claim to be.

Yasmeen slipped the gun back under the edge of the bed, softly raining kisses on the back of his neck until he rolled over and took her into his arms.

Payne was gone off the Henny and weed but couldn't help feeling superior, having been the one to survive over the likes of a real street nigga like Epic. The shit at Mimosa Grill had been surreal. He'd almost lost his mind when Yasmeen Acousta rolled up on them. That was pure craziness. He couldn't even bring himself to feel guilty about Epic's fate, as he convinced himself that what happened wasn't because he had not been slick enough, but because Epic had somehow messed up the lick and left clues that allowed the Acoustas to find them.

Payne passed the blunt to Big Moe as he worked on influencing the young street goon to be his new partner in crime.

"Yo, dog. It's like this. You're the muscle, and I'm the brains, so let's get this money," Payne finished, giving Big Moe a fist bump.

Chapter 11

Asimi had yet to hear back from Epic about how the meeting with the grandmother had gone. His troubles and stressful situation were weighing heavily on her mind, and she wasn't so sure now whether what she had set in motion was a good idea.

How could she even begin to explain to Epic what she'd done, and how would he react when he knew the whole story? It all seemed so simple and was working out as planned, but how could someone tell the love of their life that they were also in love with someone else, and that they'd been set up?

Her thoughts were interrupted as the bathroom door opened, and the other love of her life stepped out, naked, setting her heart to racing, only as Epic ever had before. The two had started as friends and classmates, but the late-night study sessions and all the time spent together led to much more than they expected. She had been so lonely, away from Epic, and one light kiss had blossomed into a two-year, secret relationship, one she couldn't believe had happened, but she could also not deny the fact that she was deeply in love with both of them.

Asimi decided that, for better or worse, she would tell Epic everything and let the chips fall where they may, hoping that it all worked out. She knew it was selfish, but she said a silent prayer to God that she wouldn't lose him. No matter how strong this relationship was, she couldn't imagine her life without Epic. The warm, wet tongue probing her pussy put her thoughts on hold.

Ariella Acousta sat poolside, feeding strips of raw meat to her year-old lion that she'd named Puppy as a joke at first, finding that it actually fit him quite well. It was something she loved about the sheer power of the big cat, the danger he presented. She'd raised and hand-fed him since he was a week old and understood that just like her, he could never be tamed.

Puppy's deep growl made her aware that someone was approaching her from behind. "Easy, baby. It's only Yasmeen," she said without turning around.

"So it's done," Ari said as more of a statement than a question.

Yasmeen stood silently, causing Ari to look back at her with questioning.

"Well? Why are you standing there like when Papa caught you sneaking a smoke from one of his Cuban Cigars?" asked Ari, a little concerned.

Understanding that there could be repercussions for her actions, Yasmeen answered her sister's question. "No, Ari, he is not dead. I did not kill him, although you ordered me to do so, and I will if you order it, after I've spoken my idea to you about a way we may benefit by not doing so." Ari's only answer was a raised eyebrow, so Yasmeen continued. "If what Payne told us about Epic is true, then would it not be smart of us to use him to go into the black neighborhoods for us?"

Yasmeen's idea was a very weak one, but that was what most intrigued Ari, and this was the first time Yasmeen had failed to obey an order from her.

"Okay, Yas. I will meet with him and decide if he should live or die, but first. I want you to tell me why you didn't just kill him like so many before," Ari said to her younger sister.

Yasmeen thought for a while about how to answer the question. "I have had to live my life with a certain amount of viciousness, merciless to any and all who would harm our family or business. Just this once, someone made me believe that I could be more than merciless. Instead, I could choose to be merciful, give someone a second chance, a chance to someone who made me feel special, made me feel fear that I thought no longer lived within me." Yasmeen fell silent under her sister's gaze.

"Send Miguel and Santo to collect him immediately and bring him to the plane. We need to be in Miami tonight."

"Alive and unhurt?" Yasmeen questioned.

With a sigh, Ari gave a small nod while Puppy used his sandpaper-rough tongue to clean her fingers.

Epic awoke to find Yasmeen gone, his iPhone dead, and a slight headache from the single malt whiskey. He slowly dressed, thinking of his to-do list for the day, and the first thing he had to do was call Asimi and lay the groundwork for the difficult conversation they needed to have about their relationship. He then thought about Sarah and ending that relationship while he tried to prove to Asimi how sorry he was for cheating on her and how much he loved her. Epic knew that, for them to have any chance at a real life together, he had to come clean with Asimi, even if it cost him everything.

He was still trying to think of what to say when the elevator doors opened to the lobby of the hotel. Stepping out, he noticed two men in dark suits speaking with the desk clerk. Passing them by, he stepped into the early morning sunshine, deciding that he'd stop by the office first to chop it up with Payne, then get on the road to Yale to see Asimi and end things with Sarah.

Screeching tires caught his attention as a black Mercedes-Benz G Wagon slid to a stop in front of him. Epic started to reach for his pistol when he was struck in the back of the head by something heavy and hard. The last thing he heard before losing consciousness was, "Sleep tight. You've got a rendezvous to keep."

The deep growl of powerful engines and a steady rocking motion woke Epic from his forced oblivion to find himself in a king-sized bed in a very nice stateroom. Teak-paneled walls and gold trim filled the room, along with full-length mirrors, a sliding glass door on the opposite side, and a sunken custom flatscreen. Artwork covered the rest of the walls.

He got to his feet a little shakily and unstable. He used his right hand to gently rub the tender lump on the back of his head, which only pissed him off as he began to remember what happened. Epic didn't know where he was, but somebody was going to get their ass whooped. He looked out the glass door and only saw water as far as he could see, which he guessed explained the rocking motion.

'What the fuck is going on?'

The only way to find out was to find out who was fucking with him and why. He walked to the door and tried the handle, expecting it to be locked, and was shocked when it wasn't. He made his way down the hall, opening each door he came to, only to find all the luxury staterooms empty. He continued until he came to the main salon, which had an elevator that led to a sky lounge and a pilot's deck.

Bypassing the elevator, he stepped out onto an open-air balcony overlooking a pool and jacuzzi, and couldn't help but think, 'Damn, how big is this boat?'

The clearing of a throat behind him made him spin around, reaching for the gun he no longer had. The short man dressed in a lightweight, white cotton shirt and slacks spoke in broken English.

"Sir, jor presence is expected below, so if ju would please follow me."

Epic stood a few more seconds before falling in step behind his guide and following him down a winding glass and gold-plated staircase. As he entered the luxury gallery filled with expensive furniture, artwork, Satellite TV, and Wi-Fi access, a beautiful woman he first thought was

Yasmeen but, on closer inspection, realized even Yasmeen's beauty paled in comparison, sat, sipping a fruity-looking drink. Epic almost forgot about being pissed—almost.

"Hola, and welcome to my yacht, The Valkyrie. I'm sure you are wondering why you are here and who I am, but all you need to truly know is that your life is in my hands," she said.

"Fuck is you talkin' 'bout, yo?" replied Epic, thug grilling her. "But you got me bent or mixed up with someone else 'cause I don't even know you, ma."

A smile crossed her face, and Epic wasn't sure if it was sexy or sinister. That was until four big muthafuckas with AK-47s stepped from each corner of the room.

"Sit. Epic, there are some things we need to talk about and some decisions we need to make." She looked back over her right shoulder and said something in rapid-fire Spanish that he couldn't understand.

One of the men left, only to return a few minutes later with a five-gallon bucket of bloody meat, fish guts, and some other shit he couldn't describe if he tried to. Epic watched as the man with the bucket started to scoop the nasty ass mix out and throw it into the water.

"What the hell is he doing?" asked Epic.

"He's chumming the water, but you don't need to worry about that right now. What you do need to worry about is why I have brought you here and for what reason," she said, holding his attention with her hard stare.

Epic thought for a minute before answering. "Well, ma, the first one is easy. You brought me out here to get a read on me, and if you don't like what you find out, that's too much damned water for me to drink. The second could be a number of things. I ain't no angel, so at some point in my life, I've done something to get your attention. Now, whether it's for better or worse is what I can't figure out yet." Epic finished and sat back, sinking into the chair.

The fact that she just sat there quietly, as if he'd said nothing at all, shook him more than if she had told him he was wrong or laughed in his face. Instead of speaking, she stood up, turned, and walked toward the pool near the back of the yacht. She didn't ask him to follow, and she knew she didn't have to.

Epic followed while trying to keep an eye on the security team.

She looked back over her shoulder with a seductive smile and began to remove her skirt and blouse, leaving nothing to the imagination. Epic watched her golden-skin-toned ass slip into the crystal-clear pool water as she sank down to her shoulders before turning around to fold both arms on the pool side.

Her security team stayed a discreet distance away but formed a protective ring around the pool. Epic stood, waiting, while the man with the bucket continued to chum the water behind the yacht.

After taking a sip of champagne, she began slowly. "I find myself in a moral dilemma, which is not a place I often land, yet here I am. You see, certain expectations, such as protection and compensation, are a promise given to any and all that work for me, and fortunately, I'm the only one who decides what these will be. Possibilities and solutions are before me."

Epic didn't care much at all for the sound of any of that, but he said nothing.

"Esco, has our guest arrived for dinner?" she asked the man chumming the water.

"Sí, Jefa."

"Bring out their meal.'

Esco hurried off into the interior of the ship as she went on. "You are here because you robbed and killed a member of my cartel family. Although he was a low-ranking member, he was still a member. And there lies my moral dilemma. So, maybe you could help me with my decision. Maybe you killing him was justifiable. Let's say that hypothetically speaking, he was stealing money, and you found out, so you did me a favor and killed him."

She waited for him to speak. "First, ma, you gonna have to put a name on this shit because I've put in too much work to just assume who it is you're talking about gettin' merked," Epic replied.

"Kyrie Nieto. Does that name ring a bell? Please remember, before you answer, that your life depends on your answer," she said, rising out of the water enough for him to glimpse her sun-kissed brown nipples.

"No disrespect, ma, but if a muthafucka out there doing too much or being extra, and I catch him slippin', then it is what it is. So, to answer your question, yes, I popped that nigga Kyrie's top," Epic said, standing up a little taller.

She tilted her head to the side in thought before she spoke. "I think that many people in life have underestimated you, and I will be sure not to make the same mistake. That is, should I choose to utilize your talents."

There was the sound of scuffling behind him as the man named Esco muscled a man with his hands tied behind his back out onto the deck. There was a wild look in the man's eyes, and only the gag in his mouth kept him from begging as Esco held him still at the back of the yacht.

"Finally. So good of you to join us, Doronato. The guests have been waiting for the meal I promised them."

Epic could see the fins of sharks thrashing around and churning the water into white foam.

"Esco, remove the gag from his mouth," she ordered, which he did, and as soon as it was out, Doronato began pleading for his life.

"Please, Jefa, I'm sorry! Please, don't kill me. Allow me to make it up to you. I'm sorry!"

"Not as sorry as you will be," she said, then gave a small nod as Esco shoved the terrified man into the shark feeding frenzy. Doronato hit the water with a splash and a scream as the water turned bright red from his blood.

Epic watched without cringing as the sharks tore into Doranato's body with razor-sharp teeth, several of them fighting over every scrap of meat. The water was chaotic as the sharks made quick work of the body that would never be found.

She emerged from the pool, grabbing a pair of Fendi sunglasses off the poolside table, then walked to the back of the boat to watch the last of Doronato get consumed. Epic stepped up beside her, causing every one of the security team to raise their weapons in case he got any stupid ideas.

She glanced at him out of the corner of her eye. "So, what's it to be? Are you in, or are you dessert?" She stopped him before he could answer by saying, "I will expect you to do whatever you're told without question or hesitation. Or we take another boat ride. I will not tolerate insubordination of any kind. To quote a very wise man: insubordination is the lack of respect a coward gives to those he wishes were dead. That wise man was my father, Ernesto Acousta, the former head of the Acousta Cartel."

She stood there, butt ass naked, facing him eye to eye, before she threw her two-thousand-dollar Fendi shades into the water.

"Esco, I seem to have dropped my sunglasses overboard. Fetch them for me. Now!"

Without a word or hesitation, Esco dove into the water and was not seen again for at least two full minutes before he resurfaced with Fendi shades in hand, swam back to the stair platform, then pulled himself from the water.

"Here they are, Jefa," he said with no animosity in his voice whatsoever.

Epic couldn't front. He was impressed by the display of power, but she was out of her damn mind if she thought he was going to dive in that shit.

"Are you a coward?" she asked with a sardonic smile playing across her face.

"Naw, ma, never that, but only a fool would waste their life for a pair of Fendi shades," he said, a little heated by the question. "But let me tell you the words of a wise man. A coward dies a thousand deaths. A soldier dies but one. Tupac said that shit, and it's the shit I live by," Epic replied.

She smiled at him as she corrected him. "Cowards die many times before their deaths; the valiant never taste of death but once—William Shakespeare." She finished with a satisfied smirk.

"Fuck ever, ma. Tupac was a true street poet, and I'm a real street nigga, so that's what it do," he said with a shoulder shrug.

After that, she was right back to business. "I have a few things for you to take care of here in Miami. You will be given everything you need to complete these tasks."

"That's what's up, but check it. I've got a few things to take care of in Cleveland before I can commit to what you need me to do down here. You feel me?"

A dangerous look crossed her face. "You're cute, but if Payne Nevins is what you need to handle in Cleveland, then you can forget about that. He now works for me, and you know how I feel about that subject."

Epic was fuming but kept his face neutral. "A'ight, ma. We'll do it your way."

"Always," she replied.

He didn't say it aloud, but he promised himself that he would kill Payne, no matter what boss lady said, and if she got in his way, then she could get it too. Epic knew, for the time being, he had to play the hand he'd been dealt with because there was no way he could bring this kind of danger around Asimi.

Ariella stepped in close to Epic so that her wind-chilled nipples were touching his chest as she trailed a manicured hot-pink nail down his stomach. "Now that we've had the chance to come to an understanding, we can have a bit of fun," she said, dropping her hand to the bulge in his jeans.

"I guess you're not worried about being sued for sexual harassment, or is sleeping with the help standard operating procedure in the cartel?"

"You are fearless, aren't you?" she asked. "But to answer your question, no. I've never slept with any who works for me, but whatever you did to my sister made her not only disobey me, but made her come beg for me to spare your life, so now I'll see for myself if Yasmeen has gotten soft or if you truly have the magic stick."

Epic leaned into the kiss. The boss was so strong that Epic actually felt his heart skip a beat, but the half-dressed woman had his mind on lock.

He glanced at his watch and realized he still had an hour to go before the muthafucka who'd won himself a death sentence was going to be there. Feeling naked in the club without a strap, and like so many niggas were looking like they wanted smoke, had him slightly on edge.

Club Vortex featured every baller's dream—bad bitches, expensive drinks, designer drugs, and a private VIP section. The entire VIP area was behind a two-way mirror that allowed those VIPs to see out but kept the regular club goers from seeing how the rich and famous lived, or the rich and infamous.

Epic sat in a corner, watching the dance floor and the flow of people coming in and out of the VIP. He was sure that smoking this muthafucka wouldn't be too hard. He just had to get past the man mountain of the VIP entrance.

Once he was inside, he could put his murder game down without worrying about being caught on camera because the VIP was the only place besides the bathroom that didn't have any. More time passed as Epic nursed his glass of Cîroc while taking slow drags on a Newport one hundred.

He'd caught the eye of a lot of the women in the club, but he'd turned down all those who came to keep him company while he waited. Ten minutes before the hit was to happen, a thick Spanish ma rolled up to his table and sat down without being asked to.

"Hola, papi."

"What it do, ma? Any other time, I'd be glad to kick it, but I'm waiting for my girlfriend right now, and she loves drama," Epic said, trying to get rid of her without causing a scene.

She smiled as she leaned closer to him to whisper. "I came here with your girlfriend. Her name is Nina, right? Kinda quiet, but she can get loud if she wants to?" she asked, slipping a 9mm Glock 17 with a silencer on it into his lap under the table. She then leaned forward to give Epic a kiss on the cheek while whispering in his ear, "Five minutes, so be ready to move."

Epic slipped the Glock into his waistband as she left the table, headed for the dance floor.

A few minutes later, as Epic watched a fight break out near the bouncer at the entrance to the VIP, he knew it was his opening. As the two men crashed into the bouncer, all hell broke loose when another group of men started fighting near the bar, and the chaos became a juggernaut that the club security couldn't handle.

Epic quickly entered the VIP section, scanning those inside to find his target. Paco Mena sat at the last booth in the back with four women and two bodyguards around him, looking through the two-way mirrors and out into the club. Epic had no idea what issue the Acousta Cartel had with Paco, but legitimate or not, Paco's ass was about to be merked.

The men guarding Paco weren't lethargic when it came to their duty. As Epic pulled the Glock 17, the first bodyguard dived on top of his boss, shielding him with his body. The second man rushed Epic Kamikaze style, pulling his weapon at the same time. Epic calmly put two 9mm rounds into his chest, then moved forward, firing at Paco and the other bodyguard as havoc ensued. One of his rounds tore through the jugular of the second bodyguard, sending a bright-red spray of blood arcing into the air. Those in the VIP room began to run, screaming and falling into the line of fire. Epic caught movement to his left as a stupid muthafucka in a loud ass neon-yellow shirt tried to be a hero and came running at him with a Patrón bottle cocked back like a club. Epic put one slug in his head for his dumb ass bravado.

By this time, Paco was on his feet, close to the last mirror, looking for a way out while using one of the women at his table as a human shield and sweating profusely.

Epic fired one round into the slim redhead's stomach, causing her to drop. The next two rounds, he put in Paco's head and chest. The impact sent Paco's body crashing through the two-way mirror and out into the club. He then exited the club with all the other running and scared-shitless people fleeing for their lives. The job was complete, and Epic was ready to return to Cleveland and take care of the other business he had on the back burner.

However, Ari Acousta had other plans, and those did not include going to Cleveland or anywhere else except where she needed him to go, so an hour after the hit at Club Vortex, Epic was being dropped off at the Miami Airport in front of the Delta Terminal with a plane ticket for a flight to New York due to land at LaGuardia early Sunday morning. While waiting for his flight, Epic bought a can of Red Bull, some Jack Links Teriyaki beef jerky, and to top it off, an Oreo cookies and cream Bar.

He watched as a woman who slightly reminded him of Asimi dragged a rolling Samsonite carry-on through the concourse. He was well aware he'd not talked to her in two days but wanted to have his shit together before he tried to start to explain any of these new, life-changing developments to her—if he ever did.

The shit with Payne was another problem he swore to himself he'd deal with, no matter what the fuck Ari Acousta said, because, evidently, this bitch didn't understand this was the streets, and snitches got left in ditches. For now, he had to play his cards right, and that meant doing whatever to stay alive and keep this drama and danger away from Asimi at all costs. To Epic, that was imperative.

Chapter 12

Payne decided the best way to clean the amount of money that the Acousta Cartel would need cleaned would be to pull the bait and switch. It was an old trick, but Payne had a new twist to add that would keep anyone looking at it from linking it to the old trick. By setting up a dummy business in South Africa he named Legion Digital Solutions, he'd be able to take money in from legit investors, then invest those funds in other companies, like Tesla, Microsoft, and Amazon, as long-term investments.

Then he'd run the cartel money through his fake company, Legion Digital Solutions, showing a large profit return on the cooked books after the money had run through the South African banks and paid a two percent tax, while all money returned would be clean and legal.

His legit investors would make a little money at first with these legit businesses, then Payne would talk them into investing in Legion Digital Solutions, which would then go belly-up, consuming all or most of their capital. At that time, he'd supply a half-percent share with Epic Investments so no one took a total loss, but would still be thankful, therefore not reporting him to the Better Business Bureau as he reinvested the lesser money through Epic Investments. Funds Recuperation went a long way after someone took a big loss, so anything that helped them get back on the right track was very much appreciated.

Payne pulled on a My Blu vaping cigarette while sitting outside of Jared's Jewelry store, waiting for Candy to come out after picking up the custom sapphire and diamond bracelet he'd bought her to prove that shit between her and Epic was nothing to him. Even if he couldn't convince himself of the lie, he wasn't pleased that Ari Acousta hadn't killed Epic, as she said she would.

He was happy with the fact that she had promised that Epic wouldn't touch him, but Payne had an insurance policy on deck if he tried anything. The twenty-six-hundred dollars he'd dropped for the bracelet would go a long way with Candy showing her appreciation in a sexual way later tonight.

While sitting there, he even toyed with the idea that maybe, just maybe, he and Epic could come together one more time to finish that lick on Mr. Incognito. After all, money was money, and even Epic could respect that, right?

Epic wasn't sure exactly who Ari Acousta had sent him to New York to deal with, but he knew this wasn't going to be a fun-filled vacation. As he exited the jetway and cleared the baggage claim, he wasn't surprised to see an Acousta Cartel cut-out waiting for him. It was as if all sense of humor eluded this man. Epic couldn't care less, because he wasn't one for jokes either, especially when it came to being in a city he didn't know and for a reason he'd yet to find out.

"Follow me!" barked the cartel cut-out with more than a hint of animosity in his tone before turning and walking away without waiting to see if Epic would follow. He was about twenty feet away before he realized that he wasn't being followed. The man turned back with a look of astonishment on his face, unbelieving anyone would disobey or question the authority granted to him through Ariella Acousta. But knowing this was not a place for argument with the audience of airport travelers.

Epic had no idea what Ricky Recardo's problem was, but after the long flight, he wasn't in the mood for anyone's bullshit, especially not some low-ranking, wanna-be tough guy. Attitude met attitude as the two of them stood there, mean-mugging each other.

The man's attempt to intimidate Epic was a waste of time, and any thought of superiority was similarly wasted. Irritated even more now, Ricky Recardo walked back to Epic, mumbling in Spanish. Epic's demeanor didn't change with the arrival of his guide.

"What? Are you waiting for an invitation?" he asked. "Or are you hard of hearing?"

"Aye, check it, my dude. This respect-my-authority-shit might work on other niggas you deal wit', but that shit don't carry no weight with me," Epic spat at him. "You might wanna ask yo' boss lady about my pedigree before it's too late to realize you don't want no smoke."

The Acousta soldier reached inside his jacket pocket to remove his iPhone and hit speed dial, never breaking eye contact with Epic. After a few seconds of rapid-fire Spanish, the combative look on the soldier's face suddenly changed. The color drained from his face as he listened without speaking. A minute later, he handed the iPhone over to Epic, who took it.

"What it do?" asked Epic into the phone.

"Buyo is there to ensure that you have everything you need to complete what you need to do while you are in New York, so you need to follow his instructions," Yasmeen Acousta said.

Epic listened before responding to the underboss of the Acousta Cartel. The fact that he'd beat her back out didn't change the discussion or the reason he was in New York right now.

"I could really care less if this muthafucka is here to show me around or get what I need, and showing me around doesn't mean bossing me around. You feel me?"

Epic couldn't miss the look of disbelief on Buyo's face as he spoke aggressively to the second-most powerful person this clown probably knew. Yasmeen's voice brought him back to the moment.

"There is a person there who has become quite a problem, and problematic people don't live long when dealing with my sister or me—something you should keep in mind."

Epic wasn't feeling the weakly valued threat, so he didn't even try to hide the menace in his voice. "Ma, you caught me slippin' once, and that's on me, but I can promise you those days are over. So, let's kill the weak ass rah-rah shit so I can do this and get back to the land."

"Are you finished now?" she asked in a frustrated tone of voice.

"Naw, ma, I ain't. See, unlike Ricky Recardo, standing here, I know my self-worth, and I know if I'm here for this, that means y'all need me to do this, not just anybody, but me. Therefore, can we get on with it? Supposedly, there is a problem that needs a ballistic solution and not merely mean mugs from the likes of this lame," declared Epic.

There was only silence on the line.

"Return the phone to Buyo," said Yasmeen.

Epic pitched the phone toward Buyo and started walking out of the airport.

Buyo caught the phone, and after a few quick words and a sí or two, he followed Epic out, ready to be rid of this arrogant ass nigga. Epic stepped out under a cool, steel-gray, New York, threatening rain, yet it wasn't the weather that had him in a foul mood. His mind wasn't on the reason he'd been flown to New York, whatever it might be. He was thinking about how to get clear of the Acousta Cartel, deal with Payne, and the talk he needed to have with Asimi.

He'd not even dared get in touch with Asimi for fear he would give the cartel another way to control him, and that, he would never do. Ariella Acousta was a woman born to exploit any and every weakness to get what she wanted, and it was something Epic understood, seeing as he was the same way.

The anxiety that Asimi felt wasn't coming from the regular stress of law school or even the conversation that she needed to have with Epic. It was more of the fact that she'd not heard from him, and although he'd been known to change plans at the last minute, he'd always at least called. Asimi left yet another voicemail for her missing man, feeling even lonelier than ever.

It was these same lonely feelings that first led to the late-night study groups, which led to late-night talks, which led to emotions being discussed, and before she completely realized it, she found herself in bed, in a relationship with someone other than Epic. Asimi's heart belonged to Epic, but where did it say that the heart couldn't be shared with more than one person?

Damn, not even she could believe that she was thinking like that. She wasn't some unfaithful hood rat that cheated on her man. She couldn't count how many episodes of 'Jerry Springer' and 'Cheaters' she had watched while talking junk about those who cheated. To make things worse, she had deceived the one she loved on more than one level.

She'd decided no matter what the outcome, maybe once she'd told Epic about her other relationship, win or lose, she'd pay him back for all her law school tuition after she passed the Bar Exams and got on her feet. Asimi was fully aware that her secret was a ticking bomb that could blow up in her face, so it was in her mind prudent for her to explain to Epic before that happened.

Picking up her phone, she tried calling Epic one more time before leaving for her study group.

Chapter 13

Essence sat in the dressing room of Exotic Toyz, doing line after line of cocaine, sweat running down between her surgically-enhanced, forty-four double D breasts. Either the coke or the bright lights had her sweating like a ho in church.

"Damn, it's packed out there," said Sexy Black, coming into the dressing room.

"Shit, any real money out there?" asked Essence.

"Hell no, just a lot of five-dollar niggas, pump faking like million-dollar ballers."

"And that's why I'm back here," Essence said, snorting a fat line.

"I came back here looking for my Altoids for this stank-breath nigga in VIP, but since I'm back here, let me get a bump or two?" asked Sexy Black while pulling a wedgy out of her coochie. After doing two lines of powder, Sexy Black said, "If I was a real grimy bitch, I'd push up on Candy's nigga and get some of that paper." Satisfied that she had a little pussy lip showing, Sexy Black went back out into the club.

Essence did one more line before putting her stash away while thinking, 'If that shit wasn't an invitation to get at Candy's nigga, she didn't know what was, and if the bitch was truly on her game, she wouldn't let him be up in this bitch around all this hot pussy without her.' Essence walked through the club, radiating sexual confidence with every step.

The pulsating beat sent vibrations from the soles of her feet, up her thighs, and to her wet wet. Cigar smoke hung thick in the air, mixing with every kind of cologne known to man. Touching the dancers at Exotic Toyz was not permitted, but neither was it stopped if a nigga as spending that money on the girl he was touching.

She watched as Lexi worked the pole on center stage, bumping and grinding to 'Wet and Wild,' the new strip club anthem by J. Rave. Her skin was glistening, and when the light hit it just right, the body glitter made her skin glow. Shit, even she had to admit that Lexi's ass was looking pretty hot and tempting. She was tantalizing to the point that she made a mental note to explore what was going on with Lexi and some girl-on-girl action at a later time.

Essence spotted Payne in his normal spot, sitting front and center stage, sipping a drink, while Lexi put that work in, making her ass cheeks clap. Yes, she was definitely going to lick that kitty. None of the girls really messed with Payne, knowing that Candy had her hooks in him, but Essence was about that bag. To her, this nigga was dollar signs, and she was willing to suck and fuck to get that buck.

Right before she slid into a chair beside Payne, Essence perked up the double D's and casually made sure her tight nipples brushed his shoulder as she sat down. Payne turned to look at her as she leaned in to speak loudly and clearly in his ear.

"So, I see ya girl let you out by yourself tonight," she teased. "You must be completely loyal or pussy-whipped to the point that she ain't worried about you puttin' dick to nobody else," she said with a little flick of her tongue on his ear. Essence grabbed the bulge in his pants. "Are you sprung? It sure doesn't feel like it."

Payne's heart was pumping all the blood for his brain right into the hard muscle that Essence was squeezing on. Every molecule in his body was on fire, and he was unsure how much more he could endure before he came in his Sean

John briefs. He'd never been rejected by Essence, but he never pursued her either, but at the moment, none of that mattered as to why she was stroking his dick through his jeans. He couldn't stop or believe the words that next came out of his mouth.

"But what about Candy?" He wheezed.

"What about her? I won't tell if you don't." She added a little more pressure to heighten the sensation. Anticipating his next question, Essence said, "Meet me in the ladies' room in five minutes, and be sure to bring this hard dick with you."

With one more glance out of her peripheral to Lexi on stage, Essence rose from the stool, headed toward the bathroom, ignoring some of the club patrons trying to get her attention for a lap dance.

Payne was barely able to wait five minutes before heading for the women's bathroom. He was feeling himself, and therefore felt every bitch out there was feeling him too. All bitches knew a real nigga when they saw one—a nigga getting that paper—and he was definitely getting that paper.

As Payne pushed open the door to the ladies' room, he was a bit shocked at how different it was from the men's bathroom. Not that the men's room wasn't up to standard and then some, but the ladies' restroom was A1.

To his left was a long counter with sinks and separate places for putting on makeup. To the right was a wall with full-length mirrors and a couch. There were tampon dispensers and a wall-mounted unit for seat covers, six identical, double-wide stalls, two wall-installed hand dryers, and hair dryers.

"Essence, you in here?" called out a nervous Payne.

By the way of answering, Essence stepped out of the last stall, ass naked with a smile. The fire that was smoldering in his pants burst into an inferno that threatened to consume him where he stood.

"Are you coming to get this?" she asked, patting a pouty-lipped kitty with the pubic hair shaved into an arrow pointing down.

Payne started to unbutton his pants as he walked toward her.

Fuck. He remembered he didn't have a rubber with him, but she he wasn't going to stop because of a lack of prophylactics.

"Damn, ma. I don't have any rubbers wit' me," said a visibly upset Payne, acting like this was a deal breaker.

"I'm straight, and I'm on the pill, so unless you got some STD, bring me that dick." She licked her lips while running her finger between her lower lips. The gesture alone was enough to have precum dripping from his primed and ready tool. Essence backed into the stall and sat down on the toilet as Payne stepped in and closed the door, leaning up against it.

He could've sworn he could see her exposed clit sticking out.

"You ever had a Trump?"

"What the hell is a Trump?" asked a confused Payne.

"It's when you get that secret service blow with one in the back door."

Before Payne could grasp her full intent, she had his dick in her mouth and a finger two knuckles deep in his no longer virgin asshole. A loud moan escaped his throat as he put his hands on her head and began to fuck her mouth. Payne's knees were shaking.

Essence sucked his dick like a vacuum gone wild as her finger worked his anus, her other hand making sure his balls weren't neglected. Essence twirled her talented tongue around the crown of his sensitive penis head, which was very effective and did the trick, as Payne shot a thick jet of cum down her greedy throat. Essence continued to suck every last drop of him as he quivered and swayed on his feet.

Popping his semi-hard dick out of her mouth, Essence told him, "That was a free warmup. Now, if you ready for the main event, you gotta come off that paper, boo boo." She finished by sinking her middle finger the rest of the way in his ass, causing his going-soft dick to jump back to a full erection.

In a strained voice, Payne asked, "How much?"

"That was a free thousand-dollar blowjob, but this here is some two-thousand wet gold between these thighs," Essence said, fingering her super-wet pussy.

"Bet."

Essence rotated Payne around to sit on the toilet before his knees gave out. Payne was pushed back against the toilet as Essence mounted his lap and pressed those beautiful double D's in his face.

"Now, let me show you why this is the best two thousand dollars you've ever spent," said Essence, lowering herself onto Payne's throbbing erection. Although he didn't have the biggest dick, it was big enough for her to work with. Ironically, it was perfect for rubbing her inner walls, and she released a satisfied sigh as she leisurely pierced her molting center.

Her slow rhythm built up speed as Payne's flesh-covered rod slid in and out of her lubricated tunnel. Sweet agony rose as Essence came closer to climax, and Payne began to thrust upward with powerful strokes, jarring her. Essence met his savagery with a savagery of her own as her first orgasm tore through her at the speed of light, welding them together to merge.

Payne lost the battle he'd been fighting within his tightening balls as spurt after spurt splashed into Essence's depths to mix with her release. Mercilessly, Essence continued to grind their lower regions together, knowing his penis was a sensitive as her clit.

Payne struggled to catch his breath as Essence stood up off his deflating dick with a mischievous smile on her face.

"Now you know that Candy is good, but Essence is the very substance distilled from great sex," she said while counting her money.

******

Spanish Harlem was turned up, and Epic could almost like New York—almost. There were thick, Latino honeys in short shorts, the smell of cooking food, and the blaring sound of reggaeton, all combining in a dense mixture to give the neighborhood of Washington Heights the feel of another country. Numerous kids ran up and down the blocks, playing in the streets, in and out of the bodegas on the corners. Motorcycles, dirt bikes, and four-wheelers were doing burnouts and doughnuts in the street. It wasn't so different from Cleveland except for the fact that the NYPD wasn't fucking with them.

Epic stood, looking out of the second-story window of a brownstone, deep in thought about what he had to do and how to get it done. He was dressed in what seemed to be the standard dress in the hoods of the city—camouflage pants, a black wifebeater, butter Timberland boots, and a durag.

His babysitter, Buyo, had given him he low-down on what Ari Acousta wanted done, and he understood why she wanted him to do it. It also explained why he'd been sneaked into this apartment and told to stay out of sight. This shit required an outsider because, success or failure, the shit was going to hit the fan, and the Acousta Cartel wanted to have full deniability.

Epic couldn't figure out the entire picture yet, but he would because, at some point, he would no longer be useful to Ariella Acousta or become a loose end. She'd try to end him. Right now, all he could do was wait for nightfall, so he decided to check over his equipment and try to come up with how he'd gone from a stick-up kid to a cartel killer and fun dummy.

Whatever Payne had done had drawn the cartel to them, but Epic didn't know the whole story yet, which meant not only was he expendable, but they might try to hurt him through Asimi, which he had to assume they knew about through Payne. If for no other reason, that was enough to make him merk Payne's bitch ass. Once this popped off, self-preservation was going to become a primary concern.

Chapter 14

Epic checked his watch, wishing he could have called Asimi at least one last time to tell her how much he loved her in case this went wrong, and he never got the chance. He could've just bounced, and the absurdity of that thought actually made him smile.

Epic weaved the powerful GSXR 1000 motorcycle through New York's heavy traffic, the black jacket, jeans, and boots all blending in with the jet-black machine. The deep growl of the bike bouncing off the massive New York Skyscrapers seemed like the cry of Hell's denizens rising. Not only was the bike a perfect getaway vehicle, but it also allowed Epic to wear a black helmet with a tinted face shield. Because everybody in the world now had a phone with a camera, he could guarantee this was going to make the news throughout the whole United States.

Twenty-One Ten was the hottest new restaurant in the city with a reservation waiting list a year long, but Assistant United States Attorney, Jason Dennett, had a private table, thanks to the owner, whose son he'd cut a sweet deal with to stay out of Federal Prison on drug-trafficking charges. Tonight, he was having dinner with a source inside the NYPD, a source about to give up the names of all the dirty cops and judges on the cartel's payroll.

The two deputy US Marshals, assigned protection detail, wore dark suits and were looking forward to the expensive meal that would be picked up by the government. A.U.S.A. Dennett looked at the wine list, thinking about a $180 bottle of Pinot Grigio to go with his meal, when Detective Mike Marales sat down across from him.

At first sight, Dennett could tell the detective was nervous. His eyes never stopped roaming over everyone in the restaurant, causing the two deputy marshals to look around.

"Relax, Detective. I was just about to order wine to go along with our meal tonight. Do you have a favorite?" asked Dennett.

"No. I'm more of a beer or shot kind of guy unless they have orange Fanta."

Figures, Dennett thought.

He had no idea what had happened between the dirty detective and the cartel that would make him willingly betray them and the rest of his dirty brothers in blue, but Dennett thanked his good fortune that Marales had come to him with it. This case would be a career maker.

"Does anyone know we were meeting her tonight?" asked Marales, looking around and scanning the crowd again.

"No. The only person who knew where I would be tonight is my personal assistant, and she didn't know that I'd be meeting with you. This meal will go down as a legal consultation slash negotiation, so calm down. Let's eat, then we'll talk shop, okay?"

Marales looked around one more time before he nodded.

Epic pulled the bike into the alleyway behind Twenty-One Ten and took a minute to scan up and down the narrow passageway. There was plenty of traffic passing at both ends of the alley's openings. Epic leaned the bike over on its kickstand as he got off and unzipped his jacket to pull out his Glock 21, quickly pulling back the slide to make sure there was a round chambered.

He then walked up to the dumpster, lifting the lid to retrieve the hard-sided, black case inside. Taking a knee, he set the case on the ground, popping the latches to remove the BushMaster MGS 96 chambered for 7.62mm NATO rounds coated with Teflon to penetrate body armor. Epic's gloved hands worked quickly, slapping the full thirty-round magazine into the weapon's magazine well. Yanking back the bolt, he seated one of the black-tipped mini rockets in the chamber. He then stuffed a second magazine into his waistband.

The cartel wanted to make a loud and clear statement. They wanted carnage and a high body count, along with the intended targets. Even though they would have plausible deniability, the underworld would know who was responsible for the massacre.

Epic took off his black jacket to expose his arms so the video cameras inside would see that the shooter was African American, therefore causing a smokescreen for law enforcement, keeping them from automatically pointing their investigations at the cartel. Epic checked the time on his watch, then stepped over to the rear kitchen door and lightly tapped on it.

It was opened immediately by a young Latino male in a white apron and thick, black rubber gloves up to his elbows. The dishwasher gave a slight nod to Epic and slipped out the open door before the mayhem to come would ensue.

The kitchen was a swarming hive of activity, and Epic was well into the midst of the cooks and servers before anyone paid enough attention to panic. It wasn't until a chef with a meat cleaver and a hero complex decided to do some dumb shit, which got his ass knocked out by a butt-stroke of an Epic MGS 96. At that time, chaos broke out in the kitchen, sending the whole staff running.

Assistant United States Attorney Jason Dennet looked up from the wine list toward the commotion as both U.S. marshals stood and began to draw their weapons. Detective Mike Marales dove out of his chair to the right side of their table just as Epic unleashed the first stream of 7.62mm rounds into the shocked crowd of diners.

Epic emptied the first thirty-round magazine, spraying indiscriminately at first, then prioritizing his fire on the table where he knew his targets were seated. A barrage of Teflon-coated death tore through the two deputy marshals and a number of innocent bystanders.

When his weapon cycled on empty, Epic smoothly pulled his full magazine from his waistband, ejecting the empty magazine, and slapping the full one in the empty well. People were running, screaming, and falling all over each other.

Epic's next nine rounds shredded Jason Dennett where he sat. The impact from the rounds knocked him over backward in his chair. An accumulation of spent shell casings lay around Epic's feet. Dead and wounded individuals were littered all throughout the restaurant, but Epic wasn't finished.

The boom from a weapon, not his own, had Epic pivoting left as the glass in the kitchen door behind him was obliterated. Epic fired in the direction the shots had come from, sending bullets ricocheting off the black-onyx-covered wall.

His MGS 96 clicked on empty again, and Epic let it drop, held by the weapon's shoulder sling. The Glock 21 was out in a flash as he scanned the area from which the danger had come, but there were no more shots—just the quiet after the storm. The beating of his heart, the surge of adrenaline, and the usual spike of euphoria at surviving another gunfight were loud in his mind.

Epic eased around the table with the Glock leading the way to find Detective Marales lying on his back in a pool of blood, but still alive.

"Please, don't kill me. Tell Ari I won't say anything. I promise," he begged while holding up his hand like it could stop a bullet.

Ignoring his words, Epic fired two heavy 45 Caliber slugs into the detective's head. He then quickly moved around a few overturned tables to where Dennett had fallen. Epic knew at first sight that the Assistant U.S. Attorney was dead, but fired two more rounds into his head as well.

He then checked his watch. A minute and ten seconds passed from beginning to end, and calculating the response time of the NYPD, he should've had about another three minutes to egress.

A sound behind him had Epic spinning, finger taking up slack on the Glock's trigger, ready to neutralize the threat. He only found a woman rocking back and forth hysterically, a man in a suit and tie dead on the floor at her feet.

Outside, Epic could hear the wail of sirens as New York's finest made their way to the scene of this city's latest carnage. He ran back through the now-empty kitchen and out the back. He tucked the Glock, then went over and threw the MGS 96 into the dumpster. He jumped on the GSXR and headed for the street and freedom.

An upscale New York restaurant was the scene of a mass shooting where a gunman, or gunmen, ambushed diners, seemingly killing at random.

Ariella Acousta hit the mute button on the television, effectively cutting off anything further the news anchor would have said about the unfolding events. She already knew all she wanted and needed to know.

Twenty-seven dead, nine wounded, and among the dead, Assistant United States Attorney Jason Dennett, along with veteran New York detective Mike Marales, and the two deputy marshals assigned to the protection detail.

The Federal Bureau of Investigation had taken the lead in the case, claiming domestic terrorism, and the deaths of an Assistant United States Attorney and two federal deputy U.S. Marshals made the case theirs. A spokesperson for the FBI had refused to elaborate on the ongoing investigation, and forensic teams collecting evidence had cordoned off the restaurant.

Ariella wished she could have been there to witness the complete pandemonium, the look of surprise on the Assistant U.S. Attorney's face, or the moment of death on the snitching ass coward as Epic pumped round after round into them. It was truly going to be shameful when it came time to kill him. No matter what she'd said, no one could be allowed to steal from the Acousta Cartel and live. It would've been viewed as a weakness.

Chapter 15

Asimi was one more day from getting in her car and driving to Cleveland to find Epic herself, law school be damned. Instead, she took a Xanax and decided to wait until her and Epic's next scheduled FaceTime, but if she didn't see his face or hear his voice, hell nor high water would stop her.

It was five minutes to six, and Asimi sat holding her breath until she realized what she was doing and took a very deep breath before exhaling it through her nose. She couldn't help but think about her obligations as a girlfriend. Epic had always been there for her, and no matter what was going on in his life right now, she promised herself she would be there for him. That was if he could forgive her for what she'd done and was still doing.

Epic had to take a cab from the Cleveland airport back to the hotel to pick up his car. The valet couldn't believe that someone had left a Bentley there for two days without so much as calling to check on it. He also couldn't believe the four-hundred-dollar tip he received.

Epic drove through downtown, enjoying being back in the land. He had a lot of thinking to do and even more planning before he could make any moves. Regrettably, he couldn't kill Payne just yet, but Payne would die for the left-hand shit he'd done. He was thinking of a way to provoke Payne into doing something stupid enough to make him kill the asshole without pissing off Ariella Acousta.

Common sense dictated that whatever Payne was doing for the cartel had to be money-related, so he would just have

111

to change the paradigm. Epic hated to think of Asimi as a liability, but as long as Payne or the cartel could get at her to hurt him, that was exactly what she was.

Passing the run-down tenement buildings, the sensation that shit was about to get even more problematic wouldn't pass, and if things were about to escalate, he needed to be ready for whatever.

Epic had destroyed the burner phone that Buyo had given him and had his own confiscated iPhone returned to him, but he had yet to turn it on. He knew there would be a thousand voice messages and texts from Asimi and a couple of hundred from Sarah, his little snow bunny nymphomaniac. Damn. Yet something else he had to take care of.

He was under no illusion that just because somebody wanted shit to go their way, that didn't mean it would. And as fun as it was to fuck the lining out of that tight ass, white pussy, he wasn't willing to give up Asimi for anyone. Epic used to consider himself a pussy connoisseur; that was until he and Asimi became Facebook official. Yeah, he still did a little creeping on the side, but his heart completely belonged to Asimi.

He fired up the blunt of Sour Diesel as he logged on to his computer. He hadn't spoken with her since he'd shown up unannounced at her door two weekends ago, aside from a few minutes. Epic knew that her curiosity would be killing her, but he also knew she wouldn't press him on it when he told her he'd been on a business trip.

That was one of the things he loved about Asimi. She wasn't about all that drama like most chicks out there would be if their man had gone missing for a full weekend without a word. Epic blew out a cloud of potent smoke as Asimi's smiling face came to his screen.

The combination of Sour Diesel and seeing Asimi equalized him. "Sup, bae. What it do?" asked Epic by way of greeting.

"Oh my God, bae! I've been trying to reach you all weekend long." The concern in her voice touched that place in his heart that only she could.

"Sorry, ma. Some really important business came up, and shit got hectic. I would have called you, but I couldn't. You feel me?"

Asimi hesitated a second before responding, realizing it would be futile to ask what business he was talking about because they didn't discuss his business.

"Okay, I was just worried—so worried that I almost called Payne to make sure you were alright."

The thought of her calling that snake ass nigga had Epic seeing red, but he controlled his emotions. "Look, ma. Remember what I told you. Don't call Payne for nothing, a'ight. And that was when we were business partners—not that we're not working together anymore— but please stay away from him, and let me know if he or anyone else you don't know tries to get at you."

"Wait. Why are y'all not partners anymore?" Asimi asked since he opened the door.

"Sometime shit happens, ma," Epic said evasively.

Asimi didn't push. She was too happy to be talking with Epic.

Epic was smart enough to know that it didn't make someone any less of a man to ask for help, and the only thing that stopped most men from seeking help was their pride. He had plenty of pride, but not enough to make him stupid.

The GSXR 1000 in New York that he'd ridden was nothing compared to his own GSXR 1300 Hayabusa he'd named the Gundam, after one of his favorite Japanese cartoons. It was completely customized with a built engine, bored and stroked to 1589 cc. undercut transmission, ported and polished heads, two stages of nitrous oxide, an air shifter, and an aircraft aluminum single-side swing arm. It was midnight blue with phantom-gray ghost graphics, a

Carolina-blue mother-of-pearl clear that made the color flip under the light.

The power was insane, and Epic could feel every cc. wanting to be unleashed as he sped down I-77 toward West Virginia and what he hoped would solve some of his problems.

One of the reasons he had bought a bike was that Ohio didn't have a helmet law, so he could feel the wind on his face at 110 miles per hour with nothing but a pair of Oakely Razor shades on.

He shot past an unmarked state trooper car, doing over 165. When the blue lights came on, he geared down one and hit the first stage of nitrous, pushing the bike to 180 in the blink of an eye, while he lay down on his tank behind the windscreen.

As the second stage of nitrous light blinked at him, daring him to push the button, he didn't need it, as the state trooper car fell further and further behind. Once out of sight, Epic took the first exit and pulled behind a Waffle House for about an hour. No matter how fast a bike was, it wasn't faster than their radio.

******

West Virginia

Felony was a nigga that lived by the name he'd earned at twelve years old and had been refreshing it ever since. If anyone was familiar with him, it was the psychotic twins he ran with and the only muthafuckas he'd trust with his life, and for him, that said a lot.

Havoc and Chaos were known to put that work in with those pistols for the right price or just for the fun of it. The three called themselves the Wild Boyz, but those who enforced the law called them menaces to society. The hood knew them as street soldiers. No matter what you called them, what they were was stone-cold killers.

Epic had met Felony in the boys' home in Ohio and quickly learned he was another nigga that didn't take shit from anyone. The two had become friends when Epic went into the bathroom to find two bigger boys beating the ever living shit out of the smaller kid. Epic quickly jumped in to help the underdog, and it was just one of many fights the two would endure during their time there, but they never again had to fight alone.

Epic rode into Shady Pines Trailer Court, looking for the old, double-wide the Wild Boyz called home. You really had to exaggerate to call it a home. Dirty kids, flea-ridden dogs, and trash roamed the streets of the trailer park, which could only be described as an economic sinkhole.

When Epic stopped in front of the address he was looking for, he could only shake his head in disbelief at the brand-new, canary-yellow NSX twin turbo, an Audi R8 Spyder, an all-black Nissan GTR with black rims and tinted windows, a white Jeep Grand Cherokee, and last but not least, a Mercedes-Benz G Wagon. These crazy ass niggas had over four hundred thousand dollars in cars parked in front of a twenty-five-dollar trailer, in a two-dollar trailer park.

There was a big ass, ferocious-looking Pitbull chained to the side of the front porch, watching Epic with great intent as if expectant of its next meal. The beast stood as Epic approached the door, but instead of growling, its tail started to wag a million an hour. Epic still didn't trust that, stepping wide of the dog. Feisty wasn't going to fool him.

Epic knocked on the thin, metal door as one of the small kids walked up to his motorcycle, which fit in perfectly with all the other expensive rides out front. He was about to tell the little boy not to touch the hot exhaust pipe, but then thought, 'Some things in life, you have to learn on your own.'

Just as the door opened, he heard a sizzling sound, followed by screaming and crying. The smell of high-powered weed smoke rolled out the open door as a woman

115

with long, blonde hair, blue eyes, big titties, and a pair of Daisy Duke cut-off shorts stood in the doorway.

"Yes? May I help you?" she asked with that West Virginia twang. Two pretty dimples flashed as she smiled.

"Yeah, ma. I came to holla at Felony."

"And who might I tell him is here to see him?"

"Epic."

"Oh, I just love y'all street names," she said, bouncing her big tits in his face.

From behind her came a deep voice Epic knew all too well. "Amber, who da fuck at the door?"

With a shrug of her shoulders, she called back into the trailer. "Some sexy chocolate, calling himself Epic!" she yelled.

"Who da fuck you say?"

"He said his name is Epic!" Amber repeated.

A second later, Amber was pushed aside, and Felony had Epic in a bear hug, his head only reaching the middle of Epic's chest. What he lacked in height, the deranged muthafucka made up in strength. Havoc or Chaos appeared in the door behind Felony, taking in the scene on the front porch, and Epic wasn't sure who was who, not being able to tell them apart. The only things distinctive about them were the weapons they chose to carry and their attitudes.

Havoc was known for the Magnum 500 riot control tactical shotgun, and Chaos carried twin Desert Eagle .357 auto-mags. Whichever twin it was had a cigarillo of that gorilla-in-the-mist, loud ass weed from the Congo.

"Damn, my nig'! What up, brah? Yo' name ringing bells all the way down here in West Gin! Dang!" exclaimed an excited Felony.

"That's what's up!" replied Epic.

"Man, come on up in this piece, brah."

If Epic thought the cars outside the trailer were crazy, then the inside was insane. These niggas had a damn six-person hot tub in the middle of the living room. Sixty-four-inch, flat screen TVs mounted on all four walls with X-Boxes, PlayStations, DVD players, and anything else one could think of when broke and couldn't afford it were connected. Now that they had money, these niggas bought any and everything they could think of at the time.

Epic looked around the living room as a little Latino baby crawled by. He was wondering which one of these niggas might have brought a Mexican baby.

Felony saw what held Epic's attention before saying, "That's Lil' Trigger right here." He picked the baby up. "He mine, but I ain't his real daddy. His moms was pregnant when I met her. She was homeless, dog, and was going to put lil' man in the system, so…"

"Look. Say no mo', my nig'," said Epic, understanding how Felony wouldn't let that happen if he could help it. No kid should have to go through what they had.

"TeTe?" called Felony while bouncing the happy baby.

A few seconds later, a short, sexy, dark-haired Latino goddess walked into the living room to collect Lil' Trigger from Felony. Epic could see the love in his homie's eyes for the baby and his mother. It was the way he looked at Asimi. No doubt, Felony had found something in life to live for and maybe a reason to change if given time.

Right now, their way was living by the gun and dying by the gun, and what he'd gone there to see Felony about may be the very thing that expired the extra time he wished for Felony.

TeTe took Lil' Trigger from Felony and turned to leave, but not before looking Epic up and down. There was nothing sexual about it. If anything, it was a look of total suspicion, which he couldn't blame her for in the least.

"So, what you need? Because I know you didn't ride all the way down here to catch up?" asked Felony through a cloud of weed smoke.

Epic sat, smoking weed and laying out his plans with Felony and the twins late into the night.

Chapter 16

Currency was flowing, and Payne was swimming in the green wave. He was able to keep his obligation to the cartel and still make moves on the side. There were plenty of licks to hit, and he was about to get back to it. Shit, who needed Epic? Epic was nothing but muscle, and Payne knew money could buy you all the muscle you needed. His only regret was that he didn't get to kill Epic himself—not yet anyway. But each new day was another chance to make that happen, and he would make it happen.

Payne wanted everything that life owed him, and he was prepared to use any and everyone to get it. He was still deep in thought about how to make his dreams a reality when Candy opened the passenger door and flopped into the leather seat of his Range Rover.

As soon as he saw the look in her eyes, any thoughts or illusions of having an easy day and getting laid went out the window. Candy threw her white, iguana-skin purse to the floorboard at her feet.

"How the fuck are you going to cheat on me with that stank ass bitch Essence at the club?" she yelled, then launched into another tongue-lashing. "Out of all the loose bitches in this city, you fuck the one ho that I hate the most! A slut that couldn't wait to throw that shit in my face!"

Payne thought about lying to her, but decided not to.

"Look, ma. Don't play at being jealous, because it's not a good look and only makes you look thirsty as hell," he said. Payne continued, "Check it. You my bitch, and no matter

118

who I slide dick, you're still number one. So don't let a fun thang and some trivial gossip fuck up what we got going here." He finished with a scowl.

Candy sat there with her mouth shut, knowing that any words that escaped would come out venomously. The fact that he felt there was no need for deniability only served to torment her more. And her failed attempt to seduce Epic had her struggling not to pull her straight razor from her purse and end this sorry ass nigga sitting beside her. But Candy's momma didn't raise no fool, and Payne's mother must have if this nigga thought that what was good for the gander wasn't good for the goose.

Two could play that game. She would just play it better than he could. Hell had no fury like a woman scorned, and no man could match a conniving woman's intent to get even. Payne could feel the menace rolling off her, but he knew all it would take was a shopping trip to keep shit from escalating. If she really thought monogamy was mandatory, then she would find herself doing a lot more sniveling before all was said and done.

Done with the emotional shit, Payne pulled away from the curb. Epic found the number for his grandmother and hit the green phone icon to place the call, but it was sent straight to voicemail. After listening to her message, he decided not to leave one and ended the call.

His phone rang before he could put it down, and he knew who it was without looking by the ringtone. It was Sarah.

"Who dis?" he asked as if he didn't know already.

"Hey, stranger. Long time since I've talked to you. Are you mad at me or something?" she questioned, and he could hear the genuine worry in her voice.

"Naw, I'm not mad at you. I just had some things come up that I had to handle that kept me outta touch all weekend."

There was a little purring sound before she asked if it was as fun as the weekend they'd spent together. The simple mention of that weekend gave him a hard-on and reminded him of the conversation he was going to have to have with Asimi and Sarah. Epic was not about to go there over the phone.

Sarah was speaking again when he tuned back in. "So when can I see you again?" she asked.

Epic thought for a minute, calculating, then replied. "If everything works out, I'll be that way this weekend."

"You promise?" Sarah asked, jumping at a chance to see him.

"Can't make you no promises on that for sure, but if I can get that way, then best believe I'ma get at you, a'ight!"

It wasn't a guarantee, but Sarah would take whatever she could get. She also knew not to harass him about it because her position as a side chick really carried no weight, but hopefully, that would all soon change.

Epic took a quick shower, then dressed in a pair of Diesel jeans, a black, snug-fit Under Armour shirt, and Timberlands with a silver-link Diesel belt. He slipped his Glock into his waistband. He was about to leave the room when he looked at his nightstand and the gold cross and chain sitting beside the flash drive. They were the things that belonged to his mother. Epic fastened the chain around his neck, letting the weight of the cross comfort him. On a whim, he pocketed the flash drive.

An hour later, Epic sat across the street from his and Payne's old business, Epic Investments, contemplating how to get at Payne without Ari Acousta knowing. He was about to leave when a white Econoline van and two black Mercedes G-Wagons pulled to a stop in front of Epic Investments.

Armed guards got out of the G-Wagons, scanning in all directions for any threat that might appear. Once they were satisfied, one of the men beat on the van's side door to signal the all clear. The door slid open, and out came four more men with large, black duffel bags. Each man carried two bags. Epic didn't need to be told that there was money in those bags. The amount of firepower on display spoke volumes, and he knew exactly whose money it was.

Well, if he couldn't make Payne bleed from gunshot wounds yet, he'd come up with a plan to cause him to hemorrhage cash. At this point, he was looking for a way to hurt, if not destroy, both Payne and Ariella Acousta. Epic was confident it could be done; he just had to find a way that allowed him to walk away when all was said and done.

Chapter 17

This was the first time in weeks that she'd had a chance to clean Mr. Bower's office without anyone around watching her. Still, her heart was a hammer striking an anvil in her chest as she moved around the office, dusting as she went. When she got to the large mahogany desk, she stalled there, dusting while looking over her shoulder toward the open door.

It was now or never if she planned on finding anything out about the murder of her daughter. God knew it had been a cold case for too long.

The fact that she'd reunited with her grandson, the only child of her murdered daughter, lent a new type of urgency to her finding answers. With one last glance at the doorway, Erica Bates, at the age of sixty-two years old, broke the law by breaking into the desk of the man she'd worked for, for years.

It was the desk that belonged to his father before him, a desk that she had a key to. Three of the drawers were unlocked and filled with old bills, car titles, land deeds, and business records. None of these things caught her eye as helpful, not that she knew what to look for, but maybe she'd get lucky.

Sliding the key into the bottom drawer that was locked sent a chill down her spine, but she had come too far to let fear stop her now. She took one last deep breath and turned the key. The lock gave with a soft click. To her ears, it sounded like a clap of thunder in the silent office.

Although she was hesitant, Erica pulled the drawer open and looked inside. *Empty.*

'Why would anyone lock an empty drawer?' she wondered. As she began to close the drawer back, a piece of white tape caught her eye. It was only a small piece—a corner taped to the underside of the drawer above the one she had opened.

Easing the tape off the drawer, she then turned it over to look at the numbers written on it: 1-8-26-49. The numbers meant nothing to her. There weren't enough for it to be a phone number or a bank account, but the answer came to her out of the blue. 'Combination to a safe.'

Erica read the numbers to herself a few times before replacing the tape under the upper drawer, then closed and relocked it. On the floor, she noticed a scrap of paper beneath the desk, which caused her to get down on all fours to reach. When she stood up, Erica gasped as she came face-to-face with Dorindo Castillo, the head of Mr. Bower's security team. His emotionless eye took in everything with one glance. Her fear spiked to an all-time high as he stared at her without speaking, as if he already knew what she'd been doing in the office.

Finally, with a slight tilt of his head, he asked, "Mrs. Bates, what are you doing in here under Mr. Bower's desk?" His accent was barely noticeable.

In answer, Erica held up the scrap of paper in an open palm and the feather duster in the other. Dorindo plucked the piece of paper from her palm and looked at it closely, also keeping an eye on her. He turned the scrap so that she could see what it was.

"A true waste of money," he grumbled as she looked at the old lottery ticket she'd found on the floor. After another tense second, he returned it to her, saying, "Forgive me for keeping you from your duties. You may carry on with them now." The reptilian smile he flashed never warmed his cold, dead eyes as he stepped aside to let her pass.

******

Epic was in deep thought about Asimi when the fire-engine-red Ferrari LaFerarri pulled up in front of the townhouse he was watching. This was what he'd come for, but this wasn't the time or place yet, because if he knew nothing else about the nigga behind the wheel, he knew that dude wasn't some bitch ass nigga like Kyrie had been.

The door of the townhouse opened, and out stepped one of the baddest bitches Epic had ever seen, and that was saying a lot, seeing as not many women could hold a candle to Asimi. Lisa sat down in the passenger seat, loving the crest of the expensive leather on her bare thighs as her minidress rode up high to expose a lot of her thigh.

She'd worn the dress just for that reason, knowing it would distract Neville enough not to blank about not answering his calls the night before. But, damn, if she knew Neville copped a brand-new Ferrari LaFerrari, she sure as hell would have picked up that call.

The only reason she knew what it was, was because she'd seen it in the new Jay-Z video. To keep it real, Neville was a little too crazy sometimes, and everybody knew the Jamaican rude boy that had the dope game on smash didn't play when it came to money and Lisa.

The look on his face said it all. He was angry, and the rapid-fire Patois told her how angry.

It was always hard for her to understand what Neville said because of his heavy accent, but when he was pissed, like then, it was damned near impossible for anyone not Jamaican to understand.

Neville looked at Lisa, not smiling, and said, "Wah dem-gyal no come when mi call dem?"

"Is da gyal too fraide-fradi, fi wa? 'Cause shi gwaan see dat mi deh badmon round 'ere." Neville pulled out a chrome .40 Cal, and pointed it at her face.

124

Lisa didn't even flinch at the sight of the gun in her face. Instead, she leaned forward and ran her tongue down the length of the barrel, swirling and sticking her tongue in the hole at the end. Neville jerked the pistol away from her and cocked it, putting a round in the chamber.

Lise put her hand on his, holding the gun, and pushed it down into her lap. She then spread her legs, causing her minidress to ride up even more, revealing her shaved sex.

Neville was loving this shit and could barely talk when he asked, "Wah gwaan do noh?"

In answer, Lisa slowly eased the barrel of the big gun to her wet pussy while licking her lips. She arched her back to take more as Neville started to pistol fuck her in the front seat of the Ferrari. His finger on the trigger only added a new level of excitement and danger.

Moments later, Lisa had a soul-shaking, violent orgasm, sending her female cream all over the now sticky weapon. Neville slipped the gun from inside her and stuck it in her mouth, watching as she licked her juices from it.

"Ras clot a no joke, ya sah gyal mi no vexed no more," he said, rubbing the bulge in his jeans. Neville put the .40 Caliber in the center console, took out a blunt, and fired it up. He slammed the car in first gear, popped the clutch, and spun it around in a tight circle, making smoke rise from the tires on the way out.

Epic fell behind the speeding supercar as it weaved in and out of traffic across the city. He wasn't worried about being spotted if the little scene he'd witnessed earlier was any indication of where old boy's mind was. Ten minutes later, Epic stopped in the parking lot of a Denny's, across the street from the Red Roof Inn on Rockside Road, not believing how cheap this nigga was.

He must have spent all his paper on that rolling rob-me sign he was driving, but for Epic, this shit was about more than a simple ass jack move. It was the first step of a much larger play.

After watching the lustful, happy couple check into a room on the upper floor, but on the back side of the hotel. He grabbed a bag of balloons, then went into Denny's bathroom and filled three of the balloons with water.

Neville was making sweet love to Lisa's sensitive clit when the alarm on the Ferrari started to go off. Neville groped for his keys and used the key fob to turn off the car alarm without missing a single lick. Lisa was now moaning and thrusting on the bed, close to orgasm, when the car alarm went off again.

"Fuck!" yelled Neville, jumping up to look out the window at his car, but there was nothing to see.

Chirp, chirp, and the lights and horn stopped flashing and blowing for a second time.

Neville started to go out the door, but then looked back over at the bed where Lisa lay there, legs spread wide, finger fucking herself and begging for him to come back and finish what he'd started.

Epic moved a little closer to the wall beside the door and threw another water balloon, striking the Ferrari's hood and setting the alarm off again. The inevitable happened, just as he knew it would, and he was ready, ski mask down, gun out.

"Mi, 'bout to dead somebody to fuckin' wit mi poom poom rida," Neville said, tearing the room door open.

Before Neville could clear the doorway, Epic smashed his Glock into the side of his dreadlocked head, sending the pissed off Jamaican flying back into the room, lights out.

Lisa opened her mouth to scream, but shut it tight when the masked gunman aimed his weapon at her. Epic looked down at the unconscious rude boy, then kicked his fallen gun into the corner of the room and out of reach in case he woke up. Epic could see the edge of a bulletproof vest peeking underneath the collar of Sleeping Beauty's shirt.

Making eye contact with the naked woman on the bed, Epic took out his phone and pressed the button for a number already programmed and spoke. "I'm here now, but he was with a woman."

Epic could see the fear in her eyes as he said those words, and after listening for a few seconds, he said, "She's not a problem. I understand. I'll take care of it, and tell Ari Acousta that after this, we're even." He ended the call.

On the bed, Lisa's mind was racing to come up with a way to stay alive by any means necessary. She slowly spread her legs, offering him what she thought was her most valuable asset.

Epic took in the sight. Hell, who wouldn't? But that wasn't what he was there for. Instead, he told her to cover herself and stay quiet. He then removed a .380 from his hide-it-holster and aimed at the man who lay at his feet and turned to the scared woman.

"Keep your mouth shut, or Ari Acousta will know that I disobeyed her orders and didn't kill you, too!" He then fired two shots into Neville's chest before dashing out of the room.

Lisa sat on the bed in shock, unable to move from the spot. She was unsure of how long she'd been stuck before she crawled to the foot of the bed to look down at Neville's body with tears running down her face.

Lisa was still in shock when Neville suddenly sat upright, coughing, and the last thing she heard as the room began to spin was Neville cursing.

"Dem a dead mon. Weh gon' kill dis boy soon. Mi wanna show dem a real shotta!"

As Epic drove away, he could almost hear the clock ticking.

Chapter 18

Payne moved from one room to the next in the new office, planning how to best use the new space he'd rented. The built-in vault was reason enough to take this office with the amount of cash he was cleaning for the cartel.

His phone vibrated in his pocket, and the caller ID made him smile.

'Now, how much better could this day get?' he thought, pushing the talk icon.

"Speak," Payne answered the phone.

"Check it, boss man. I'm across the street and waiting to see if shit good to go right now or not. I could run up in the spot if you want me to," replied Blacq in a deep voice.

Payne thought for a minute. "Naw, we wait a sec on that. All I want you to do is keep your eyes on the prize so when the time comes, I'll know exactly where and how to get my hands on shawty."

"A'ight, say no mo'," finished Blacq, ending the call.

"Excuse me, Mr. Williams, but I'm going to need your final deposit and signature on the deed for the property to finalize the deal," the realtor said, coming into the room with Payne.

Payne pulled a cashier's check from his inside pocket and waved it in front of her, watching her honey-colored eyes follow it from side to side as if it were a doggie treat. This new building was some next-level shit.

Kanye's track *Through the Wire* was playing low as Epic drove the rain-slick streets of Cleveland, running his next move through his mind. He was well aware that the shit he'd set in motion was about to get real on the battlefield, and nobody could guess at how shit would play out.

Asimi draped the expensive wristwatch over her much-too-small wrist, admiring how the light danced across the inlaid diamonds. It was magnificent, the perfect Valentine's gift for her man. Valuable suited her just fine because she knew Epic would spare no expense when it came to her Valentine's Day gift. She could only pray this wouldn't be the last Valentine's Day they had together.

Her life had just, in one day, become way more complicated than she had calculated it would, but not everybody could help or control who they fell in love with. Asimi knew deep within her heart that she wanted to spend eternity with Epic and was surprised she also felt the same about her other relationship.

With school coming to an end, her future was no longer way down the road, but now at her doorstep. Asimi could more than accept the fact that she may have made the biggest mistake of her life when she set up Epic. Maybe he'd understand, or maybe he'd be done with her, feeling betrayed.

She was still deep in thought as she sat inside Fancy Tips Nail Salon. One way or another, it would all come to the light.

******

The three Hayabusa super bikes screamed down the highway with each of its riders carrying five kilos of coke a piece in backpacks. Neville, Cutu, and Major were only running about eighty miles an hour when they saw the state trooper.

Cutu and Major both geared down, dipped low behind their windscreens while opening the big bikes up. The two were gone in a flash, but Neville, feeling extra reckless since his near-death experience, slowed down to wait for the souped-up Dodge Charger to catch up to him.

As the trooper pulled up beside him, Neville pointed down to the chrome, hundred-shot-nitro bottle tucked close to his frame as if asking the trooper, 'Really, dude?'

When the overzealous cop continued the chase, Neville's heart rate spiked as he gave the throttle a savage twist, launching the uber cycle, a dark-blue streak as he shot away from the flashing blue lights.

Neville lay down on the tank as the front wheel reached for the sky. Wind could not offer enough resistance to stop the precision machine from cutting through with an angry *swish* sound as it blew by cars that seemed to be going in reverse. The moment his front tire touched the asphalt, Neville pushed his nitrous button, feeding the highly combustible gas into the high-performance engine.

A wide spectrum of blue flame shot from his exhaust pipe as the monster between his legs made a mad dash for freedom. The dark bike seemed to disappear as Neville hit a special switch that cut out all the lights on the Busa.

Life surged through his veins like the nitro through his motor. He was unstoppable, untouchable, unkillable, and soon, he would show Ariella Acousta just who she was fucking with. He had things to do but prioritized the dealing with Ariella Acousta as priority number one. The fifteen kilo's they'd stolen was just the beginning, they would make the Cartel bleed until Ariella Acousta showed herself.

Epic cut the headlights on the nondescript Honda Accord as he pulled into the back alley behind one of three clubs that he secretly owned. He then sent a text message to JuJu, who ran this club for him, to open the rear door so no one would see him enter. Club Insanity was a rave club in the warehouse district on the west side of the flats.

"Sup, Boss man?" questioned JuJu as Epic walked in. "Come to check up on the finances and transactions?" JuJu teased, going with the long-time running joke he had with

Epic, knowing for a fact Epic wasn't worried about any of that.

He left the running of the clubs to his managers, not even worried if they would steal from him. To him, that would be like them stealing from themselves. Plus, stealing from Epic was a surefire deterrent and an easy way to get killed.

"Naw," Epic replied as he sat down behind JuJu's desk. "Just needed a spot to chill for a moment without being seen. And I don't have many worries about that here with this crowd."

A smiling JuJu said, "Damn, and here I thought that you just liked Insanity better than Clubs Insatiable and Insomnia."

Now it was Epic's turn to smile, knowing JuJu took immense pride in running the club, and he could see it as a sort of competition with the other club managers. Epic owned all three clubs through shell companies and an offshore bank account he'd set up years ago as a nest egg or rainy-day account, but it had since grown into a very lucrative retirement fund. Not even Asimi knew he owned the clubs, and Epic never went to his own clubs to party. He only went to Insanity when he needed time to think and a peace of mind.

JuJu poured two glasses of Cîroc, handing one to Epic as he took the visitor's seat in front. He removed a small pill bottle from his pocket and shook it in an offer to Epic. Epic raised a single eyebrow at the offer of Xanax, to which JuJu shrugged, tucking the bottle away.

Without having to be provoked, JuJu dived right into what was going down in the streets. "Check it, dog. Da street is talking, and word is, yo' boy Payne don't fuck wit' you no mo', and that he big time now off that cartel money. Shit must be true 'cause he spending like that shit counterfeit, even moving into a new building at the end of this month." JuJu finished and sat back, sipping his Cîroc.

Epic fired up one of JuJu's pre-rolled Sour Diesel blunts and released a mushroom cloud of loud smoke at the ceiling of the office. He was running what JuJu had said through his mind, letting the pieces fall into place. He'd known some of the information JuJu had, but he didn't know about the new building. JuJu, not understanding Epic's silence, offered to smoke Payne for his blasphemy of Epic's name.

"If only it was that easy," said Epic.

"Shit, boss man. It is. Just holla at yo' boy. You know I'm about that life," JuJu spat, making his fingers into a gun.

"No doubt!" answered Epic, feeling the loyalty from JuJu. "But shit is more complicated than it should be right now."

"Well, I'm here if you need me, and that's my good word!" JuJu exclaimed, meaning every word.

Chapter 19

This would be the last drop at the old office, and Payne was already sweating because the van was ten minutes late. Ariella Acousta had mentioned some friction with the rude boys in the city robbing some of her Guatemalan clients.

What would compel those crazy assed island boys to try the cartel? He didn't know, but what he did know was that, regardless of whatever they had going on, he wasn't going to take any losses on his end.

Payne made sure that Blacq hired some more goons just in case the rude boys, Epic, or anybody tried to steal the cartel's money in his possession. He understood that no one could ever underestimate someone else's ambition. As the first G-Wagon pulled into the parking lot, Payne released a deep sigh of relief. When all was there and accounted for, Payne gave Ari's man in charge an inquisitive look.

"Traffic," the man said, and that was it.

They were all unaware of the young woman with dreadlocks sitting on the bench across the street, waiting for the bus with her iPhone recording them.

******

Epic had two stops to make before he could get on the highway, heading to see Asimi for Valentine's Day. He was still thinking of his other stop as he entered Broadway Diner off McBride Street to see his grandmother sitting in a booth near the back. Epic took in the entire place with a glance as he approached the booth and took a seat across from the only blood family he had left in this world.

Once seated, his grandma gestured toward the menu on the table, but he declined the offer. Epic could see the concern in her eyes, but could do nothing to change it.

"Epic."

"Mrs. Bates," he replied.

She raised her hand as if to say something, then just let it fall back to her lap. A small quaver shook her bottom lip as she began to speak. "I've been looking for proof of Mr. Bower's involvement with my daughter's death!" she blurted out.

Epic sat motionless as she told him about snooping around in his office and desk drawers. She assured him she was being very discreet and sensible with her movements, but Epic knew she was in over her head and maybe in mortal danger if her boss was a killer and found out she'd been digging into the past.

Epic saw her tired eyes examining the gold cross around his neck, knowing she recognized it. He only shrugged. She was speaking about how she felt the safe combination she'd found could hold substantial evidence about the murder. As reluctant as he was to use her in this way, Epic knew there was nothing he could do to stop her.

Her determination filled his heart with gratitude and fear. He'd just started to get to know her, and the thought of something happening to her tied his intestines in a knot. He exuded an outer calm he didn't feel inside, then, on impulse, he took his grandmother into his arms for the first time.

As he stepped back, she laid a warm hand on his left cheek. There was sorrow in her eyes and something Epic had never expected to see—love.

Epic hit a preprogrammed number in his iPhone.

"What's up, mi Jefe?" questioned White Mike. "Long time, no hear."

"Shit been hectic 'round my way, but I need you to work some of your magic for me," said Epic.

Computers and electronics were White Mike's bread and butter, and he was ruthlessly efficient at both. He wasn't sure what Epic had for him, but if he was enlisting his help, it had to be important.

"Pull up. I'm at the spot, and could you stop on the way and grab some beef jerky links and a DiGiorno's Pizza!"

Epic looked at the phone like it had come alive in his hand, but only asked, "Anything else?" in a dry tone.

Epic pulled into the driveway of the house that looked as if it belonged in a retirement community in Florida, instead of a middle-class neighborhood in Cleveland, Ohio. The bright-orange 1971 Pontiac GTO 455 HO convertible spoke volumes about the person who drove it. Noxious, yes, but White Mike could circumvent just about any firewall encryption used to protect most data.

White Mike answered the door wearing a lime-green T-shirt with the word Kamikaze in hot-pink letters, cargo shorts, and a pair of flip flops. Looking at him, one would be hard pressed to believe, under all that teased-up, spikey hair was an extremely brilliant mind.

Not much had changed since the last time Epic was there. The old, cold pizza on the coffee table even looked the same, and after closer inspection, he believed it was the same one from last time.

Epic handed the bag over as White Mike unnecessarily tried to pay him for the items he'd been asked to pick up. Computer monitors dominated most of the walls, and coax cables snaked across every inch of the floor. Unused exercise equipment became keyboard and printer shelves. Several terminals beeped and flashed lights as they ran whatever programs White Mike had tasked them with.

"Come to exorcize your demons?" joked White Mike.

"Something like that," Epic replied, eyeing the PlayStation 5 off in a corner, only to be overshadowed by the makeshift altar in the other corner.

White Mike noticed Epic's astonishment. "What?" he asked, sounding somewhat offended.

"I thought you didn't believe in God!" Epic stated.

"Oh, I believe in a divine being—God if you'd like. It's just his fan club that I dislike," mumbled White Mike around a mouthful of beef jerky.

Epic pulled the flash drive from his pocket and passed it to an extremely hyper White Mike. With all the etiquette in the world, he released a huge burp, looking the flash drive over.

After a minute, he commented, "Well, it's old. What's on it?" he asked.

"If I knew that, we wouldn't be having this conversation right now," Epic shot back. "Can you open it?"

White Mike didn't even dignify the question with an answer. Instead, he went over to his main tower and plugged the drive into a data port. White Mike ten issued an exclusive command, at which time his entire screen began a countdown that led to a frenzied amount of keystrokes and directives. Line after line of codes and numbers flashed on the screen as White Mike's fingers flew over the keys.

After a few minutes, White Mike sat back and exhaled, looking at the monitor. He scanned the screen so long without speaking.

Epic finally asked, "Well?" Almost as though he were afraid to volunteer any information, Epic got an ominous feeling in the pit of his stomach.

White Mike typed in a few more lines of coding before the screen reconfigured into numbered accounts from top to bottom, the minor accounts being in the hundreds of thousands, and the major accounts being over several million dollars. White Mike slouched back into his chair. The color had drained from his face, leaving him an ash-gray complexion in the glow from the screen.

When he'd composed himself enough to speak, his voice was monotone. "They're offshore bank accounts with millions and millions in them. I'm talking Steve Jobs money, never-work-again money. Hell, your grandkids wouldn't have to work again money. Epic, this is fatal income money."

Epic stood quietly, trying to digest this world-shaking bit of information. He could tell there was a tremendous amount of money without adding it up.

"Epic, how long we been friends?" questioned a stunned White Mike.

"More than five years," answered Epic. "Why?"

"Well, one, because you never told me you had this kind of money. Two, if you stole this kinda money, someone is, I assure you, looking for it. Last but not least, whoever this came from will now know that it's back in play."

The ramifications of that were pretty self-explanatory. Epic's mind caught up with what White Mike was saying, and on reflex, he reached forward, yanking the flash drive from the computer.

"Wait. Can they trace this back to you? Are you now in danger because I bought this to you?" asked Epic."

White Mike rolled his eyes. "Please. These guys' programs were top of the line twenty years ago, but now I know amateurs who could evade this outdated tracking software."

His assurance only made Epic feel marginally better, seeing as White Mike was one hundred percent right in guessing that this was fatal income type money, and he was sure he knew who it had been fatal for. He was stuck on that thought when he realized White Mike was saying something to him.

"Hold up. What did you just say?"

White Mike looked up but continued speaking. "You're rich but not. See, you have all the accounts and account numbers. What you're missing is the routing codes and transaction password. Basically, you only have one half of the puzzle."

"So, it's useless?" asked Epic.

"Well, I wouldn't say useless. I would say it's more problematic, if that will make you feel better."

It didn't.

In an office across town, a computer gave up a soft chime.

Chapter 20

Asimi stood in front of her full-length mirror, turning from side to side, looking at the little black dress she wore. The Versace had been a gift for her birthday from Epic, and she knew he loved it on her. Cartier two-carat diamond earrings and a matching necklace were the only ice she wore, and with one final look, she stepped into her red bottoms. One swift spray of Crave perfume was her last added touch.

She'd decided that tonight would be their night, no matter what the morning would bring regarding their relationship. She was walking through her living room when she remembered the vase with twelve long-stemmed roses on the mantle. They were beautiful and meant more to her than she would have liked to admit, but she could never allow Epic to see them. With one last, longing look, she took out the roses, vase, and all of, and put them under her kitchen sink.

At the ding of her doorbell, Asimi's heart skipped a beat or two. Upon opening the door, Asimi jumped into Epic's arms, loving the strength he enfolded her in. The kiss they shared dissolved her very bones, making her weak in the knees.

Epic stood with a devilish smile on his face, the smile she loved so much—charming, sexy, and devastating. Asimi's panties would have been wet, had she been wearing any. Epic produced a single red rose from behind his back to stroke softly down her cheek, along her neck, and over her cleavage. Little sparks shot through her entire body, which had her trying to pull Epic into the condo, but he knew that if he went in, they were not coming back out.

At dinner, Epic hand-fed Asimi coconut shrimp with white wine. The strawberries and whipped cream, he saved for after. All through the night, Asimi took shots of them that she would never post on Instagram, but it was the picture of the four-carat canary-yellow diamond and platinum engagement ring that damn near made her faint. Epic could feel Asimi's joy when he'd proposed, but he was observant enough to know that something on her mind was casting a shadow on this moment.

Before he could give it much more thought, Asimi stood before him naked, all but for her expensive red bottom shoes. Her skin sparkled as light danced off the glitter spray on her flawless skin. Asimi gave herself fully to Epic. She allowed every bit of love she had for him to flow free, praying it would be what he remembered when the happy bubble burst.

Slowly, she sank onto Epic's flesh-covered rod, taking him slow and deep. Her wetness coated his tool. The heat that rose from their lovemaking seemed at times an inferno that threatened to consume them both. Passion drove her to her limits as she rolled her hips in a circular motion, grinding on the dick.

Epic allowed Asimi to ride until she was thrashing and bucking through her first orgasm. He then rolled her onto her back, positioning his swollen bell head at her molten-hot entrance. Grabbing his thick shaft, he lightly tapped her throbbing lover's lips, sending shock waves after shock waves pulsing through her.

His first thrust bottomed out deep within her core, causing her to dig her nails savagely into his back. Asimi moaned as long stroke after long stroke caused her inner walls to clench tightly on the spike impaling her. She was wild beneath him, thrashing and bucking as the tension built deep within her coil, promising to release liquid fire with her climax.

Epic continued to pound away at the hot, velvet tunnel. Slick, wet heat covered his hard dick. The more he grew, the more she stretched to accommodate him. A starburst of color and lights exploded behind her closed eyelids as multiple orgasms ripped her apart.

Epic's arms gave out on him as he erupted, spraying jet spurt after spurt deep enough to coat her cervix with his hot, sticky seed. The two collapsed, exquisitely drained and exhausted but satisfied. Epic never noticed the quiet tears slipping from her eyes.

Asimi awoke to soft kisses on the nape of her neck and shoulders.

Her heart swelled at the love she felt for Epic before her mind returned to what lay ahead today, when she'd have to sit and face the music. The thought alone brought with it a sharp stab of agony beyond any she'd ever known.

Two hours later, Epic was focused on Asimi sitting across from him at the Firehouse Subs shop, anticipating but unsure what had Asimi acting like there would be no tomorrow. Maybe there wouldn't be—not after he came clean.

"We need to talk," they both said at the same time. Then, "You first."

Asimi would have laughed had the situation not been so serious.

Epic took both of Asimi's hands in his and began at the start of first meeting with Sarah, and how he'd been creeping on the low with her. Asimi listened while Epic took the blame for what she had set in motion. As Epic finished, the last thing he expected was Asimi shaking her head no and saying it was all her fault.

Her next words stilled him on the spot.

"I set you up!" blurted Asimi. "It's all my fault. Sarah was my first-year roommate. Then we became more. I love you both and thought that maybe we could be a triple if you liked her and she liked you. The day we went shopping was my

141

idea, but she got carried away with her little show." Asimi took Epic's silence for anger.

Epic sat quietly, thinking about how beneficial the relationship could be and how much it cleared both his and Asimi's consciences. To him, it wasn't a true betrayal to find out his girlfriend was bisexual. What guy wouldn't want his cake and eat it too?

The consequences of his cheating on Asimi could have ended all the plans he had for them, but if she was willing to make room in their lives for Sarah, then he was down with it. Get in where you fit in.

Asimi called Sarah.

******

The Bell 429 helicopter touched down at a small airfield outside of Lost Nation, about forty miles from Cleveland.

Ariella Acousta, her sister Yesmeen, and four bodyguards moved from the helipad to the three waiting Mercedes-Benz G63 custom-armor-plated G-Wagons. They were all black with dark-tinted windows, and black rims with no chrome were on them, plus another six heavily armed bodyguards.

The cold, icy wind followed Ari and Yasmeen into the rear seat of the middle vehicle, reminding Ari of how much she truly hated the cold weather. Ari pulled twice on a My Blue vaping cigarette as the convoy left the airfield. She was more than upset at having to come to this winter wasteland to deal with some island niggas robbing her clientele and disrupting the shipping of her product.

The Cartel had the last eight soldiers to work with the Rude Boys so far, and more than 790 kilos of pure cocaine. This was a problem that Yasmeen should have been able to handle, but this was a direct challenge laid down in the streets for Ari and Ari only.

That didn't mean she wasn't calling in all the weight she could bring to bear, yet she had to move carefully with the feds on hyper alert since the New York hit. She couldn't afford to be pulled into a messy headline, getting law enforcement a clusterfuck of a street war. She had been called out, so now she would rectify the situation quickly and quietly.

Ari decided on a more surgical strike to remove the problematic island fleas nipping at her heels.

"Yas, contact our asset here in Cleveland and have him meet us at the hotel as soon as possible," Ari ordered, checking her makeup in a small handheld mirror.

Payne's negligence had already allowed one of the smaller sums of laundered money to be stolen in transport, not that he couldn't have replaced the four hundred thousand dollars stolen, but his greedy ass decided to charge the loss to the Acousta Cartel.

Hell, maybe he could even shift the blame to Epic and have Ari Acousta take care of that problem once and for all. Blacq ran stacks of hundred-dollar bills through the counting machine, too preoccupied to pay much attention as Payne paced back and forth in the office.

Ever since the stick-up of his shipment, he'd hired as many guns as he could to protect future shipments, and if truth be told, he'd trade the whole lot of them for Epic—if only he could put the fact he'd tried to fuck his bitch aside, but he couldn't. Every time he looked at Candy, he thought of Epic fucking his bitch. Hell, he was even feeling hostile right now, just thinking about it. The animosity was real in his heart, the envy was true in his soul, and the hatred was fuel for his revenge.

What really unnerved him specifically was the fact that the streets were silent when it came to Epic, and if he wasn't getting his money in the streets, then where was he getting it? Practically paranoid now, Payne felt like the whole hood was lying to him, like the city had taken sides between the two rivals.

Epic's mood was one of controlled chaos at being summoned like some chain-kept pet, at Ari's beck and call. Although he knew the call would come, the timing couldn't have been worse. He'd had to leave before he could come together with both Asimi and Sarah. So rushed was he that he had to have Asimi drop him at the airport, promising to be back as quickly as possible.

Epic understood that dealing with Ari Acousta didn't leave him with a vote, not when he was under a dictatorship. Six hours and twenty-four minutes after Yasmeen Acousta's text, Epic entered the lobby of the Hilton and took the elevator up to the penthouse.

As the elevator doors opened, Epic saw two cartel soldiers stationed to the left and right of the door with MP5 machine guns at the ready. If he had any delusions that Ari Acousta trusted him, those quickly ended as he was forced to relinquish his weapon before being searched a second time. He was sure that Ari had her suspicions, but had nothing definitive to base them on.

Confident in this knowledge, Epic casually strolled into the room with his chest out, head up, into a dominant room full of domineering personalities.

"Sup, boss lady?" asked Epic upon seeing Ari Acousta lying lavishly on the couch, eating peaches and cream.

A masseuse stood off to the side, happily forgotten for the moment. With a glance over her shoulder, the masseuse was excused and left without a word.

There were no greetings. "What took you so long to get here?" she questioned.

"Traffic," said Epic with a straight face.

"Epic, never keep me waiting again, or you'll never have to worry about traffic again." Epic took the open threat in silence, waiting for her to get to the business at hand. She continued. "Unfortunately, a problem here has gained my attention. Someone has been foolish enough to think that stealing from me is very lucrative, and you will find them and show them the error of their ways."

"I'm willing to comply, but I'm going to need more to go on than that," said Epic.

Epic listened as Ari laid out the case and misdeeds of the Rude Boys against the cartel. She, however, couldn't find a justifiable reason for their lunatic actions. Had it just been money or product, there were easier ways to get both.

"You will hunt this dog down for his inexcusable repass and put him down in such a way that any and all will know to never run afoul against the Acousta Cartel again." Glaring, she finished by demanding, "Do you understand?"

A spike of adrenaline made his lip twitch, but he kept his cool, replying, "Say no more." When the doors opened in the lobby, Epic found that Yasmeen was waiting for him. The beauty he'd first seen in her was gone and now replaced with a darkness he hadn't seen when he was thinking with his dick.

She licked her lips before speaking. "Maybe you could come back later or meet me somewhere else?"

Enticing as the offer was, there was no way in hell that he was going down that rabbit hole again, but he refused to miss an opportunity this good. "Hit me up later if you can sneak away from Boss Lady. I get the impression she's not happy with you sleeping with the help."

In response, she grabbed the bulge in his jeans and whispered, "later," before slipping into the elevator.

Chapter 21

"Move forward! Cover right! Watch the left flank!" yelled White Mike into the mic of his online gamer headset. His Ghost Recon team was putting in some heavy work, and the outcome of this game would give them a world ranking online. He had a 360-degree view made up of six fifty-two-inch plasma screens and four twelve-inch subwoofer towers for the real surround sound effect.

Crushed cans of Red Bull and slices of half-eaten pizza littered the tables and floor.

"Mediocre, my man. Mediocre," he said as he fired an anti-tank weapon and destroyed the hiding place of his video game enemy. If I could blacklist you from Call of Duty Urban Warfare, you would have been gone months ago," he joked while he continued to lay waste to every and all.

"Stalker 922, I am your father," said White Mike, impersonating Darth Vader. "Come over to the dark side."

It was about to be game over when all the power to his home was cut, leaving him in complete darkness. As he walked over to the banister for a look downstairs into his living room, he could see the many red lines of laser light snaking through his windows. For a brief second, he thought the feds were about to knock down his door, but the feds would come with a warrant and flash bang grenades.

He had to fight to keep from going into panic mode. When his brain finally did reboot, he sprang into action, first hitting a hidden switch that dumped acid on all his hard drives.

Others had criticized his extreme measures, but who was laughing now?

Now, he could hear glass breaking downstairs. A second button triggered a hydraulic lock in his closet to reveal a secret passageway from the house. Red lights started to flash all over the house in each room. Hacking was lucrative, and he'd spared no expense in rigging his house to blow up, making it look like a natural gas explosion. The blinking lights were a final warning.

No one could identify him, and all the paperwork for the house and land was fake and couldn't be traced back to him. Then again, they shouldn't have been able to track him down then, but somehow, they had. No law-abiding citizen could have run a reverse trace through all the servers he'd bounced the information through. If anything, they should've been chasing an old lady in Thailand.

White Mike didn't know who the men in his house were, but he did know whoever that flash drive belonged to was very enthusiastic about getting it back. Fortunately, he was very enthusiastic about not getting caught. *Envious.* The word just popped into his head as he fled down the stairs. As implausible as it was, some hacker had found him in less than three days.

He was a block and a half away, opening the driver's door on a hunter green Honda Accord, when there was a loud swoosh, followed by a bright orange fireball climbing high into the evening sky. He stood, mesmerized, as pieces of the house were blown in every direction, and big pieces morphed into smaller ones. The kinetic energy broke windows of the surrounding houses, and with one final look toward his old house, he started the Honda and drove away.

Cerrano watched from across the street as his team moved in on the house where the flash drive search emanated. Whatever had compelled them, after all these years, didn't matter to him. The business of finances and transactions didn't matter to him. What did matter to him was recovering that flash drive and putting an end to this long overdue chapter of his life—a failure he'd had to live with for more than twenty years.

"Echo, this is the team leader. We are breaching the home now," came the voice of the eight-man team leader.

The splitting of wood could be heard, along with the tinkle of raining glass. He lit a Cuban cigar, looking at the cherry glowing tip. He'd just stepped off the curb, thinking how inconsiderate it was of whoever made him come way over there to kill them. He could hear his team clearing rooms over his earpiece. That was discipline, and he loved discipline.

A devastating boom destroyed the house in front of him. He was picked up as if by an invisible hand and thrown across the street and into the bushes. Dazed and surrounded by burning debris, Cerrano didn't bother to check on his team. They'd all been inside when the house disappeared. Nothing was ever simple.

Yasmeen had sent a text to Epic a little over an hour before, with a time and place to meet her. As much as she hated to admit it, she'd become more than a little obsessed with Epic, which her sister could never find out about. She was well aware of the fact that the feelings were not mutual, but she always got what she wanted.

Yasmeen and two bodyguards passed quietly through the lobby of the Sheraton Hotel. She paid very little attention to the lavish interior or the full-length, gold-leaf-trimmed mirrors lining the walls of the lobby. Her mind was set on the hedonistic pleasures ahead. The corridors were well lit, and her room was beside the one for her security team. Now, all she had to do was wait for Epic to arrive.

Dressed in a black silk shirt and tie with matching dark slacks, he had no problem fitting in. Only the fact that he'd gone through the trouble of circumventing the hotel security cameras gave a clue that he was up to something illegal. If all went as planned, this would ignite the war between them, but she'd set them on a collision with her actions, and now it was time to pay the reaper.

He'd impersonate hotel management to gain access to the room, then discreetly take care of business—if this wasn't a trap. The text had given him the two room numbers, and as luck would have it, the door to room 213 was open, with a guy hanging out while talking back to someone in the room. There were no cameras in the hallways for the privacy of the customers.

He never broke stride as his silenced 9mm came up in line with the back of the man's head. The voice from inside was ordering B.L.T. and Coke, and that was as far as he got when a 9mm hollow point ripped through the back of his friend's head and out of his face just below his left eye. The same bullet blew through his jugular as he watched his friend's body fall back into the room.

Gurgling and choking sounds filled the room as he made a quick sweep of the living room and bathroom, paying no attention to the dying man. So far, his information was on point, but it meant nothing if he didn't get the main prize he'd come after. Outside the door of room 215, he scanned the corridor. Still all clear.

He'd taken an extra key card from the bodyguards and was just about to let himself into the room when the elevator doors dinged open. The hotel security guard stopped and looked toward the man dressed all in black who stood in the hallway, holding a silenced pistol.

The guard went for his sidearm as the assassin raised his weapon. Two quick pops followed, with one bullet striking the door jamb of a room and the other hitting the guard in the left shoulder. Seconds later, there was the loud boom of the guard's Beretta 9mm in the hallway. Those shots were followed by a wide spray of shots now from the wounded guard.

Neville was forced to retreat down the hallway toward the south stairwell, sure that the guards' shots had alerted anyone inside the room now. Yasmeen heard gunfire outside of her doorway. She knew that she needed to get downstairs to the car. It was going to be bad enough to explain to Ariella why she was at the hotel in the first place.

Cracking the door, she poked her head out to see the security guard lying on the floor, bleeding. Yasmeen slipped out and headed for the south stairwell. She kept her compact .380 pistol in her hand beside her right thigh as she came to the parking level where the car was left. Yasmeen pushed the remote to unlock the doors, and she felt someone behind her. In the blink of an eye, she'd rotated left, bringing her gun in line with the man's chest behind her.

Recognition made her hesitate. "My God, it's you," she said, lowering her weapon.

With casual fluidity, he fired two hollow-point 9mm rounds into her chest, knocking her back against the car. He fired one more round into her forehead, right between her pretty eyes, bent down, and retrieved her dropped phone.

Epic's phone started to blow up with text after text. Then calls started to come, all from Ariella Acousta. Looking at the text messages, urgent would have been an understatement.

He answered the next call and scowled at the phone as Ariella Acousta's voice came through loud, clear, cold, and controlled. "Get here now!"

"Give me twenty minutes. I'm down in the flats on the west bank," Epic replied. "Hello? Hello?" He looked at the phone to see that the call had ended. Twenty-two minutes later, Epic stepped off the elevator and into the penthouse Ariella Acousta had rented, but with all the armed men on high alert, it was more like the craziness of a war camp.

At least ten guns were aimed at him as two of Ariella's goons gave him a mean pat down, taking his two Glock .40 Cals from him. Now he was the only one in the room who wasn't armed. He really didn't want to relinquish his weapons but had no real choice. Epic stood there, looking at Ariella Acousta, who wore a no-nonsense look on her face that was so intense his smart reply died on his lips.

Ariella stood toe to toe with Epic when she asked him. "Where were you tonight, about an hour ago, and did you see or meet with Yasmeen?" Her eyes were searching his face for any sign of a lie.

"In the flats, at a club. Why so interested in my whereabouts tonight?" Then he remembered the second part of the question. "And no. I haven't seen or spoken to Yasmeen tonight."

He watched her face erode from a cold façade to a hurt and wounded animal and knew which was the most dangerous. "My sister is dead!" The words lingered like smoke in the air.

Epic just stood there because Ariella Acousta was not a woman you threw your arms around and tried to comfort. He watched as she paced from one side of the room to the other. At this point, he was well aware of the fact that she was damn close to a psychotic break, and he was the odd man out.

Ari spun back around to face him, condemning him with a look, like a predator locking onto its prey. Yet Epic stood there under the glare of all those in the room. If she was expecting him to squirm or break out in a cold sweat, then she'd gravely underestimated the situation. The cold reptilian look in her eyes was a visual promise of death. After several heartbeats, Ariella Acousta, the most powerful woman in the drug world, seemed to deflate right before him. Epic was in no way a psychic, but he could foresee much death in the future. He just had to find a way to make sure it wasn't him.

Payne and Blacq sat in a corner off to the left side of the stage in the Platinum Pole Strip Club with two untouched drinks on the table while the foot-sore dancers swayed to the boss's heavy soundtrack filling the club.

For Payne, this was a rarity. Being in a strip club other than Exotic Toyz was almost like cheating on your side piece with your other side piece, not that he gave a damn over any betrayal he committed. He was more than a little on edge in East Point. This was not his stomping grounds anyway—too close to the territory of the weed-smoking, gun-toting, dread heads. Although he and Blacq were strapped, he didn't really feel any better, seeing that so was everybody else in the spot.

If Exotic Toyz was where Atlanta's cream of the crop went to see and be seen, then the Platinum Pole was where those who lived the ski mask way went to plot and play. What Payne needed was a pair of top-notch shooters that couldn't be tied back to him if shit didn't go down right.

Pop One and Drako slid into the Platinum Pole as if they owned the place and pulled up on the table before Payne and Blacq had a chance to even take notice. It wasn't until the cold kiss of their pistols touched the sides of Payne and Blacq's head.

"Fuck," Payne swore, looking at Blacq as if this was all his fault. Blacq sat very still, keeping his hands on the table in front of them.

"Sup, dog? Y'all lost? Y'all must be lost to be up in this place without a thousand goons, guns, and the balls to use them," said Pop One, putting a little more pressure against Payne's head with his pistol.

A few more seconds passed with the tension building. Then Pop One cracked a smile, showing off a mouth full of gold fronts and telling Drako to chill out and grab them some drinks as he pulled a couple of chairs from another table and sat down with his gun on the table in front of him.

"Now, nigga, what you wanna holla at me and man about?" Pop One questioned him with aggression.

Payne released the breath he'd been holding, then took a shaky-handed drink to settle his nerves and wet his very dry throat.

152

Blacq sat there, glaring at Pop One, more than pissed that Payne even wanted to fuck with these wannabe 'Boyz in Da Hood' drive-by shooters. Payne cleared his throat as Drako sat down at the table and fired up a stick of K-2, blowing the pungent smoke in Blacq's face. Blacq started to set it off until Payne placed a restraining hand on his shoulder to keep him in his seat.

"Look. We didn't come out here to play silly ass games. I'm here to offer the two of you a chance to get paid and the street cred y'all will ever need in the A," Payne said as he watched the greed light shine in the depths of both their eyes.

"Shit, nigga, spit it out before I decide you're wasting our time, and believe me. My nigga, wit' us, time is money!" Pop One snarled while fingering his pistol on the table.

Payne launched the reason he'd reached out to the two killers, making sure they understood he could have taken his offer to a dozen other shooters in a city full of them. Drako just sat there with dead eyes locked on Blacq, either from hatred or the K-2.

Pop One took control of the conversation. "So, you're going to pay us two hundred and fifty bands to smoke your own roll dog, Epic? The very nigga that held you down out here on the streets?" He couldn't seem to believe what he was hearing.

Payne misunderstood what Pop One was asking, thinking that they were trying to squeeze more money out of him. "Look, I know—" Payne began, only to get cut off by Pop One.

"Shit, you can stop right there. In fact, say less. I'd smoke my main man Drako right here to get that bag. Hell, I'd body Mom Dukes as a bonus for two hundred and fifty G's," Pop One said in all seriousness.

"Well, in that case, shall we toast to the business at hand?" Payne asked, raising his drink.

They all did except for Blacq, who felt some type of way about dealing with these super shady niggas.

A cold drizzle fell from the steel-gray sky over a city that seemed ready to cry itself, which Epic felt was more than appropriate in this situation as he stood graveside in silent support of Ari Acousta. I wasn't that she didn't have the support of the other thirty or so Acousta Cartel soldiers standing around, all dressed in black, wearing dark shades on a rainy, overcast Cleveland day.

Besides being the black guy near Ari Acousta, Epic kept his head down, not out of respect, but in case the Feds were somewhere camped out, watching those in attendance. Even though all this had been kept on the low, one could never sleep on the feds.

Epic watched Ari out of the corner of his eye, noticing her face was almost without emotion, her eyes dry, but he knew her heart was broken, and her sourness raging for the vengeance she felt she deserved and would get. The priest was just wrapping up his eulogy for the late Yasmeen Acousta, gone all too soon. The grave porters had just started the wrenching system to lower the shining, metallic coffin into the open ground.

A cold drop of water rained down Epic's spine, raining a line of chill bumps in its wake, yet, that wasn't the only feeling of unease that had him scanning the tombstones around him. Shit just felt off, and when living by instinct, one should listen to that little voice in the back of their mind, the warning of danger.

Epic looked around, trying to figure out what triggered his survival instinct. That was when he saw the groundskeeper on a riding mower, and some more breaking ground for a new grave a few rows over. There were also two men and two women visiting a grave two rows to their left. It all seemed to be normal, except every one of them was black, and six of them had dreadlocks. Every warning bell in Epic's head went off at the same time. Epic suddenly knew what was bothering him. No groundskeeper worth a damn would be cutting grass and making ruts in the rain-soaked turf.

Adrenaline surged through his system like a shot of nitro as the man on the riding mower quickly whipped up an H & K MP-7 submachine gun. Epic moved without hesitating for a second. He tackled Ari at waist level, driving them both into the open grave and onto the slowly lowering coffin as the first rounds fired illuminated the shooter's angry sneer in orange and yellow flashes.

The three men who stood behind where Ari Acousta had been a second before were sprayed with 9mm rounds as all hell broke loose. Two stray rounds dug into the back wall of Epic and Ari's makeshift hiding place, causing dirt and small pebbles to shower down on them.

Epic snatched his Sig Sauer P-92 from his shoulder holster as Ari cursed while struggling and trying to get from under Epic's body weight. Epic took a quick peek over the side of the grave to assess the battle, only to see the cartel soldiers sprawled out in several places. He fired two rounds, both of which missed because of Ari's struggle, bumping into him and throwing his shots wide.

The quick glance he got was enough to show him the two women ducking behind marble tombstones and firing at the cartel soldiers. One of the cartel soldiers strafed the guy on the riding mower, ending his cutting days for good. Only a few minutes had elapsed, yet it was as if time slowed and was holding them all in that moment.

There were two things that Epic knew for sure. First, it was that the cartel soldiers were being decimated and frenzied after being caught in the open, flat-footed. The second and most important thing was that they couldn't stay there. The gunfire from the cartel's men had already fallen off in volume and tenacity. They had to move. It was as simple as that, yet the only way out that Epic could see was to say, 'Fuck Ari Acousta' and go with self-preservation. As much as he wanted to—hell, probably should have left her to her fate—he knew he wouldn't.

There was an easing in the savagery as both sides rushed to reload. Epic was sure he could jump out and make a run for cover behind some of the larger tombstones, but also understood that Ari Acousta, in her tight, form-fitting, black dress, wouldn't be able to. Instead, Epic sprang up and smacked the control panels of the grave elevator from lower to raise, allowing Ari to finally make it to her knees as the coffin slowly started to rise.

'So,' she thought, 'this is the betrayal she'd been expecting from Epic all along,' but she was Ariella Acousta, and she would not die easily. Ari slipped her hand under the edge of her skirt to retrieve the carbon fiber switchblade from its thigh sheath.

Just as the coffin rose enough to expose their head and shoulders, the click of the spring-loaded blade popping out caused him to turn in that direction, saving his life. As the strike, meant to land between his shoulder blades, instead plunged deep into his left shoulder. The sharp pain and impact actually helped clear his mind.

'What the fuck?' he thought, but didn't have time to worry about that as he not-too-gently grabbed Ari by the waist then rotated, throwing her out of the grave, using the rising coffin for cover.

The impact of bullets slamming into the coffin held his undivided attention. He then glanced at Ari as she lay in the wet grass behind their makeshift cover, staring at him in a disembodied way. Movement from the corner of his eye drew his attention back to the situation at hand.

As one of the two women chose that moment to break cover and overestimate her capabilities, she dashed to change positions for a better line of fire. Epic aimed, his weapon an extension of his arm, kicked back into his palm twice. Identical twin holes appeared in the woman's chest. She swayed a couple of steps more before she succumbed to the fatal two-piece served hot. The coffin was riddled with bullets.

Without even thinking about it, Epic reached out and pulled the high-heeled, red-bottom shoes from Ari's feet. As good as they looked and as much as they cost, they were shit for running, especially on rain-slick, soft ground.

One of the last of the cartel soldiers cut loose with a long line of suppression fire from an MP-5, forcing the attackers to take cover. It was enough for Epic. He reached down with his left hand to grab hold of Ari's hand. The pain that shot through his left shoulder was a clear and painful reminder that he wouldn't be escaping this without taking some personal damage. With a wince, Epic pulled Ari behind while firing at anything moving.

A few rounds knocked an outstretched wing off one of the stone angels, throwing stone chips into the air in front of Epic. Spinning, Epic remembered his training—sight, acquire, fire—sending three rounds at one of the false ground keepers just as Ari fell face-first. Not sure if she'd been hit or not, he fired two more rounds, then bent to one knee, grabbed her outstretched arm, and then scooped her up, tossing her weight over his right shoulder.

The pain from his left shoulder caused black spots to dance across his vision. As simple as the move was, it shot a blazing-hot pain down from his injured left shoulder, down to his toes. He fought through it and was up and moving again with Ari over his shoulder in a somewhat fireman's carry.

The cars were now only a few feet away, and Epic didn't stop until he reached the line of vehicles. He would have liked to have taken his own whip but thought better of that as a couple of bullets shattered the windows of the hearse and a limo as he passed them. Willing to run a little further, he headed for Ari's Mercedes-Maybach S600 Guard for two reasons. The first being that Ari's driver stood in the open driver's side door, firing an Uzi 9mm in the direction from which Epic had just come. As he neared the car, the driver threw open the rear door while still firing.

Epic had just set Ari's feet back on the ground when blood and brain matter splashed across her face. With no time to waste, Epic shoved her into the back seat and slammed the door closed. The second reason he was willing to risk the extra distance to reach the Maybach was that it had a six-liter V-12 bi-turbo, which could go from zero to sixty in 3.9 seconds, and had a top speed of more than 170 miles per hour, and the highest ballistic protection possible for non-military vehicles. Its body armor could stop hardened core bullets from an assault rifle, protect against explosive devices, and was reinforced with steel and had windows coated with polycarbonate. To put it simply, the car was a luxury tank on wheels.

Epic, at last, released the breath he didn't even realize he'd been holding. Sweat stung his eyes as he stabbed a finger into the push-to-start button, bringing the sleeping beast to life.

Bullets smacked loudly and flattened against the armored shell surrounding them. Epic put the car in drive and was pulling away when Neville, himself, stepped into the road and emptied a full magazine of an AR-15 assault rifle into the driver's side door and windows. The heavy rounds spider-webbed the glass, but no rounds passed through.

Epic pulled up in front of Ari Acousta's manner on the Lake, then got out of the car, looking at the stunned security team that met them out front. He opened the door for Ari as she quietly stepped out, putting her bare feet on the cold, wet pavement. After a minute of awkwardness, she finally raised her eyes to meet him. Without a word, he reached across to his left shoulder and took hold of the mother-of-pearl handle and, with a grimace, pulled it out, spun it around, and then gave it back handle-first to Ariella Acousta.

She stuttered and said, "Epic, I thought—"

The look he gave her stole the next words from her. She started to reach for the wound, then thought better of it.

"Yo, I know what you thought," Epic said before everything went black.

Asimi sat cross-legged in front of the coffee table, waiting for her laptop to boot up. She hadn't really spoken to Epic since the whole Sarah reveal. Whatever the big emergency had been that made him disappear for the last four days had her more than a little bit worried. Even knowing he could take care of himself didn't really relieve the stress of not hearing his voice.

Sarah had all but moved in with Asimi, and things were going great between them, as always. She just hoped that their new triple relationship would stand strong when they were all together daily. Sarah had already asked Asimi how she thought Epic would feel about her moving to Cleveland when she and Asimi finally walked the stage in cap and gown in about six more weeks. That was just one of many unknowns that Asimi wished to speak to Epic about, amongst other things.

Sarah walked into the living room, carrying two glasses of white wine, wearing a triple X-1 Dallas Cowboys jersey that fell to her mid-thigh, teasing Asimi with a little flash of silk, blue panties with every step she took. Sarah set one of the glasses down and turned to leave, but Asimi felt like she was trying to push too far, too fast into the relationship, where Asimi and Epic were concerned. Truth be told, she felt like their FaceTime chats were their thing and didn't want Asimi feeling like she was trying to take over.

Asimi watched Sarah hesitate for a second, a questioning look passing over her face so quickly that, had Asimi not been looking Sarah in the eyes when she asked her to join in on the video call, she may have missed it.

"After all, our man is calling, and he would be happy, if not expecting, to see both his woman safe and sound," Asimi said.

Sarah paused. It was the fact that Asimi had not only sounded sincere, but she was also happy to have Sarah there, and for the first time, Sarah truly understood she could never best Asimi for Epic's love. She'd have to be happy that Asimi had decided to share, but the love she felt for both of them would allow her to live with that.

As time passed, and the link didn't come, Asimi and Sarah both became even more worried. They tried reaching him on his cell phone, only for it to go straight to voicemail.

Chapter 22

Ari stood at the foot of her California king-sized bed, watching Epic sleep. Her on-call private physician had cleaned and stitched up the wound and assured her that he'd live, even though he'd lost a severe amount of blood, which was why he was still unconscious two days after blacking out. Ari watched as the nurse came in with a basin of warm, soapy water, washcloths, and towels, preparing for his sponge bath.

She watched as the nurse folded back the covers from Epic's chest, down to his waist, revealing his chiseled abs, then dipped a washcloth into the warm water and gently raised his right arm and began to tenderly wash Epic's arm and upper body. His physique made her mouth water. Her physical attraction to him was terrifying. The denial in her mind couldn't outweigh the ruth in her heart, as much as she tried to deny it.

Ariella Acousta, the most powerful woman in the drug world, had fallen head over heels in love with Epic. A nobody, common street thug, whom she once ordered killed, and she herself had tried to kill two days ago as he fought to save their lives. The look in his eyes right before he'd passed out, the accusation in them alone, had been enough to shake her soul. On a sudden whim, Ari dismissed the nurse, telling her to leave everything. Once the nurse left, Ari moved over to the side of the bed. Looking at him lying there did something to her.

Ari folded the covers lower to expose Epic's nudity in all its glory. The sight of his limp penis had her mouth watering. Deep within it kindled a fire that she wished could be quenched, yet it burned deep, threatening to consume her.

Without thinking about what she was doing, she wrung the excess water from the washcloth and began to bathe his thighs, working her way toward what held her so captivated. Taking his soft penis in her left hand, she moved it so she could wash every inch of him. The feel in her hands made her feel powerful, and the desire that slammed into her made her delirious. Ari couldn't help but rub her thumb over the soft, spongy head, and as she did, she was surprised to feel the soft velvet flesh start to harden into durable steel.

This rise in him had her stroking him now, bringing his member to full attention. Ari didn't know if it was the fact he'd saved her life or the near-death experience. Maybe it was simply his vulnerability at the moment, but she couldn't help herself as she leaned forward, taking his rapidly swelling dick into her mouth. Rationally, she knew that he needed to rest, yet as he hardened more, she applied more suction while pumping up and down, frenzied by his reaction to her tongue swirling around his blood-filled, enlarged head.

Ari stopped long enough to hike her skirt up around her waist before climbing up onto the bed and straddling Epic's prone form, doing her best not to jostle him too much. Her fingers came away wet as she pulled her panties to the side before lowering her creamy, hot slot onto his mahogany-colored rod.

Ari threw back her head as she impaled herself with every inch of him. Heat rushed through her in micro waves at first, quickly building into a supersonic release as she ground on his dick, forcing it even deeper into her scorching depths. Several more bounces had her shaking through an amazing, mind-blowing orgasm that radiated from the very center of her, drawing a satisfied moan from her.

Her wild passion as she reached her climax shook Epic, causing him to grow while still out of it, but as she started to climb off of him, he mumbled something she could barely hear. She leaned forward to bring her ear closer to his lips as he mumbled again, and this time, she heard what he said.

"I love you, Asimi."

Anger and rage shot through her as he proclaimed his love for another woman while still buried deep inside of her, but she quickly got her emotions in check. She had no idea of who this Asimi woman was, but she would not be allowed to stand in the way of what Ariella Acousta, queenpin of the world, had now claimed as her own.

The darkness slowly began to recede as Epic fought his way back to lucidity. His mind felt stuck in a dream state, Asimi at the forefront of his thoughts. As his eyes cracked open, the bright light in the room ignited a brain-numbing headache, and the fact that his surroundings were completely alien to him didn't help either.

Migraine aside, his other senses started to come in line, like the smell of a cigarillo emanating from right outside the open patio door and the enticing aroma of coconut shrimp and salmon steak with lemon juice coming from the serving cart near the foot of his bed.

With effort, he sat up, feeling stiff and a bit weak. Slowly but surely, everything that had happened started to come back to him—the whole ambush at Yasmeen's funeral, the mad dash for the car, and Ari Acousta stabbing him in the back. If he had any doubt about where he was, the elaborate furnishings and cartel soldier outside on the patio, armed with an AK-47, confirmed to him that he was at Ariella Acousta's. but for how long had he been here?

Epic threw back the covers on the bed so he could get up. Despite being naked, he stood up and went to the platter on the food cart. The grumbling of his stomach outweighed the rules of etiquette as the delicious-looking food caused him to put all else on pause for the moment as he dug into the offering ravenously.

On the nightstand, there were bottles of painkillers and sedatives, but he decided the tidbit of pain he was feeling was a good thing and used it to focus his thoughts. Once he'd eaten, he looked around for his clothes, but the Vier suit he'd worn to the funeral was nowhere in sight. However, he did find a pair of Nike sweatpants, and that was good enough. Epic made his way through the lavish mansion, looking for someone who could tell him what was going on.

He finally encountered a maid in what he guessed was the central hallway and was more than shocked when she led him to his ruined suit and a handwritten letter from Ari. Epic opened the envelope to find one sheet of paper with Ari's neat script on it.

Epic if you are reading this, then please know that I'm sorry that I couldn't be there when you awakened from your injuries. I've taken the liberty of having your vehicle retrieved from the graveyard, and the situation has been sanitized as fas as law enforcement is concerned. We will come together and discuss what must be done to rectify the trespass and treachery committed against me. There will be no exceptions on this. Those who are responsible will get what they deserve. There is so much that I would like to say to you, but this is not the way to do it, so know that when I return stateside we will sit down and have that conversation. But, for now please let me say thank you for saving my life. P.S., you will find a small token of my appreciation in your vehicle.

It was signed Ari.

Before the maid could disappear, Epic asked her the date and was shocked to find out that he'd been out of it for three days. He was very aware that he'd missed his set FaceTime with Asimi, who was probably going crazy about now after hearing from him.

By the time Epic reached the front door, his Bentley was out front with the driver's door open and the car running. A Calvin Klein mid-size tote sat on the passenger seat, and after a quick count, he returned the tote to the passenger seat and couldn't help but think, 'Does she feel like her life is only worth two hundred fifty thousand dollars?' Hell, he felt like the knife wound in his shoulder was worth twice that amount by itself, but she was right about one thing. When he saw her again, they were going to have a long, serious conversation.

Chapter 23

Payne was pretty much a no-show on the streets and at the club. Shit was too live right then, and with what occurred at Yasmeen Acousta's funeral, her sister was looking for anybody that she could pin to the wall that may have had something to do with it. The only reason he wasn't on the hit list or a suspect was that he wasn't a rude boy, and he was in South Africa, setting up another shell company to move money through.

He'd also told her about it a full week before Yasmeen had been killed, so his absence at the funeral from hell didn't seem so suspicious, just lucky as a muthafucka. The only thing that could have been better was if Epic's punk ass had caught a bullet or two. Instead, his lucky ass ended up saving boss lady's life. As commendable as that was, it still pissed Payne off. Just knowing that Epic was still out there was enough to give him nightmares.

He thought to himself, 'Soon, that loose end will be tied up tight.'

For now, Payne pulled out his cell phone to fire off a text message to Candy, letting her know that he missed her and was thinking about her. He switched his phone to the camera mode, then pulled out his hard dick and snapped a couple of pictures to send along with his text.

P.S. Be wet, wild and ready.

El Angel de la Muerte sat across from Ari Acousta, his dead, sharklike eyes analyzing the entire room. El Angel de la Muerte or, in English, The Angel of Death, did not like

166

being summoned like some stray dog. Regardless of the fact that he was on the mend after breaking his collarbone in the explosion, which had wiped out twelve of his men. He'd made his report to Cal Bower, who had informed the big boss, which was why he was now sitting there instead of tracking down the asshole who'd killed his team and had the banking account numbers he'd been looking for, for more than twenty years.

It was a rarity he was ever called in to meet face to face. His job was to fulfill the last wishes of the head of the family, not to come running every time something happened. So, no, he was not happy to be there. He'd been told to stay away, so what had changed?

"Well, you summoned me here. What is so important that you would have me step away from my promise?" he questioned.

"Actually, there are two reasons you are here now, and both are more important to me than you honoring a promise to the dead, a promise that would mean allowing an enemy of this family to go unchecked. So, I've decided to double down."

Cerrano just sat, watching and waiting.

Finally, the plan was laid out before him, a plan that he didn't like at all, so he said as much.

"It is not for you to like; it's for you to do."

After a minute of tense silence, he gave a curt nod and replied, "As you wish, as always." Cerrano, understanding that the conversation was over, began to rise from his seat to leave.

"And, Cerrano, if you fail this family again, the loyalty you've shown this family will not protect you. I will rectify the mistake my father made by letting you live."

Without a word, Cerrano turned and walked out.

Epic sat in his favorite leather recliner. He'd just called Asimi and was told to send a FaceTime link. With a deep sigh, he sent the link. Asimi, along with Sarah, accepted the request immediately, smiling. Then, the sight of her man wiped that smile away to be replaced by her mean mug, the face that Epic found cuter than threatening.

Asimi and Sarah both gasped upon seeing him. Due to blood loss, his skin had a pale, waxy sheen to it. His usual swag was missing as he wore a pair of Nike shorts, a wifebeater, and a pair of throwback Jordans. He'd removed the white bandage from his shoulder to allow his wound to get some fresh air. It had been four days since Yasmeen Acousta's funeral, and he was feeling better, but not yet a hundred percent.

Before he could even say a word, he was hit with a deluge of questions from both Asimi and Sarah.

"Bae, what happened? Are you sick? Did you have an accident?" Asimi asked, worry etched on her face.

Sarah was no less shocked or inquisitive with her questions. "Oh my God, what happened? Did you get food poisoned? 'Cause we can sue the place if so," she said in full-blown lawyer mode now.

"Now, it was nothing like that," he said, turning to expose his left shoulder with his stitches to the camera for them to see.

Asimi snapped when seeing his shoulder. "Bae, what happened to your shoulder? Who in the hell hurt you?" she shouted at the screen. "Where are you? We're on the way. Just let me know who I need to lay hands on."

Sarah felt the same way and was down to ride with Asimi no matter what. Epic smiled; the love he felt from them did more than the painkillers did to have him feeling better.

"Bae, I don't know why the hell you're smiling, 'cause I'm dead serious as a heart attack," spat a heated Asimi.

Using his good arm, Epic patted the air in a calm-down gesture while saying, "Chill, baby girl. It's all good." He ran a hand over his jaw. "They still couldn't touch my pretty," he said jokingly, trying to lighten the mood, but he could still see the tears brimming in Asimi's eyes.

Asimi, not wanting to cry in front of Epic, jumped up and dashed to the bathroom. Sarah started to follow, but Epic's voice stopped her as he called out to her.

"Yo, let her be. Just give her a minute," he told her, then asked if she was okay.

Sarah took two deep breaths to calm herself. She really wanted to know what had happened to him, but decided to wait for Asimi to come back so that if Epic told them what had happened, he'd only have to do it once.

"So, Barbie, are you taking care of our girl? Or after this, are you having second thoughts about this whole relationship you find yourself in?" Epic questioned. He went on to explain that their job was to take care of each other, while his job was to take care of both of them. Epic's words touched Sarah's heart and had it swelling with love.

Still, she couldn't stop herself from thinking, 'Whose job was it to look out for and protect him?'

Asimi returned a few minutes later. She'd splashed some cold water on her face and pulled her shit together. It didn't stop her from worrying, especially since Epic and Payne had fallen out. Without Payne, who had her man's back out there?

Sarah wrapped her arms around Asimi as soon as she sat back down. Asimi squeezed out a soft, "I'm sorry," to Epic as she faced the screen and was more than thankful when Sarah came to the rescue.

Jokingly, she said, "Thank God," which caused Asimi to snap a look at her in disbelief. Sarah continued, "Thank God! Do you know how hard it was, trying to keep up with your never-ending perfection?" she asked, her tone serious, and face deadpanned. "Now that you've got a scratch or two on you, me and Asimi may have a chance to be noticed when we're all out together." She went over to Asimi, laughing out loud. "Besides, I'm a strait-laced, white chick, looking for that thug love, and now you look a little dinged up, so maybe my street cred will go up a notch or two," she finished, joining Asimi laughing.

Epic shot one of his own mean mugs at the screen, causing Asimi to say, "Aww, bae, everyone has a soft spot for the lil' scruffy puppy."

And just like that, tension drained out of them, and Epic went on to tell them about some of what had popped off. He made sure to downplay most of the danger he'd been in. Their conversation switched to Asimi and Sarah's upcoming graduation and what was to come afterward, and adding Sarah into the mix just raised the game to another level. Epic was well aware that they wanted to see him in person—hell, almost as bad as he wanted to see them—but it wasn't the time for that. And no matter how bad he wanted to get that threesome jumping off with them, he'd never willingly endanger either of them.

With the city being turned up, he didn't want Sarah or Asimi anywhere near the pandemonium that was his life, so to put an end to their complaints of not getting to come baby him, Epic promised to do something big for both of them for their graduation. In fact, he decided to let them pick whatever they wanted to do. He also didn't miss the fact that neither one of them mentioned that Valentine's Day was in two days. Right then and there, he made a silent promise to himself that he would be there on V-Day for them.

Chapter 24

Payne felt good as he sat across the table from Candy in the most expensive restaurant in Cleveland; 17th on Broadway had a waiting list over a year and a half long, and he'd had to pull out the stops to cop a spot the day before Valentine's Day. He'd given the owner five thousand in cash and a promise to move some of the assets he was trying to hide from his wife in their upcoming divorce.

Candy couldn't stop talking about how great the food was, and why he didn't take her out like this all the time.

"Maybe I will now that I see how much you enjoy it," he replied. But he was really thinking, 'Bitch, you've gotta be out of your damn mind—as much as this shit just cost me.'

Candy, not knowing his true feelings, smiled back at her man and said, "Tonight, you can do it anyway you want to."

Payne was instantly hard, ready for the check. As they waited for Blacq to bring the Range Rover up front so they could leave, Candy snuggled up to her man and slyly rubbed a hand down to give a little squeeze to the bulge in his pants. Blac switched lanes while keeping his eyes on the rearview mirror. He let out a soft grunt as the old-school box Chevy two cars back also switched into the same lane behind them.

He really hated to break up boss man's fun, but he was a hundred percent sure they were being followed. Slowly, he reached over to the passenger seat and slid the A.P.C. 223 assault rifle into his lap. The folding stock made it easy to handle in the close confines of the driver's seat.

For a brief second, he thought that this might've been that nigga Epic tryin' to creep up, but if it was true on how that nigga gave it up, then that wasn't him. The M.O. didn't fit. From all Payne had told him about old boy, it wasn't his style at all. Epic was said to be incognito, and whoever it was was the exact opposite of the word.

Payne loved Candy's head game. Shit, there was nothing like getting some good head from a bad ass bitch while your right-hand man played the chauffeur role, some shit Epic would have never gone for. He was only minutes from trying to get Candy's throat pregnant when the sound of Blacq calling his name cut through the suction-induced tranquility.

"Payne, yo, boss man," Blacq called from the front.

"Yo, boss Man!" he said again, louder this time. "We got company tryin' to slide up behind us on some jack-move type shit."

The dick popped out of Candy's mouth as she turned to look out the rear window of the Range Rover, but that last pull of suction had Payne nutting all over the front of his four-thousand-dollar Vier tailor-made, double-breasted suit. He was about to curse her out when what Blacq had just said registered.

Blacq made eye contact with Payne in the rearview mirror and could have sworn he saw fear. Payne looked back in time to see a box Chevy sitting on twenty-eight-inch chrome rims swing into the left lane and come racing up beside them.

Payne, in fear for his life, grabbed Candy and spun her around toward the driver's side rear passenger door and pressed her bare double D's against the window, lying across the seat and putting a foot in the center of her back to pin her there. Payne thought, 'Shit, better her than me,' as he used Candy like a bulletproof vest.

Suddenly, a cold blast of air washed over him as Blacq hit the power window button, lowering the windows. The foot that Payne had pressed deep in Candy's back caused pretty, chocolate titties to pop out of the window, exposing her dark-chocolate Hershey's kiss-shaped nipples to the cold Cleveland night air. The cold winds of Lake Erie turned them hard as dark-smoked diamonds.

The box Chevy pulled up beside the range with a hitter in a ski mask hanging out of the front passenger window and an AK-47 finger ready to squeeze the trigger. The sight of Candy's beautiful titties popping out of the window caused him to hesitate for a split second instead of pulling the trigger.

That gave Blacq the chance to slam on the brakes, causing the box Chevy to pass them as he opened with the APC out the driver's window, spraying the whole passenger side of the Chevy and the would-be killer. The ski-masked assassin took two in the chest and one to the top of his head as he fell from the window, only to be run over by the large rear wheel of the Chevy. Payne just about shit himself when Blacq opened fire with the A.P.C. assault weapon.

The box Chevy bounced off two cars waiting to make a left turn as the driver made a desperate attempt to get away from the sudden hail of hot lead. Spent shell casings rained into Blacq's lap and the floorboard as the .223 made its presence known.

Blacq then cranked hard right on the steering wheel, cutting across a lane of traffic, causing a Toyota Prius to slam on his brakes, only to be rear-ended by a city transit bus.

Blacq looked in the side view mirror, his view blocked by a set of pretty, bouncing double-D titties, as he got them the hell out of there.

As soon as Payne removed his foot from her back, Candy jumped on his ass like a wildcat, swinging and trying to scratch at his face, yelling, "You sorry muthafucka!" That was all he could understand as she attacked him in a murderous rage.

Chapter 25

February the fourteenth was usually one of Asimi's favorite holidays, and she had been looking forward to it being really special this year. She'd thought that she'd be able to spend it with the two people she loved, but it seemed that with Epic hurt and still in Cleveland, it would just be her and Sarah. She was fine with that, but she also wanted to be with her man.

Asimi thought about the expensive watch she had brought as a Valentine's gift for him. She guessed, like her, it would have to wait until they were together again. Asimi had also noticed Sarah was pretty much bummed out, too, so the two decided they'd stay home tonight and at least videochat with Epic. The doorbell rang just as Sarah walked into the living room.

The two of them looked at each other, puzzled. The look said neither was expecting anyone. Hope flared in Asimi's eyes as she sprang from her seat and shot to the door. Sarah, caught up in her excitement, followed closely on her heels.

Asimi reached the door and snatched it open, fully expecting to see Epic standing there. Instead, she was let down at the sight of a short white guy dressed in the worldwide-brown uniform of UPS, standing there with an electronic signature pad and two small packages.

"Um, are you Ms. Asimi Samato or Sarah Wellington?" he asked.

"Yes, I'm Asimi Samato," she answered.

"Could I please get you to sign right here?"

Sarah stood watch over Asimi's shoulder as she signed for the two packages. Asimi thanked the UPS driver and closed the door. She was in the process of handing one of the two boxes to Sarah when the doorbell rang again.

This time, standing there was a small, Asian woman from Forget-Me-Not Flowers, holding two very elegant vases filled with red and white roses for them. Sarah set the flowers on the table as Asimi opened the card that came with the flowers, while Sarah opened her box. The gasp from Sarah made Asimi turn to see what caused it.

Sarah stood frozen as she saw what was inside the box, lying on a blue velvet pad. Looking up, she met Asimi's inquiring look. As she turned the box to give Asimi a better look at what it contained, the light sparkled off the platinum chain with a diamond-encrusted charm, a matching tennis bracelet, and two-carat diamond earrings, all by Cartier.

Asimi tore into her package to find the same ridiculously expensive jewelry as Sarah's. They were both stunned and silent, and then the doorbell rang again. When the door was opened this time, there was a delivery from FedEx waiting with even more boxes for the two astonished women.

The door was still ajar when the next carrier arrived from the travel company—World Travel Mates—with two tickets to Tahiti and reservations at the nicest resort. Asimi and Sarah both screamed with overwhelming excitement and then started talking at the same time, making plans for their upcoming trip.

Asimi grabbed her phone and hit the speed dial to call Epic as the doorbell rang again. Sarah opened it to a large bundle of heart-shaped balloons—so many that they completely covered the person delivering them.

Sarah was reaching for the balloons as the song *Love of My Life* started to play. At the sound of the ringtone, Asimi swung around, facing the door, her phone all but forgotten as it fell to the floor. Sarah reached for the balloons and was completely shocked as Asimi ran passed her and almost tackled the balloon guy in the doorway, throwing herself into his arms.

"Sup, baby girl? Does this mean you missed me, or are you just happy about all your Valentine's gifts?" Epic asked with that cocky smile Asimi loved.

Before he could say anything more, Sarah almost knocked them both over as she joined the hug fest on the front porch.

"Oh my God, bae! What are you doing here? I thought you were wounded and laid up," Asimi said.

"Should you be up and moving?" questioned Sarah as she began to untangle herself from the pile.

The question suddenly reminded Asimi that Epic was hurt, and she immediately released him and stepped back, checking to see if she'd hurt him. "I'm sorry! I'm sorry!" she repeated as she rained kisses all over his face.

It sent a jolt of pain through Epic's wounded shoulder, but it had been worth it for their surprise, so he answered, saying, "Nah, ma, it's all good. And as to what I'm doing here, did you really think that I'd miss spending Valentine's Day with my two sweethearts?" He flashed that heart-stopping smile again. "So did y'all like your Valentine gifts?" he asked, smiling, knowing the answer all along.

They both took hold of a hand and pulled him inside, intending to show him just how much they loved their Valentine's gifts. It started in the living room with a whirlwind of clothes flying off, pulling, tugging, and tearing to get to skin-to-skin contact. All the material presents were forgotten as Sarah and Asimi unwrapped the gift that was Epic, the gift that would keep on giving.

Epic kicked off his cumbersome jeans and Timberland boots while he unsnapped the silk bra Sarah was wearing, freeing her beautiful, tan-lined breasts. Sarah then slid Asimi's lace panties down her thighs as she kissed Epic passionately. Epic's hard dick sprang from his Tommy boxer briefs as Asimi took his flesh pole in her hand, stroking him to an even harder length.

The shock and surprise showed on his face as his gaze came across Epic as he swept the crowded room. The other patrons parted before him like seals from a great white shark as he headed toward Epic's table. Without seeming to, Epic casually shifted to allow himself easier access to this Glock 27, .40 Caliber tucked in his waistband at the small of his back. He watched every move that the newcomer made as he stepped up to the table.

Talk about a fish out of water. His attempt to blend in with the crowd was all wrong. Although it was a sports bar, the triple XL Cleveland Browns jersey, sagging jeans, Timb boots, and red bandanna hanging from his back pocket were warning enough to any and all who had any sense of self-preservation.

"Sup, gangsta?" asked Bloodrush. "What da hell you doing out here in Cracker land?"

Epic waved a hand at the table, indicating his food. "Just stopped in for some wings and a drink."

Bloodrush started to take a seat, then thought better of it and asked, "Mind if I pull up?"

"Feel free," Epic replied.

Epic watched as Bloodrush's eyes continually scanned the room. He knew the look all too well—the look of somebody looking for a come-up. The waitress, noticing Bloodrush at the table, came over to take his order, asking, "What can I get for you?"

"Yeah, let me get a Red Bull, twenty-five hot wings, and a Grey Goose with ice in it," he said.

"Atomic or Infamous Fire? And can I see some ID, please?" she asked with a disarming smile.

It was the wrong move on her part, as Bloodrush thug-grilled her before saying, "Bitch, just go get my shit 'fore we got a problem up in here, a'ight?"

Epic shook his head, making a mental note to leave a big tip.

As soon as the waitress was gone, Bloodrush said, "Damn, dog. If I hadn't run into you way out here in Snowville Land, I wouldn't have believed what the streets was saying."

"Is that so? And just what are the streets saying that you find it so hard to believe?" Epic asked.

Bloodrush glanced around like someone might've been trying to eavesdrop on their conversation before he continued. "Check it, gang. Word is, yo' man Payne kicked you to the curb and put a hundred bands on yo' head of that cartel money. But yo' rep was so strong that the niggas that took the down payment tried to smoke his ass instead, feeling like he was easier food than you. And since ain't nobody seen you in a while, and you ain't been making no noise, you know how it goes, blood. The king is dead—long live the king." He finished saying, just as the waitress arrived with his food.

Bloodrush took a sip of his Goose before he continued.

"Shit, my nig', you the real truth when it comes to Black Ops, so I can't understand how you lettin' this nigga live, puttin' bullshit on yo' name. Hell, it's niggas out there believing you don't want no smoke."

"And what do you believe?" Epic asked, his tone calm, deceiving of how he really felt.

Bloodrush had the same sixth sense that most real killers possessed, knowing they were close to the edge.

He raised both hands, palms up, in a gesture of peace, saying, "Peace, Blood. I meant no offense—just telling you what the word is on the streets."

Epic gave a slight nod to acknowledge that he understood that Bloodrush was just relaying information, and there was no harm done. To change the subject, Epic asked, "So, how you living?

"I see you out here with that hungry look in your eyes."

178

"Shit, dog. I'm out here looking for easy food, and you know I'm willing to get it the lethal way," Bloodrush growled as he looked around the room full of yuppies.

Epic thought for a moment before he spoke.

"Check it, dog. I know you hungry and gnawing on the bone to get that paper, but I need to ask a favor of you," Epic said.

"What's that, gang?" Bloodrush questioned.

"Drop the hunt out here tonight, or at least look elsewhere to put down your stick-up game." Epic watched as a few different expressions played over Bloodrush's face as he tried to decide if Epic was asking or telling him to fall back, but in the end, it really didn't matter. Bloodrush released a deep sigh before he answered.

"Now, that may be easier said than done, Blood, seeing as I have to have six thousand dollars by tomorrow or find a new spot for my BM and kids to lay their heads. She let the rent lapse month after month and didn't tell me until the eviction notice got tacked to the door."

"Say less," Epic said. "I got you, a'ight, and no, this isn't a handout but a hand up, brah. Look at it as a payment for the info. Plus, I can't have you merking one of these white folks out here after everybody in this piece done seen us choppin' it for the last hour, so I'll push you ten racks for your time and info."

"Damn, dog. That's yo' good word?" asked a very excited and relieved Bloodrush. "That's what it do, my nig'. Show one fo' the po' one." He smiled as he reached across the table to give Epic some dap.

Epic's phone vibrated with an incoming text and pictured from his grandmother. The text read, *Epic, I'll call you later when I get home.*

Epic tried her number but got no answer, so he tried again, only to have her voicemail pick up. He decided not to leave a message, guessing she must've been tied up.

After Bloodrush left, Epic sat at the Winking Lizard for another hour, thinking over everything he'd been told, and coming up with a plan. 'It's time,' he thought, pulling out his phone and scrolling through the directory, finding the number he was looking for. He hit the speed dial. His call was answered on the third ring.

"What's up, my nig'?"

"It's time. Let me know when you touch down," Epic said.

Chapter 26

Payne sat in a dark corner in the smoke-filled room of his new favorite strip spot of the Silk Room. It wasn't Exotic Toyz, but it was somewhere to pull up on some new pussy, seeing as every bitch in Exotic Toyz now treated him like a parasite, even the damn bouncers and bartenders. Ever since Candy's hoe ass shot her damned mouth off about how he'd used her like a bulletproof vest, none of the bitches at Exotic Toyz would fuck with him, not even when he was waving stacks around.

Those stupid bitches would rather give Blacq lap dances for free than to take money from him. It was bad enough he'd lost his main piece, but not being welcomed at Exotic Toyz was like losing his home. He was still deep in self-pity and contemplation when LaLa, one of the better-looking dancers, stopped beside his table and asked him if he wanted a table dance.

He almost said no, but Blacq was still in the VIP with the lil' dark honey he'd slid off with, and hell, maybe shorty could take his mind off of Candy's ratchet ass. Instead, he put his bulging money clip on the table and asked her what she'd do to earn it. She pushed him back into his chair while unsnapping her top with one hand and throwing it on the table.

Payne's dick hardened automatically when the strobe lights reflected off the barbells piercing both of her perky nipples. LaLa slipped a wet, toned leg over Payne's and slowly lowered herself onto his lap, grinding and gyrating slowly, feeling his hardness put pressure on her clit, moaning as she lay her head back on his shoulder with her breasts thrust into the air.

Payne was definitely feeling shorty, but she was going to have to do a lot more than tease his dick through his pants if she planned to get the money on the table. As if reading his mind, she leaned forward and grabbed both of her ankles, giving him a perfect view of her barely covered, puffy pussy lips, and an even better shot of her G-string bisected asshole.

'Now, this was like it,' Payne thought while pulling out a condom from his pocket, slipping a finger into her wet and ready pussy, knowing she was with it as she started to push back on his probing finger, forcing it deep.

Even when the song ended, LaLa continued bouncing on the thick finger in her wet box, refusing to let anything stop her from getting that bag. Shit, if she had to give up some pussy for paper, she didn't mind. It was better than all those dumb hoes out there fucking for free.

Payne was so turned up that he pulled his dick out and shot his first load on the floor between her legs, looking around to make sure no one was paying them too much attention as he used her top to wipe the nut from his still-hard dick.

LaLa watched as the thick jets of cum splashed on the floor, almost catching her in the face, not that she would have tripped if it had. She'd had cum on her face for less money than was on the table right then. Payne ripped the condom wrapper open and rolled the rubber down his stiff member as LaLa pulled her G-string to the side to give him easy access to her wet gold. She came as soon as his swollen head parted her lush lips, sliding easily into moist depths coated by her female ejaculation.

As LaLa rode Payne for all she was worth and then some, he couldn't help but think, 'Fuck Candy. Money talks, and bullshit walks, and right now, it's saying everything I want to hear.'

R. Kelly's *Bump and Grind* was playing as he and LaLa came together, her soaking his balls and him filling his condom.

Three days had passed since Epic had been sent the pictures and texts from his grandmother, and she had yet to answer her phone or respond to any of his return text messages. He had no home address for her that he could go by and check up, and from the content of the pictures he'd received, he was sure something had happened to her.

He was so worried he was having a difficult time staying focused on what White Mike was saying as he sat across from him in the Next Level sports bar.

"So, how does it feel to now be one of the super-duper rich and infamous?" he asked jokingly. "Because, as of right now, you're the richest friend I go—or have ever had, for that matter."

"Well, truth be told, I think it may have cost me more than it was worth," Epic replied.

Not understanding his meaning, White Mike waved a hand at him and said, "Please. The three million I deducted as my fee didn't even make a ding, let alone a dent," he said, smiling.

"Naw, that's not the problem. I think someone I've come to care for, and who also found the numbered codes and routing numbers, may be in a world of shit now, and the only way I can see this playing out, if she's still alive, is by returning the flash drive."

The shock on White Mike's face said it all. "Wait. You mean as in, turning over Bill Gates, Warren Buffett, Rihanna type of money, for one person?" he asked incredulously.

Epic gave a slight nod then added, "She's my grandmother and the last living link I have to the mother I never had a chance to know."

"But what's to say that once you give the money and the flash drive are back, they won't just kill you both anyway?"

"That's just a chance I'll have to take, unless you have a better idea."

"Hell yeah. Do what you do. Find the motherfucker, and go in guns blazing," he said, turning his hands into pistols and firing air shots in every direction.

"I wish I could, but like I said, I think they have my grandma hostage, so there will be no wild bullet orgy if I can help it."

White Mike banged his fist against his head, trying to come up with a better solution to the problem. Finally, he asked, "Okay, okay. How about you give them back the flash drive but not the money?"

In answer to this, Epic pulled out his Glock and set it on the table.

"Whoa. Wait, wait! You didn't let me finish," he said, in a rush to get the words out. Epic rolled his wrists in a go-ahead type of motion. White Mike took a deep breath before continuing as he mentally put together the plan. "Alright, I got it," he said, slapping the tabletop and spilling his drink, which he quickly used his napkin to mop up so none of the liquid reached Epic's Glock that was still out of the table. Giving the menacing-looking weapon the side eye, he asked, "Could you please put that away? It's hard to think straight with that lying there."

Epic returned his weapon, to White Mike's great relief. "Okay, so what's this great plan that you have, genius?"

"Alright, they want the flash drive, so you give it to them."

Epic began to reach for the Glock again.

Panicking, White Mike said, "Hold on a damned minute, will you?" He was a little too loud, drawing unwanted stares toward them.

"Okay, here's my plan. We give them back a ghost drive."

When Epic just sat there, looking at him, the small muscle in his jaw ticked from him clinching it so tightly.

White Mike hurried on to explain. "See, we transfer all the bank account numbers onto an identical flash drive, only this one is special because it has a Magic Mike embedded in its coding," he said, like that explained everything, which it didn't.

After a second, Epic simply said, "Mike, let's pretend for a minute that everybody in the world isn't a computer geek or hacker. So for us computer illiterate people, i.e., me, could you explain this shit in terms that I can understand?"

White Mike thought for a second, then launched into his so-called less-complicated explanation.

"First, we have to get passed the bank's security, but that won't be a problem because once whoever logs into the bank's mainframe, it will allow my coded worm to slip through their security firewall. Once the worm has infiltrated the bank's system, it will kick it into a system-wide maintenance update status, rebooting the routers, but whoever is attempting to access the accounts will actually be manipulating a bogus transfer of funds and will even receive an authenticity code. You see, it's all ones and zeros."

"I'm guessing whoever is transferring this money is going to be more than suspicious when there's no money in their account and more than a little pissed off," Epic said.

"You don't get it," White Mike said. "The money will be in their account for a split second, then bounce back to the bank's accounts and into yours once more, and since the money is still there when the maintenance update finishes, there will be no alarms going off."

He smiled, taking a mock bow. His smile was infectious, causing Epic to smile back.

"Mike, if this works, pay yourself another five mill'," Epic said.

"Money in the bank," White Mike replied, giving Epic some dap.

Just then, Epic's phone vibrated. Looking down at it, he smiled as he recognized the West Virginia area code and number.

"What it do?" he answered.

"Same ol', same ol', brah," Felony growled. "Damn, my nig', we at the gate. I thought you was cappin' when you was talkin' 'bout yo' crib and shit."

"Never that, my nig. You know me better than that. Hold on a minute while I turn off the security system and punch in the gate code. When it opens, just go on up to the house and make yourselves at home, a'ight?" he asked, disarming his security system and opening the gate for them. "I'll be there in about an hour, so chill and hold it down for me."

"And you know this, man!" Felony said, mimicking Chris Tucker's character 'Smokey' from the movie *Friday*.

"Yo, check it, Mike. I gotta be in the wind, but get that flash drive done for me as quick as possible, even though nobody's reached out to me yet, I'm sure they will."

"A'ight, my nig'," replied White Mike.

Epic froze, looking at White Mike like a Smurf had just popped out of his ass. "I know you didn't just drop the 'N' bomb up in here, did you?" Epic snarled, mean-mugging him.

White Mike started to stutter. "My bad, Epic. I just thought we were like brothers, you know?"

"What the fuck made you think some shit like that?" questioned Epic with a serious face.

White Mike was speechless until Epic burst out laughing and pointing at White Mike, saying, "You should have seen yo' face just now. You 'bout shit yo' pants!"

White Mike released the breath he was holding. "Not funny, man. Not funny at all," he said.

Chapter 27

Blacq pulled into the parking lot of Exotic Toyz on a bullshit mission for Payne to beg Candy to come back to him. Hell, he couldn't blame her for leaving, especially after he used her as a vest, and that thought made him smile as he thought about those pretty ass titties hanging out the window. He couldn't lie to himself; it felt good to be back at Exotic Toyz, where the baddest bitches in the land worked. Shit, the whole vibe in there was A-one, and the club was packed with real niggas that understood the G-code.

The eye candy was even better in there than he remembered after being stuck going to the Silk Room because nobody in there wanted to fuck with Payne. Forced exile was how Blacq saw it, but tonight, it was his time to shine on boss man's dime while he asked a ho to be a housewife for a ho ass nigga.

He ordered his favorite—Hypnotic—with a Sprite chaser and then fired up a pre-freaked Black & Mild, ready to watch some dancers shake it fast before taking care of boss man's business, which he was sure was going to be the end of his night when she blanked the fuck out.

A lot of commotion beside the main stage caught his eye, drawing his attention to three niggas with at least fifteen stacks piled up in front of them on the stage. He didn't recognize these dudes, but he knew their type by the clothes and jewelry they wore. They were loud, obnoxious, and wild as hell, just the type of niggas Blacq would click with.

He watched as one of the dancers pulled up on one of the three to ask him if he wanted a private dance. After he looked her up and down, he started laughing before he grabbed one of the bottles of Three Aces off the table and poured it over her head, giving her an old-school thug bath while laughing with his boys.

As she stormed away, surely to get the bouncers, one of the other dudes grabbed a band from the stacks and threw it at the white girl on stage, smacking her in the face and damn near knocking her ass off the other side.

He then yelled out, "Get this slack-ass white bitch outta here, and bring on some thick ass sisters!" He dapped up his dudes while the white chick scooped up the band of money and left the stage in tears.

Blacq shook his head, laughing at their antics, but he noticed the four big ass club bouncers moving through the crowd, headed toward the group. He took one more sip of his drink, then got up to move closer to see how it was going to play out.

These niggas were so turned up that they didn't even pay the club security any mind whatsoever as they made a semi-circle around them. It wasn't until the biggest bouncer reached out and tapped the shortest dude of the three on the shoulder to get his attention. Blacq had to admit, dude may have been short, but damned if he wasn't built like a tank, and the hostile look he gave the bouncer made the larger man take a step back before he could stop himself.

"Fuck you want, nigga?" he asked the bouncer, his aggression on max.

Staying calm, the bouncer said, "Sir, the owner has sent us over to inform you that your business is no longer welcome here tonight or any other time, so if you could gather your things, we'll escort you gentlemen out."

"What the fuck you mean, escort us out? Our money ain't no good up in this hole in the wall?" he shot back.

Still calm and trying to keep the situation from escalating, the bouncer said, "Maybe you guys will find one of the many other clubs in the city more to your liking."

"Naw, we like this one just fine," said one of the other dudes, speaking for the first time.

Blacq could see that the bouncers were losing patience, and shit was about to go from verbal to physical any minute now. Just as the bouncers decided to take it there, the three niggas produced guns out of nowhere like it was some kind of magic trick. Any bravado the bouncers were feeling went out the window.

"Yo, check it, nigga. I'm a hundred percent sure yo' boss don't pay you enough for this type of shit," snarled the heated lil' thug nigga. "See, you muthafuckas is playing Checkers, while we playing Chess—same board, different moves and rules."

Blacq was feeling this hit and wasn't willing to miss an opportunity to maybe recruit some real soldiers, maybe even some niggas to smoke that muthafucka Epic. Taking a chance, he stepped in. "Yo, excuse me for rolling up in y'all's business, but maybe I can help y'all solve this situation without this becoming the scene of four homicides," he said. "You fellows look like the type of livewire niggas I roll with, and this is definitely an opportunity that could be mutually beneficial to all of us."

After one more mean mug from the bouncers, lil' dude gave a nod to one of his boys, who Blacq realized were twins, turned, and grabbed up the money from the stage. They then made their way to the door with Blacq following as they hit the parking lot. The three men went over to a blacked-out G-wagon, as Blacq jumped into the Range Rover. He smiled as they followed him to another club.

Sunlight warmed Blacq's face as much as its bright glare stung his eyes. His neck and back were stiff due to the position he'd slept in last night. His memory was hazy, and his mind felt sluggish as he took in his unfamiliar surroundings. Where in the hell was he, and why the hell was he outside?

The last thing he remembered from the night before was doing lines of cocaine out the ass crack of some stripper bitch and then hitting that funny-smelling shit those twins were smoking. It wasn't until he tried to stand up that he realized he was handcuffed to a wrought black iron patio chair he had sat in.

The sliding glass door behind him slid open, and Felony came into view with a box of Cap'n Crunch and a box of Fruity Pebbles, Quick Strawberry mix, milk, and a bowl of blueberries.

"Yo, what da fuck's going on nigga?" Blacq asked, pulling against his restraints.

Felony gave him no answer as he went back into the trailer, and came back out with a medium-sized bowl, which he then poured half of each box of cereal, then added four scoops of the Strawberry Quick along with blueberries, then milk.

Blacq started to speak again, but was interrupted by a deep growl down by his right thigh. Looking down he was completely surprised to find the block head of a drooling pitbull.

"Sssshhh," Felony said. "Beast don't like when someone he doesn't know disturbs his daddy's breakfast."

"But, don't worry, you'll have all the time in the world to talk when my mans get here, so just relax and enjoy the sunshine."

Blacq watched as the twins Chaos and Havoc pulled the plug on the above-ground swimming pool, causing a flood of water to cascade through the backyard.

Blacq didn't know why they did, but was sure that he wouldn't like it.

One of the twins went back into the trailer and came back out with an animal cage in each hand. He sat them down and went to retrieve another, all the while, Felony chomped away at his breakfast.

Chaos came over to Felony, smoking a stick of that mean ass Death Grip K-2, the same shit that had knocked Blacq out last night.

"Yo, Felony, brah just pulled up out front," he said, exhaling a cloud of smoke.

A few minutes later, Blacq heard the thumps of Timb boots on the wooden patio deck.

Felony stood up, greeting the newcomer, "Yo, what it do, my nig'?" he asked. "And where did you find this sweet ass spot? I could use a spot like this."

The double-wide trailer was out in bum-fuck Egypt, in the woods outside of Zanesville, Ohio. It was a property he'd bought some years back as an emergency fallback spot. The trailer sat on four acres of land, most of it wooded.

"I'ma cop me a spot like this one, somewhere my shorty and Trigger can feel safe," Felony said.

"Naw, you don't have to cop a spot like this, dog, because this one is yours now."

Shock registered on Felony's face, then an emotion that on anyone else would have been called gratitude and love, but it was gone so quickly that he wasn't sure he'd seen it.

Felony yelled back over his shoulders to the twins. "Yo, this our spot now!" He laughed as the twins high-fived.

Blacq didn't know who this new nigga was, but whoever he was, he made Blacq sweat like a muthafucka, and the fact that no one had called him by name made him even more nervous.

Finally, the two turned to look at Blacq, who wished that he'd been forgotten about.

"Everything go as planned?' asked the newcomer.

"Oh, hell yeah, brah. And not that I doubted your mental cognition abilities, but how in the hell did you know that ol' boy would show up last night?" Felony inquired.

It always amazed Epic when Felony said shit like, mental cognitive abilities.

"Naw, dog it wasn't any special mental powers involved. Just someone returning a solid I did for them once."

When Felony continued to stand there, waiting for an answer, he said, "My dud Bloodrush just signed on with that lame ass nigga Payne as a bodyguard and shooter. So when he was given babysitting duty, so this one cold gon' beg for Payne's triflin' ass bitch back, Bloodrush shot me a text, and I sent y'all in, knowing he couldn't miss out on the chance to recruit some more live wire niggas."

"Damn, Epic, I'm not worthy," said Felony, offering a mock bow.

Hearing Epic's name almost made Blacq shit on himself. Epic gestured to the empty swimming pool, still completely ignoring Blacq. He looked over at Beast and the other pet cages and asked, "What, you 'bout to have some pit fighting going on out here?"

"Naw, gang, dog fighting is for savages, especially after the feds knocked sarks outta Michael Vicks ass. Us West Virginia niggas now participate in a real gentleman's sport for nigga's that wanna bet big," Felony said.

"And what sport is that ?" Epic asked.

"Bloodsport," Felony replied. "Check it, dog. You put a rooster, a rabbit, and a raccoon in an enclosure with a Pitbull, but you bet on how long it will take the pit to kill all three, and whoever is the closest to the time wins the pot. Like I said, dog, a gentleman's game, real civilized," he said.

"I bet the rooster, the rabbit, and the raccoon don't think so," Epic shot back.

Felony only shrugged in reply. "You in on the betting or not?"

"Maybe some other time," Epic said. "I need to have a chat with our silent guest right now."

Epic couldn't help himself, and had to ask, "Where in the hell did you niggas find a dam rooster, a rabbit, and a raccoon at?"

"We brought 'em with us," Felony answered, looking at Epic like everybody traveled around with a rooster, a rabbit, and a racoon.

Epic finally turned his attention to Blacq sitting there quietly, handcuffed to the wrought iron patio chair.

Bypassing all formalities, Epic said, "Why should I let you live?" he questioned.

To his credit, Blacq looked Epic in the eyes before he took a deep breath and answered, "Because when Payne wanted me to kidnap yo' bitch, Asi—"

Epic struck quicker than a Black Mamba, as he pulled the Desert Eagle .50 caliber hand cannon out of his waistband and pistol-whipped the shit out of Blacq while snarling, "Please, I dare you to say the word bitch and Asimi's name in the same sentence. Naw, fuck that, in the same paragraph muthafucka."

The force of the impact had knocked Blacq backward in the chair, causing it to flip over backward, damn near dislocating both his shoulders.

The sound of the .50 smacking the side of Blacq's head was like a baseball bat making contact with a ripe melon, and the rise of a long speed knot proved the power behind the strike.

Blacq was fortunate that the blow didn't fracture his skull, as he realized that shit had just got real as he sat there, looking pathetically up at the business end of Epic's Blue Steel .50 caliber.

The dark-black hole was like looking into the depths of an endless abyss large enough to swallow his whole head.

"Check it. Yo' next words better be careful, nut ass nigga,"—Epic growled—"or they will definitely be yo' last."

193

Epic's outward appearance was calm and in control, but inside, he was a raging storm of emotion, just thinking about Asimi being in any kind of imminent danger.

Once sitting back up, Blacq, seeking any leniency possible, said, "Sorry, I misspoke, dog. I'm ghetto as hell." After collecting himself, he said, "I talked him out of it because this isn't about the women in y'all's lives; this is between you and Payne."

Although all of the problems between him and Payne had started behind Candy's ratchet ass cappin' about Epic tryin to push up on her. After a minute, Epic said, "I asked you why I should let you live, and you give me reason to end you ass right here and now."

"Wait, wait, I know something that could get Payne put away by the cops forever."

Epic aimed at Blacq's head and spat, "Fuck ass nigga, we real street niggas, and we don't ever put the police in our business. I'll put a nigga in the ground before I put 'em behind bars."

Blacq bowed his head in shame.

Epic continued, "If you think that I give a fuck about Payne's felonious cock sucking with intent to swallow, then you got me fucked up, my nig'."

Blacq could feel the gravity of the situation and knew that he had to play his ace in the hole card, and the .50 caliber, plus the look in Epic's eyes was more than enough motivation. "I got a video of Payne bustin' his cherry merkin a bitch," he blurted out.

This information gave Epic pause, so much so that he said, "If its what I think it is, you get to keep on drawing breath. That's my good word."

"I need my phone," Blacq replied.

Epic could see the top of a tattoo barely peeking from Blacq's shirt collar. Pulling down the collar, he read the word Loyalty. As if Epic couldn't read, Blacq said. "It says loyalty."

"I can read, nigga. You do know that the niggas that have to tat the word loyalty on themselves usually aren't. They do it trying to convince others that they are. Loyal niggas don't jave to show it in ink. They show it with their actions."

Blacq answered, "Contrary to what you believe, I am being loyal. To myself," he said.

Chapter 28

Epic sat across the street from the four-bedroom, three-bath home in Maple Heights, watching the five-year-old boy chase a Pitbull puppy around the fenced-in yard. He was unsure which of them was having the most fun at their game. Looking at the covered porch of the house, he also saw NuNu keeping a watchful eye on Tyrik Jr.

He seldom came here, but he felt that with the way things were going, he might not have another chance, not anytime soon anyway.

After a deep sigh, he reached over into the passenger seat and grabbed the three full bags sitting there, and climbed out of the car.

He made it all the way to the front gate before lil' Rik even noticed him. When he finally did, he released a squeal of pure joy and ran to greet Epic as fast as his five-year-old legs would carry him, with the little Pitbull pup in hot pursuit.

Epic smiled as at the last minute lil' Rik pulled up short and shot a worried glance toward the porch. He'd stopped so fast that the puppy ran into the back of him, nearly knocking him down.

Epic couldn't help but smile at the little boy's mean mug at the puppy, as the small pit started to growl and bark at Epic.

"What it do, lil' Rik?" Epic asked while reaching into one of the bags with his free hand to grab a pack of mini Oreo's for TyRik.

The look of indecision on the little boy's face made him laugh out loud, as lil' Rik answered by saying, "I'm not 'posed to talk to strangers." He finished, looking back at NuNu.

"Oh, so I'm a stranger now, huh?" Epic replied. "Well, I guess I'm just going to have to eat these Oreo's myself then." NuNu looked on for a couple of seconds more before she couldn't help but burst out in a cackling laugh. Epic gave Tyrik the Oreo's as he made his way to the house. He'd just reached the bottom step when the front door opened and Ebony stepped out, wiping her damp hands on her apron, and breaking into a huge smile of welcoming when she saw Epic, and then into an instant frown when she noticed the bags that he held.

"Now, how many times have I told you about showing up here with bags of groceries?" she asked, with her hands on her hips.

"Just grabbed a few things while I was at the store, seeing as whenever I stop through, you always try to feed me," Epic commented.

Ebony rolled her eyes, knowing that anytime he stopped by, and she had food ready, then he was ready to eat it. This was an old, but usual argument between them, just as old as them trying to pay him rent for the house they stayed in, which he owned.

Ebony shook her head as she looked into the bag overflowing with all kinds of steaks, ground beef, lunch meats, breads and cheeses, while the other bag held every kind of rice, peppers, and vegetable you could almost think of, and of course, the third bag was filled with chips, cookies, pudding cups, juice boxes, ice cream, M & M, pizza bagel bites, Entenmann's Donuts, and too much more to name.

Epic looked at the bag filled with junk food, and said, "That's lil' Rik's bag," as if she didn't already know. "I'll try to keep Big Rik outta of it," she responded. "I'll let him know you're here."

"Aight, I'll be in, in a few minutes."

"Come on inside, TyRik, and wash up for dinner!" Ebony cast an all too knowing look at her mother, NuNu, sitting there quietly.

Epic plopped into the seat across from NuNu, before asking, "Sup, NuNu? Is your blood pressure still up?" he questioned, barely able to contain his smile.

"Shit, if I started to name all the shit that's wrong with me, you'd pull out yo' gun and put me outta my misery, but I'm willing to settle for some more of that fire ass sticky icky like you gave me last time. It had my whole left leg numb for two days."

"Well, if you liked that, you're going to love this," he said, pulling out a fat bag of that Gorilla in da mist hydrophonic, and a prerolled blunt.

He fired it up and took a couple of pulls, then passed it to NuNu, saying, "This shit will have your appetite right, along with everything else."

NuNu took deep pulls on the blunt and handled that shit like the true O.G. that she was without choking. After a few minutes, she looked at Epic with glazed eyes and said, "You know you're going to have to carry my old ass in the house, don't you?"

Epic gave Big Rik dap as he entered the living room with his cane and barely a limp now. Epic was glad to see the vast improvement and knew that it wouldn't be long before TyRik Sr. was a hundred percent again.

He'd been shot on accident by a nigga trying to smoke Epic outside of a club in the parking lot. TyRik had actually saved Epic's life when he'd stopped to comment on Epic's GSXR 1300 Hayabusa. By doing so, he'd inadvertently stepped into the line of fire meant for Epic. He'd taken a round in the shoulder and one in the back close to his spine. The doctors weren't sure if he would ever walk again, but he was determined to prove them wrong, and was doing a hell of a job at it.

So Epic had shown his gratitude by paying for all of TyRik's medical bills and also moving him and his family out of the crime-infested 30th Projects and into this home in Maple Heights. He refused to accept any rent from them, stating that it was the least that he could do, feeling that it was a cheap price for his life. And since then, he and TyRik had become good friends despite their age difference.

After dinner was over, Epic sat in the living room, talking with TyRik, letting him know that it might be a hot minute before he came back through, so he wanted to give him something. The words weren't even out of Epic's mouth good before TyRiek was shaking his head no.

"Whatever it is, the answer is no," Tyrik stated. "Man, you've done more than enough for me and my family. Hell, just moving us outta the damned projects was enough. I would have taken those bullets for that any day," he said, meaning every word of it.

Epic reached inside his jacket pocket and removed a document pack, trying to hand it to TyRiek, who refused to take it.

Epic sighed and said, "Look, man. If anybody knows anything about pride, it's me, but even I learned that it doesn't make you any less of a man to ask for help, or accept it when it's offered."

TyRik was still about to say no when his son came running into the room, laughing with the puppy once again in hot pursuit. "It ain't always about us," Epic said, giving a meaningful look at Little TyRik.

TyRik Sr. took the packet.

Epic was miles away before TyRik opened the packet and looked inside to see what it contained. He then almost passed out as he held the deed to the house and a cashier's check in his name for two hundred and fifty thousand dollars. Despite himself, he couldn't stop the tears that silently slid down his cheeks.

It had been over two weeks since she'd been taken by the security of her employer, Cal Bower, who'd shown up the day before with a woman she'd never seen before. But it was clear to her who was really in charge; even Mr. Cerrano was really respectful to the woman who said nothing.

Erica was worried for herself, but even more so for her grandson, Epic, whom she felt she had endangered by giving him the flash drive and sending him the pictures of all of the old newspaper clippings and ledger book. She had given him his mother's personal effects that she'd had at the time of her death, which were a flash drive and a gold chain with a gold cross that his mother had been wearing.

Erica had always been convinced that her employer, Mr. Bower's, father had to have had something to do with her daughter's murder. Erica had continued to be a maid for the Bower household in the hopes of finding proof of her suspicions. She stayed to work for the son, Cal Bower, while she kept trying to find evidence.

She had no idea what they would do with her, but she was determined not to give them any information that would lead them to Epic.

Overall, she had been treated fairly well, except for being slapped by Cal Bower in a fit of rage, when she refused to tell him who she was spying for. But surprisingly, it was the head of his security, Mr. Cerrano, who had pulled Mr. Bower away from her.

She sat there, thinking about Epic when the door opened.

Two men that she assumed were a part of the security team entered and grabbed her roughly by the arms and pulled her from the room and into a room down two flights of stairs, and into a dark, damp, musty-smelling cell.

Erica didn't like their rough treatment or the dark room, but as the overhead lights were turned on, she quickly realized that she preferred the darkness much more. The cell was a complete horror show, with dark brown stains all over the floor and walls. She wasn't sure, but she thought that these stains were the result of dried blood.

The fact was confirmed as she noticed a severed human hand in one of the corners of the room, just before they unceremoniously slammed her onto a stainless-steel operating table bolted to the floor in the middle of the room. Using leather straps, they then bound her wrists and ankles to the table. One of the men left the room, only to return shortly after with two large buckets of water, towels, and an electric chainsaw. Erica had been as brave as she could be up until that point, but the sight of the electric chainsaw scared her so much that, to her embarrassment, she peed herself.

When the door opened again and the strange woman walked in, followed by Mr. Cerrano, Erica's humiliation was again overruled by fear.

Next, they rolled in a table with several needles filled with only God knew what.

"Why are you doing this?' she stammered. But no one answered her question.

Then, at some unseen signal, one of the men grabbed one of the needles from the tray, saying, "I think we'll start with a little bit of Hydroxyzine, but just a little. It's a very strong tranquilizer, and too much will stop your heart before you tell us what we want to know." He finished with a nasty smile.

Erica felt a sharp pinch in the crook of her left elbow, followed by a cold numbing sensation that slowly relaxed her entire body.

"Now, isn't that better?" he questioned. "Soon you will be ready to tell us everything."

The questions started ten minutes later, and even with the tranquilizer muddling her brain, she still found some way to resist.

And after another five minutes of unanswered questions, the interrogator switched to more sadistic techniques, grabbing a device that looked somewhat like a C-Clamp and put her right wrist between its serrated jaws. He then began to crank it closed on her wrist, methodically inflicting pain as the sharp teeth of the device bit into her skin.

Erica tried not to cry out, but the torture was too great for her to remain silent. The linoleum floors and concrete walls echoed with her screams.

The device was loosened before she could succumb to the pain and pass out.

Without remorse, the man asked, "Who were you snooping for, and who did you send the information to?"

Erica's heart was pounding in her chest, and she actually prayed that it would stop before she betrayed her grandson. She knew that these people were utterly ruthless, and she was going to die by their hands, but she was determined not to subject her grandson to the same fate.

Erica lay there, making her peace with God, as the man took one of the towels and soaked it in the bucket of water, then gave it to the man standing over her head.

A swift nod was given, and the man placed the wet towel over her face as her interrogator poured water over it.

Erica was being drowned and suffocated at the same time. Each time she attempted to take a breath of air, water would flood into her nose and mouth, filling her lungs and setting them on fire.

When the towel was finally removed from her face, she coughed up so much water that the towel holder had to turn her head to one side to clear her airway.

She had heard of this type of torture before, when the news had reported that the government had banned the waterboarding of terrorists.

She now understood why.

"You are not a young woman anymore, and your heart can only take so much. It would be easier if you just tell us what we want to know," he said amiably.

Before she could refuse again, three beeps, followed by a vibrating sound, filled the room. The lady in the room looked toward one of the men holding her phone and asked who it was.

The man looked down at the screen and replied, "It's Epic."

Erica, hearing his name, blurted out, "How do you know my grandson?"

Ari Acousta quickly told the man with the towel to gag Erica before she answered the call, her mind racing to put all the pieces together on what was going on.

"Hello," she answered in a calm voice as she watched Erica struggling on the table in an attempt to warn Epic somehow.

"Yo, I've been trying to reach you for over a week," Epic said in a rush of words. "I need to talk to you face-to-face. It's important."

"Well, I've been out of the country and have just returned today. I was going to call you also because I need to see you, but I won't be in Cleveland until the day after tomorrow. Then I will call you and inform you where to meet me."

"Check it—" Epic began, but Ari had already ended the call and didn't pick up the next six times that he tried to call her back.

Ari told the men to release Erica, bandage her arm, clean her up, and then bring her upstairs to the living room. It was time the two of them had a woman-to-woman talk about a few things.

Epic was more than a little frustrated and pissed off right then with Ari, but figured he had no choice but to wait. It was an unseasonably warm day for that time of the year in Ohio, so Epic decided to make the best out of it as he drove home to switch out his Bentley for his motorcycle.

It felt good, pushing through the city on his Busa, with no helmet on, just a pair of Qakleys and a Nike fitted to the back. Yeah, it was definitely time for the streets to see his face again. And on a warm day like this, he knew the beach would be packed.

Although he never understood why they called it the beach, seeing as it was just sand around Lake Erie and not a real beach.

The line of cars, trucks with boats behind them, bikes, and any other form of transportation one could think of had traffic into Edge Water Park backed up for at least two miles.

Anybody and everybody who was somebody was out there.

To Epic, it seemed like every dope boy, hustler, shot caller, and jack boy was all in one place. Box Chevy, Dodge Chargers, Benzes, Vettes, Ferraris, and even a few Lambos were thrown into the mix.

He'd just made it into the park when the passenger riding in a silver and black Audi RZ asked if she could ride with him. Shorty was bad as a muthafucka, but he still declined, wanting to be able to react quickly if need be.

Even though the day was warm and the sun was shining, the water temperature had to be only about fifty degrees, and yet, crazy ass white people were playing in it.

The amount of noise was deafening as everyone with a loud stereo system attempted to outdo any other system. The park was utter chaos, and he loved it. He was just passing the basketball courts, where a lot of cars and people were all chilling and smoking, yelling back and forth at one another, when he heard his name called.

Looking to his right, he saw Kendra's ghetto ass hanging out of the passenger side window of a Pearl White Dodge Durango SRT sitting on 28s, with the system booming. Some dude Epic had never seen before sat behind the wheel, and unfortunately, traffic stopped right in front of them.

Kendra popped out of the truck and went over to Epic. She was wearing short shorts, a tank top with no bra, and a pair of pink and white Reebok classics.

She stepped up with hands on her hips and, with attitude, asked, "So you can't call me no mo' Yo', lil' main chick got you on lock now, or are you hiding out from Payne like the streets is sayin'?" she asked, rolling her neck.

"It won't even dignify that dumb shit you just said with an answer," Epic replied.

"It doesn't matter anyway," Kendra went on. "'Cause, I've moved on to big and better," she said, pointing back toward old boy in the Durango, who, as if on cue, started getting out of the truck and flexing like that would scare Epic.

Epic looked at the dude's muscular upper body and skinny ass chicken legs, the disproportionate build of most niggas' that had done some time—all upper body and skipped leg day. Epic said, "Naw, ma, maybe bigger but never better. And you might wanna take yo' monkey ass back over there wit' that nigga before he get his priorities mixed up, and put stunting for you before self-preservation," he growled, reminding her of just who the fuck she was talking to.

Kendra spun around and stomped off calling back over her left shoulder, "Whatever! Fuck you, Epic."

"Naw, bitch fuck wit' me," Epic replied, shooting fake ass.

He gave a mean mug as traffic began to crawl along again.

He clicked one down with his left foot, putting the bike in first gear, and popped the clutch on Kendra's hoodrat ass.

After another hour or so cruising, he left the park and headed for East Cleveland, deciding that he'd ride past Payne's new office building and scope it out. He figured that Payne's pussy ass would be on high alert since his right-hand man, Blacq, was ghost now, and even Bloodrush had quit, claiming that Payne wasn't looking for real security. He was looking for a do-boy type nigga. And BloodRush was definitely not a do-boy type of nigga.

Epic was focused on the future, although he knew that no one knew what tomorrow would bring, and tomorrow was promised to no man. But he also believed that those who failed to plan, planned to fail, and failure was not an acceptable option. He would make Ariella Acousta release him the easy way, he hoped, the way that didn't lead to gunplay, but by force or by choice, he was done being her on-call killer.

Chapter 29

The rhythmic steel drums of Bob Marley's song 'Road To Zion' beat in the backroom of the Island Boi Bar and Grill off Fleet Avenue. A pungent cloud of weed smoke filled the air of the small room as much as the music if not more. The vibrating of his phone interrupted Neville's tranquility as he answered the call.

"Yea Mon, wa' you callin weh fo?" he questioned, exhaling a mushroom cloud of weed smoke.

"Wa know star, dis Nemo, and mi just see da birdie weh been spotten fo."

Neville sat up so quickly that it caused Jaymia, who was in the middle of sucking his dick, to choke and gag.

"Nemo, keep weh eyes on da prize, den tell I where da bloodclot sirt tail land, so weh Rude Boys can soon come make dead," Neville said, getting hyped up.

Finished with the call, Neville look down at Jaymia and asked, "Who tell she too stoo polishing on mi' shine stick?"

Without a word, Jaymia wrapped her lush, thick lips back around Neville's rock-hard member.

Neville smiled a smile of satisfaction as he lay back, placing a hand on the back of Jaymia's bobbing head, feeding her even more dick.

Epic parked outside of the old warehouse in the meatpacking district on the west bank of the flats, unsure he was in the right place until two cartel soldiers stepped out of the doorway.

The fact that they didn't bother to frisk him or take his weapons told Epic two things: the first was that there were enough of them here to handle any problems that might present themselves, and the second thing was that if anything popped off out there, there would be no one to come to the rescue.

Of course, he was armed with twin Sig Sauer P229 Elite 9mm pistols, but he prayed he wouldn't have to use them. Yet he knew to hope for the best, but plan for the worst.

The interior was lit by standing pole work lights that cast his shadow on the graffiti-covered walls, and trash littered the floor. The strong smell of cat urine stung his nose as it mixed and mingled with the smells of years of meat processing. The sound of his echoing footsteps seemed to chase him through the warehouse.

And he'd been correct when he had assumed that there were plenty of cartel soldiers there, as he passed another group of four men, all armed with automatic weapons. Finally, he pushed through the dingy, once clear plastic divider and into what used to be the main processing floor. The wide-open space was brighter than the rest of the warehouse because of the large plate-glass windows that lined the entire upper floor.

Epic noticed that Ari Acousta had pulled out all the stops, it seemed, where her security was concerned. He couldn't blame her after what had transpired at the graveyard, so he fully understood it, although he didn't like it.

The floor was bisected by an old conveyor belt. There were metal bins on wheels that had been used to move the pounds of meat to the packaging area, into the freezers.

At least another twenty-five to thirty more heavily armed cartel soldiers filled the room with menace, but nowhere did he see Ari Acousta. He stood waiting for her to come in, and as he did, he peeped out the other two exits from the room.

When he'd tried to talk to Ari about the important matter he wished to see her about, she'd cut him off, and then completely shocked the shit out of him when she told him to bring the flash drive with him. He tried to ask his own questions, but she'd hung up.

Epic was trying to piece together how all this came into play, everything from Ari, the flash drive, his grandmother, and his mother's death. He had a lot of the smaller pieces in place, but a few major ones were still missing, and he was certain that those answers lay with Ariella Acousta.

He stood here with the flash drive in his pocket, waiting for those answers.

After ten minutes of silent waiting, Ari must have tired of her mind games as she emerged from another entrance, followed by ten more cartel soldiers, a white guy in a business suit, his grandmother, and an older Dominican cartel soldier, and if that wasn't shocking enough, Payne brought up the rear of the entourage.

Shit had just gotten extremely worse, or extremely more interesting. He felt like he knew why Ari had so much firepower on exhibit. The very sight of his grandmother in danger may have caused gunfire to erupt, but Ari knew that not even Epic could overcome these odds.

None of that stopped Epic from being heated as he saw the older cartel soldier put a .357 Python to the side of his grandmother's head.

"Fuck is you playin' at, muthafucka, with that gun to my grandmother's head?" Epic snapped.

The .357 was removed from Erica's head, then the man opened the cylinder and dumped the six rounds into the palm of his hand. He then put five rounds in his pocket, dropped a single bullet into the cylinder, and spun it. Then, with a flick of his wrist, he snapped it closed.

A demonic smile creased his face as he placed the weapon back to Erica's temple.

Epic started to reach for his Sig's but froze as every single weapon in the room was pointed in his direction.

"Let's not be hasty, Epic." Ari all but purred.

"Bitch, have you lost—" Epic started.

He stopped immediately when Ari said, "Cerrano."

The man Epic assumed was Cerrano pulled the trigger.

The metallic click as the hammer fell on an empty chamber made Erica attempt to flinch away from the gun, but Cerrano held her tight.

Epic released a deep sigh and began again in a calmer tone.

"Yo, Ari, Im sorr—"

"Cerrano," again the man pulled the trigger, causing Erica to jump as tears spilled from her frightened eyes.

Payne, smiling, raised a hand to the side of his own head, shaping his fingers to mimick a gun, like he was blowing his brains out.

Epic swore to himself right then and there that it would become a reality for Payne.

Ari told Epic, "Now is not your time to talk, but to listen.

Your grandmother has defied the odds now twice, and I personally don't think she approves of you gambling with her life, but feel free to continue if you like."

Epic nodded once to show that he understood.

"I am sure that you are wondering how and why you and your grandmother find yourselves in this situation." She paused for a minute as if to gather her thoughts before she continued. "It seems that our families have more of a history than even we knew about. You see, before you were born, your mother and father stole something from one of my father's transportation specialists, on Mr. Cerrano's watch, and because of a lack of security by Mr. Bower's father," she said, indicating the white man in the suit.

"My father, Ernesto Acousta, God rest his soul, gave Mr. Bower's father his just deserves for his incompetence, and would have done the same for Cerrano if not for his service to this family. And for a chance to rectify his mistake and regain his honor. So, for the last twenty-two years, Cerrano has been in search of the flash drive, which your mother had escaped with on the day he came to retrieve it."

The brutal truth dawned on Epic that he was looking at the very man who'd killed his mother and father.

"Now that I am head of the family, I will complete my father's wishes. So very slowly, give the drive to Mr. Bower."

Moving carefully, Epic removed the flash drive from his right front pocket and reached it out to Mr. Bower.

One of the cartel soldiers placed a laptop on the conveyor belt and stepped away, allowing Mr. Bower to step up and plug in the flash drive and set up a wireless modem. Epic sent up a silent prayer to God that White Mike's Magic worm flash drive wouldn't get him and his grandmother killed in the next few minutes.

To Epic, it seemed as if everybody in the warehouse was holding their collective breath as Mr. Bower opened a ledger and began to type in codes.

After a minute, Ari's patience wore thin, causing her to snap.

"Well, is it a legitimate flash drive and accounts?' she questioned.

After a few more keystrokes, Mr. Bower looked up, smiling. "Yes, it all here," he said.

"Cerrano, your honor is restored, and per my father's last wishes before he died, I free you from your mistake."

As Cerrano turned to look at Ari, she pulled a compact nine from behind her right thigh and fired a single shot between his eyes. Cerrano's head snapped back, the pink mist hanging in the air as his body collapsed.

"The cartel does not accept failure," she said, then swung the weapon toward Mr. Bower and pushed his wig back also.

Payne's smile was now gone, and he looked like he wanted to make a run for it.

Erica stood, shaking uncontrollably as she locked eyes with her grandson, trying to express how much she loved him with what she felt would be her last chance.

"So now, do I punish the two of you for your part in all this?" she mused aloud.

Epic decided that if he was going to die, then he would die speaking his peace.

"Yo, this shit you've got going here has nothing to do with my grandmother, who was only trying to find out who murdered her only child. Tell me, Ari, that you wouldn't give everything to find out the identity of the person who killed Yasmeen," Epic said.

Ari raised her weapon, taking aim at Epic's head as she yelled, "Do not test me! You saved my life once, so I owe you a life debt, but if you mention my sister again, I swear that you will immediately join her in death!" She finished, visibly shaking with rage.

Without hesitation or thought of his own safety said, "Then I choose my grandmother. Release her."

"No!" Erica wailed

"As you wish," Ari replied.

Ari looked deep into Epic's eyes and couldn't help but admire his courage and loyalty, the same values that she would teach the child she now carried within.

"Any last words?" she asked.

Epic thought about his ace in the hole card. He looked at Payne, shook his head, and responded, "Naw, ma, do what you do."

Ari steadied her pistol, taking up the slack on the trigger, when the room exploded in chaos.

Automatic weapons fire erupted from the upper floor, spraying two of the cartel soldiers close to Ari. While at the same time, another firefight broke out in the entryway. People began to scatter for cover and return fire on the hostile force attacking them.

Epic was in motion as soon as the first shots rang out, tackling his grandmother and pulling her behind one of the metal meat transfer carts. Drawing both Sig Sauers, he peeked around the edge of the cart to assess the situation. The volume of noise from all the assault rifles was a painful reminder of how outgunned he was. Epic didn't know who had intervened, but he would count his blessings later if he could get his grandmother and himself out of the damned bullet orgy.

A body fell from the upper floor, landing on the conveyor belt. The long dreadlocks dripping blood gave name to the identity of who was taking on the cartel.

Epic turned to Erica and said, "I know that you're afraid, but trust me. We can't stay here; we've gotta move. Stay low and behind me, okay," he said as calmly as he could.

Right then, two rude bwoy shottas ran through the dingy plastic curtain, blasting away with AK-47s. Epic fired two rounds into both men, putting them down, but this caused him to draw fire from the cartel soldiers and the rude bwoys.

Epic was on the move now, going from bin to bin, using the metal carts for cover, attempting to clear a path for them. It was total mayhem as the cartel tried to eliminate the rude bwoys and the rude bwoys tried to eliminate the cartel, and everybody was trying to kill Epic.

This shit gave a whole new meaning to the word clusterfuck, and the situation was getting worse by the second.

One of the cartel soldiers swung his still-smoking AK-47 toward Epic, only to be driven off his feet by four rounds center mass from Epic's twin Sigs.

They were now only about ten feet from the exit, but still, it might as well have been ten miles away across the open floor. He'd pulled his grandmother behind the last of the metal carts they were using for cover.

If shit wasn't bad enough, he was now caught between both factions without enough ammo for a prolonged firefight.

At least from what he could tell, the cartel was winning, which didn't really do him any good. As he took a quick look around the cart, he saw Payne break cover, running to hide behind a stack of fifty-five-gallon drums.

Epic fired at him and would have smoked his bitch ass had not a cartel soldier stepped into the line of fire.

He caught a glimpse of Ariella Acousta standing with only two of the men she'd had as bodyguards. The rest were down. They made brief eye contact as she fired more shots at the catwalk up above.

Epic saw movement behind Ari and to the left, but with so much gun smoke in the air, it was hard to tell who it was. By their stealthy approach, he could guess whose side they were on.

Most of the gunfire had slacked off now due to a lot of the combatants being dead or reloading.

This was the opportunity Epic had been waiting for as he dug his car keys out of his pocket and gave them to his grandmother and said, "Make a run for the exit. I'll cover you. Get to to the car out front, the Bentley, okay."

He could see the indecision in her eyes about leaving without him, so he found the strength to smile at her and said, "Don't worry. I'll be alright. Just get to the car and get outta here." And after a slight pause, he added, "I love you, Grandma."

With her eyes brimming with tears, she said, "I love you too, and I'm sorry for everything." She quickly leaned forward and kissed him on the cheek before running for the exit as Epic lay down cover fire for her.

Epic was about to follow her when he saw Ari's last bodyguard go out in a blaze of automatic gunfire glory, and now he could make out the person creeping up on her.

Against his better judgment, Epic broke from cover, running toward Ari with both guns raised and aimed at her. Ari was caught completely off guard as Epic came running full out toward her with both guns raised.

She was going to die.

Epic drove to his right and fired both Sigs. Ari felt the heated air as the shots fired by Epic missed the mark by bare centimeters. She couldn't believe her luck as she took aim at him. She also noticed that both of his pistols' slides were locked back on empty chambers.

Epic lay on the floor with both guns still raised and wishing for more bullets, but knew that wishes wouldn't save his life right now.

"You missed" Ari said, starting to apply pressure on the trigger.

"Naw, ma, I didn't," Epic replied as Neville dropped the machete, falling forward with a hole in his forehead and one through his neck. Ari spun at the sound of the machete hitting the floor, and watched as the Rude Bwoy Don Da Ta fell at her feet.

Ari placed her free hand on her stomach as she looked back at Epic, finding it hard to believe that Epic had saved her life again, even when she had been ready to take his.

She shook her head in disbelief, her emotions all over the place now. She couldn't believe the loyalty. Ariella Acousta lowered her pistol as Epic got to his feet, standing toe to toe with her. After a minute, she said, "Thank you! I thought that you were—"

Epic cut her off, saying, "Yeah, ma, I know what you thought. Yet again, you was wrong." He finished, wiping sweat from his face.

In response, she just gave a slight nod.

A sound to the right made them both swing around in that direction as Payne stood up from behind the stack of fifty-five-gallon drums, dusting off his suit.

He looked at Ari, then at Epic, and asked. "What da fuck you looking at, nigga? You better be glad that boss lady gave me orders not to fuck you up, or I would've had my goons black bag yo' ass," Payne sneered.

"Shit, nigga, what's wrong with right now, bitch ass nigga?" Epic questioned, stepping toward Payne.

Payne quickly dodged behind Ari for protection, smiling as she told Epic to stop.

If looks could've killed, Epic's would have added Payne's lame ass to the pile of bodies lying all over the warehouse.

"I still need him," Ari said, understanding the bad blood between the two men.

Epic took a step back and pulled out an iPhone, and turned it on.

"Who are you calling?" Ari asked, raising the gun again, pointing it at Epic.

Instead of answering, Epic pulled up a video and pushed play, handing the phone to Ari.

And asked, "You sure 'bout that?'

Ariella Acousta watched as her little sister, Yasmeen, came out of the stairwell door and into the underground parking garage, heading for her car.

When she suddenly spun around, raising her pistol as someone stepped out of the shadows behind her, but once she saw who it was, she lowered her weapon, saying, "Oh, it's you."

Before the man in the shadows fired a shot, hitting her between the eyes, the muzzle flash was enough to light up the shooter's face.

Payne was easing back away from Ari as he realized what Epic had just given her, but stopped cold as she raised the gun, pointing it at his head.

Her arm shook, barely, but Epic didn't know if it was from the shock of seeing her sister murdered or from rage.

Ari pressed her hand to her stomach again as if she would be sick.

She looked at Epic, the sadness in her eyes speaking volumes. "You may leave," she said a little above a whisper. "And thank you again."

Epic turned and walked away. He heard Payne ask, "What are you going to do to me? You can't kill me. You need me, remember," he whined.

"Oh, I'm not going to kill you. In fact, I'm going to have you retrieve my sunglasses," she said in a calm voice.

Epic kept walking.

Epilogue

3 weeks later…

Epic lay back under the giant beach umbrella, protecting himself from the blazing Tahitian sun. Asimi lay to his right in a sexy, baby-blue, two-piece bikini, while Sarah lay out in the sun on her stomach with her top off.

The two of them had walked the graduation stage a week ago, receiving their law degrees, and were scheduled to take the bar exam next month.

Epic had already purchased a six-story office building through a shell company he'd had White Mike set up for that very reason. With the capital he had, he'd decided to open a law firm for them.

Asimi would handle the criminal law side, while Sarah would hold down the corporate side of the law. They would be the heads of their departments over all the other lawyers.

Samato & Wellingon and Associates at Law, and he'd even talked White Mike into being his cyber and tech guy for any computer-related shit that might pop off.

Epic had even told Asimi and Sarah that he might even do a little private detective work when it came to beating the streets to help get a client off. Asimi and Sarah both agreed that he was their private dick and assured him that they would be getting it on the regular.

'Oh, hell yeah,' he thought. It was going to be a law firm with a Pitbull attitude.

He sipped his drink and smiled to himself. Hell, with the type of money he had, there were a lot of things he had lined up. He could even give up the streets. *Naw, you can take the boy outta streets, but you cant take the street outta the boy.* Yep, life was about to get real interesting.

He just didn't know how prophetic those thoughts would soon turn out to be.

The man stood with his back to the people he'd been sent there to watch. He ordere a fruity drink from the bartender. He was part of a four-man team, and their job was to observe and follow.

Why? For how long? Those were the kinds of questions not to be asked; you simply did as you were told.

Ari sat in the back of the G-Wagon with her hand resting on her now starting to show baby bump. Things were definitely about to get way more complicated.

Lock Down Publications and Ca$h Presents
Assisted Publishing Packages

Due to an increase in the price of services we have increased our prices. The prices below reflect the price increase as of 11/1/24.

BASIC PACKAGE	UPGRADED PACKAGE
$699	**$1000**
Editing	Typing
Cover Design	Editing
Formatting	Cover Design
	Formatting
	Upload eBooks to Amazon
	Upload Paperback to Amazon
ADVANCE PACKAGE	**LDP SUPREME PACKAGE**
$1,400	**$1,700**
Typing	Typing
Editing (line editing/content)	Editing (line editing/content)
Cover Design	Cover Design
Formatting	Formatting
Copyright Registration	Copyright Registration
Proofreading	Proofreading
Upload eBooks to Amazon	Set up Amazon Account
Upload Paperback to Amazon	Upload eBooks to Amazon
	Upload Paperback to Amazon
	Advertise on LDP's Amazon and Facebook Page

***

Other services available upon request.
Additional charges may apply

Lock Down Publications
P.O. Box 944
Stockbridge, GA 30281-9998
Phone: 470 303-9761
Email: lockdownpublications@gmail.com

Submission Guideline

Submit the first three chapters of your completed manuscript to ldpsubmissions@gmail.com. In the subject line add **Your Book's Title**. The manuscript must be in a Word Doc file and sent as an attachment. Document should be in Times New Roman, double spaced, and in size 12 font. Also, provide your synopsis and full contact information. If sending multiple submissions, they must each be in a separate email.

Have a story but no way to send it electronically? You can still submit to LDP/Ca$h Presents. Send in the first three chapters, written or typed, of your completed manuscript to:

LDP: Submissions Dept
P.O. Box 944
Stockbridge, GA 30281-9998

DO NOT send original manuscript. Must be a duplicate. Provide your synopsis and a cover letter containing your full contact information.

Thanks for considering LDP and Ca$h Presents.

NEW RELEASES

BLOODLINE OF A SAVAGE 1-3
THESE VICIOUS STREETS 1-3
RELENTLESS GOON 1-3
BY PRINCE A. TAUHID

THE BUTTERFLY MAFIA 1-3
BY FUMIYA PAYNE

A THUG'S STREET PRINCESS 1&2
BY MEESHA

CITY OF SMOKE 3
BY MOLOTTI

GET IT IN SLUGS 1 &2
BY B. STALL

STANDING ON HER BUSINESS 1&2
BY DG SANTANA

STEPPERS 1,2&3
THE REAL BADDIES OF CHI-RAQ
BY KING RIO

THE LANE 1&2
BY KEN-KEN SPENCE

THUG OF SPADES 1&2
LOVE IN THE TRENCHES 2
CORNER BOYS
BY COREY ROBINSON

TIL DEATH 3
BY ARYANNA

THE BIRTH OF A GANGSTER 4
BY DELMONT PLAYER

PRODUCT OF THE STREETS 1-3
BY DEMOND "MONEY" ANDERSON

NO TIME FOR ERROR
BY KEESE

MONEY HUNGRY DEMONS 1-2
BY TRANAY ADAMS

HUB CITY MENACE 1-3
BY J. WHITE

A THUGGISH PASSION 1&2
LAND OF DA HOOLIGANZ 1-4
KILLAZ ON STANDBY 1&2
BY IRA B.

FO'EVA ROLLIN 1&2
BY ASSA RAYMOND BAKER

THE LEVEL UP 1&3
BY LUXURY KING

Coming Soon from Lock Down Publications/Ca$h Presents

IF YOU CROSS ME ONCE 6
ANGEL V
By Anthony Fields

A THUGS STREET PRINCESS 3
By Meesha

CORNER BOYS 2
By Corey Robinson

THA TAKEOVER
By Keith Chandler

BETRAYAL OF A G 2
By Ray Vinci

SAVAGE FAMILY EMPIRE 1&2
SOULLESS GOON 1,2&3
THE DIRTY SIDE OF MONEY 1,2&3
By Prince

FOR MY ENEMY'S SAKE
AMBITIONS OF A SLIDER
FRESH OFF DA PORCH
By IRA B.

BY THE TRUCKLOAD 1-4
TIPPIN' THE SCALES 1-3
BAD BITCHES WIT GUNZ 3
PROBLEM SOLVED 2
By Christopher "Diesel" Hornezes

Available Now

RESTRAINING ORDER 1 & 2
By **CA$H & Coffee**

LOVE KNOWS NO BOUNDARIES 1-3
By **Coffee**

RAISED AS A GOON I, II, III & IV
BRED BY THE SLUMS I, II, III
BLAST FOR ME I & II
ROTTEN TO THE CORE I II III
A BRONX TALE I, II, III
DUFFLE BAG CARTEL I II III IV V VI
HEARTLESS GOON I II III IV V
A SAVAGE DOPEBOY I II
DRUG LORDS I II III
CUTTHROAT MAFIA I II
KING OF THE TRENCHES
By **Ghost**

LAY IT DOWN I & II
LAST OF A DYING BREED I II
BLOOD STAINS OF A SHOTTA I & II III
By **Jamaica**

LOYAL TO THE GAME I II III
LIFE OF SIN I, II III
By **TJ & Jelissa**

IF LOVING HIM IS WRONG…I & II
LOVE ME EVEN WHEN IT HURTS I II III
By **Jelissa**

PUSH IT TO THE LIMIT
By **Bre' Hayes**

BLOODY COMMAS I & II
SKI MASK CARTEL I, II & III
KING OF NEW YORK I II, III IV V
RISE TO POWER I II III
COKE KINGS I II III IV V
BORN HEARTLESS I II III IV
KING OF THE TRAP I II
By **T.J. Edwards**

WHEN THE STREETS CLAP BACK I & II III
THE HEART OF A SAVAGE I II III IV
MONEY MAFIA I II
LOYAL TO THE SOIL I II III
By **Jibril Williams**

A DISTINGUISHED THUG STOLE MY HEART I II & III
LOVE SHOULDN'T HURT I II III IV
RENEGADE BOYS 1-4
PAID IN KARMA 1-3
SAVAGE STORMS 1-3
AN UNFORESEEN LOVE 1-3
BABY, I'M WINTERTIME COLD 1-3
A THUG'S STREET PRINCESS 1&2
By **Meesha**

A GANGSTER'S CODE 1-3
A GANGSTER'S SYN 1-3
THE SAVAGE LIFE 1-3
CHAINED TO THE STREETS 1-3
BLOOD ON THE MONEY 1-3
A GANGSTA'S PAIN 1-3
BEAUTIFUL LIES AND UGLY TRUTHS
CHURCH IN THESE STREETS
By **J-Blunt**

CUM FOR ME 1-8
An LDP Erotica Collaboration

BLOOD OF A BOSS 1-5
SHADOWS OF THE GAME
TRAP BASTARD
By **Askari**

THE STREETS BLEED MURDER 1-3
THE HEART OF A GANGSTA 1-3
By **Jerry Jackson**

WHEN A GOOD GIRL GOES BAD
By **Adrienne**

THE COST OF LOYALTY 1-3
By **Kweli**

BRIDE OF A HUSTLA 1-3
THE FETTI GIRLS 1-3
CORRUPTED BY A GANGSTA 1-4
BLINDED BY HIS LOVE
THE PRICE YOU PAY FOR LOVE 1-3
DOPE GIRL MAGIC 1-3
By **Destiny Skai**

A KINGPIN'S AMBITION
A KINGPIN'S AMBITION II
I MURDER FOR THE DOUGH
By **Ambitious**

TRUE SAVAGE 1-7
DOPE BOY MAGIC 1-3
MIDNIGHT CARTEL 1-3
CITY OF KINGZ 1&2
NIGHTMARE ON SILENT AVE
THE PLUG OF LIL MEXICO 1&2
CLASSIC CITY
By **Chris Green**

A GANGSTER'S REVENGE 1-4
THE BOSS MAN'S DAUGHTERS 1-5
A SAVAGE LOVE 1&2
BAE BELONGS TO ME 1&2
A HUSTLER'S DECEIT 1-3
WHAT BAD BITCHES DO 1-3
SOUL OF A MONSTER 1-3
KILL ZONE
A DOPE BOY'S QUEEN 1-3
TIL DEATH 1-3
IMMA DIE BOUT MINE 1-6
DYING FOR LIKES
By **Aryanna**

A DOPEBOY'S PRAYER
By **Eddie "Wolf" Lee**

THE KING CARTEL 1-3
By **Frank Gresham**

THESE NIGGAS AIN'T LOYAL 1-3
By **Nikki Tee**

GANGSTA SHYT 1-3
By **CATO**

THE ULTIMATE BETRAYAL
By **Phoenix**

BOSS'N UP 1-3
By **Royal Nicole**

I LOVE YOU TO DEATH
By **Destiny J**

I RIDE FOR MY HITTA
I STILL RIDE FOR MY HITTA
By **Misty Holt**

LOVE & CHASIN' PAPER
By **Qay Crockett**

TO DIE IN VAIN
SINS OF A HUSTLA
By **ASAD**

BROOKLYN HUSTLAZ
By **Boogsy Morina**

BROOKLYN ON LOCK 1 & 2
By **Sonovia**

GANGSTA CITY
By **Teddy Duke**

A DRUG KING AND HIS DIAMOND 1-3
A DOPEMAN'S RICHES
HER MAN, MINE'S TOO 1&2
CASH MONEY HO'S
THE WIFEY I USED TO BE 1&2
PRETTY GIRLS DO NASTY THINGS
By **Nicole Goosby**

LIPSTICK KILLAH 1-3
CRIME OF PASSION 1-3
FRIEND OR FOE 1-3
By **Mimi**

TRAPHOUSE KING 1-3
KINGPIN KILLAZ 1-3
STREET KINGS 1&2
PAID IN BLOOD 1&2
CARTEL KILLAZ 1-3
DOPE GODS 1&2
By **Hood Rich**

THE STREETS ARE CALLING
By **Duquie Wilson**

STEADY MOBBN' 1-3
THE STREETS STAINED MY SOUL 1-3
By **Marcellus Allen**

WHO SHOT YA 1-3
SON OF A DOPE FIEND 1-4
HEAVEN GOT A GHETTO 1&2
SKI MASK MONEY 1&2
By **Renta**

GORILLAZ IN THE BAY 1-4
TEARS OF A GANGSTA 1/&2
3X KRAZY 1&2
STRAIGHT BEAST MODE 1&2
By **DE'KARI**

TRIGGADALE 1-3
MURDA WAS THE CASE 1-3
By **Elijah R. Freeman**

SLAUGHTER GANG 1-3
RUTHLESS HEART 1-3
By **Willie Slaughter**

GOD BLESS THE TRAPPERS 1-3
THESE SCANDALOUS STREETS 1-3
FEAR MY GANGSTA 1-5
THESE STREETS DON'T LOVE NOBODY 1-2
BURY ME A G 1-5
A GANGSTA'S EMPIRE 1-4
THE DOPEMAN'S BODYGAURD 1&2
THE REALEST KILLAZ 1-3
THE LAST OF THE OGS 1-3
By **Tranay Adams**

MARRIED TO A BOSS 1-3
By **Destiny Skai & Chris Green**

KINGZ OF THE GAME 1-7
CRIME BOSS 1-4
By **Playa Ray**

FUK SHYT
By **Blakk Diamond**

DON'T F#CK WITH MY HEART 1&2
By **Linnea**

ADDICTED TO THE DRAMA 1-3
IN THE ARM OF HIS BOSS
By **Jamila**

LOYALTY AIN'T PROMISED 1&2
By **Keith Williams**

YAYO 1-4
A SHOOTER'S AMBITION 1&2
BRED IN THE GAME
By **S. Allen**

TRAP GOD 1-3
RICH $AVAGE 1-3
MONEY IN THE GRAVE 1-3
CARTEL MONEY 1&2
By **Martell Troublesome Bolden**

FOREVER GANGSTA 1&2
GLOCKS ON SATIN SHEETS 1&2
By **Adrian Dulan**

TOE TAGZ 1-4
LEVELS TO THIS SHYT 1&2
IT'S JUST ME AND YOU
By **Ah'Million**

KINGPIN DREAMS 1-3
RAN OFF ON DA PLUG
By **Paper Boi Rari**

THE STREETS MADE ME 1-3
By **Larry D. Wright**

CONFESSIONS OF A GANGSTA 1-4
CONFESSIONS OF A JACKBOY 1-3
CONFESSIONS OF A HITMAN
CONFESSIONS OF A DOPE BOY
By **Nicholas Lock**

I'M NOTHING WITHOUT HIS LOVE
SINS OF A THUG
TO THE THUG I LOVED BEFORE
A GANGSTA SAVED XMAS
IN A HUSTLER I TRUST
By **Monet Dragun**

QUIET MONEY 1-3
THUG LIFE 1-3
EXTENDED CLIP 1&2
A GANGSTA'S PARADISE
By **Trai'Quan**

CAUGHT UP IN THE LIFE 1-3
THE STREETS NEVER LET GO 1-3
By **Robert Baptiste**

NEW TO THE GAME 1-3
MONEY, MURDER & MEMORIES 1-3
By **Malik D. Rice**

CREAM 2-3
THE STREETS WILL TALK
By **Yolanda Moore**

THE STREETS WILL NEVER CLOSE 1-3
By **K'ajji**

LIFE OF A SAVAGE 1-4
A GANGSTA'S QUR'AN 1-4
MURDA SEASON 1-3
GANGLAND CARTEL 1-3
CHI'RAQ GANGSTAS 1-4
KILLERS ON ELM STREET 1-3
JACK BOYZ N DA BRONX 1-3
A DOPEBOY'S DREAM 1-3
JACK BOYS VS DOPE BOYS 1-3
COKE GIRLZ
COKE BOYS
SOSA GANG 1&2
BRONX SAVAGES
BODYMORE KINGPINS
BLOOD OF A GOON
By **Romell Tukes**

CONCRETE KILLA 1-3
VICIOUS LOYALTY 1-3
BLOODY MONEY BAGS
By **Kingpen**

THE ULTIMATE SACRIFICE 1-6
KHADIFI
IF YOU CROSS ME ONCE 1-3
ANGEL 1-4
IN THE BLINK OF AN EYE
By **Anthony Fields**

THE LIFE OF A HOOD STAR
By **Ca$h & Rashia Wilson**

NIGHTMARES OF A HUSTLA 1-3
BLOOD AND GAMES 1&2
By **King Dream**

GHOST MOB
By **Stilloan Robinson**

HARD AND RUTHLESS 1&2
MOB TOWN 251
THE BILLIONAIRE BENTLEYS 1-3
REAL G'S MOVE IN SILENCE
By **Von Diesel**

MOB TIES 1-7
SOUL OF A HUSTLER, HEART OF A KILLER 1-3
GORILLAZ IN THE TRENCHES
OOPS CRY TOO 1&2
THE DAUGHTER OF A CARTEL BOSS
By **SayNoMore**

BODYMORE MURDERLAND 1-3
THE BIRTH OF A GANGSTER 1-4
By **Delmont Player**

FOR THE LOVE OF A BOSS 1&2
By **C. D. Blue**

KILLA KOUNTY 1-5
TENDER
By **Khufu**

MOBBED UP 1-4
THE BRICK MAN 1-5
THE COCAINE PRINCESS 1-10
STEPPERS 1-3
SUPER GREMLIN 1-4
A GANGSTA'S SON
By **King Rio**

MONEY GAME 1&2
By **Smoove Dolla**

A GANGSTA'S KARMA 1-5
By **FLAME**

KING OF THE TRENCHES 1-3
By **GHOST & TRANAY ADAMS**

BAD BITCHES WIT GUNZ 1&2
PROBLEM SOLVED
By **"Christopher Diesel" Hornezes**

QUEEN OF THE ZOO 1&2
By **Black Migo**

GRIMEY WAYS 1-3
BETRAYAL OF A G
By **Ray Vinci**

XMAS WITH AN ATL SHOOTER
By **Ca$h & Destiny Skai**

KING KILLA 1&2
By **Vincent "Vitto" Holloway**

BETRAYAL OF A THUG 1&2
By **Fre$h**

COUNTDOWN OF A KILLA 1&2
SEX, MURDER AND GOD 1&2
GUNS DOWN, BOTTOMS UP 1&2
By Lo-Life

THE MURDER QUEENS 1-7
By **Michael Gallon**

FOR THE LOVE OF BLOOD 1-4
By **Jamel Mitchell**

HOOD CONSIGLIERE 1&2
NO TIME FOR ERROR
By **Keese**

PROTÉGÉ OF A LEGEND 1,2&3
LOVE IN THE TRENCHES 1&2
By **Corey Robinson**

THE PLUG'S RUTHLESS DAUGHTER 1&2
By **Tony Daniels**

BORN IN THE GRAVE 1-3
CRIME PAYS
By **Self Made Tay**

MOAN IN MY MOUTH
By **XTASY**

TORN BETWEEN A GANGSTER AND A GENTLEMAN
By **J-BLUNT & Miss Kim**

LOYALTY IS EVERYTHING 1-3
CITY OF SMOKE 1-3
By **Molotti**

HERE TODAY GONE TOMORROW 1&2
By **Fly Rock**

WOMEN LIE MEN LIE 1-4
FIFTY SHADES OF SNOW 1-3
STACK BEFORE YOU SPLURGE
GIRLS FALL LIKE DOMINOES
NAÏVE TO THE STREETS
By **ROY MILLIGAN**

PILLOW PRINCESS
By **S. Hawkins**

THE BUTTERFLY MAFIA 1-3
SALUTE MY SAVAGERY 1&2
By **Fumiya Payne**

THE LANE 1&2
By Ken-Ken Spence

THE PUSSY TRAP 1-5
By **Nene Capri**

DIRTY DNA
By **Blaque**

SANCTIFIED AND HORNY
by **XTASY**

BOOKS BY LDP'S CEO, CA$H

TRUST IN NO MAN
TRUST IN NO MAN 2
TRUST IN NO MAN 3
BONDED BY BLOOD
SHORTY GOT A THUG
THUGS CRY
THUGS CRY 2
THUGS CRY 3
TRUST NO BITCH
TRUST NO BITCH 2
TRUST NO BITCH 3
TIL MY CASKET DROPS
RESTRAINING ORDER
RESTRAINING ORDER 2
IN LOVE WITH A CONVICT
LIFE OF A HOOD STAR
XMAS WITH AN ATL SHOOTER

www.ingramcontent.com/pod-product-compliance
Lightning Source LLC
Chambersburg PA
CBHW071147260626
47162CB00003B/952